MW00889496

SIR LAURENCE DIES

Christopher D. Abbott

Ocean Highway Books™
Independent Publishing Consultants

Cover Design, Richard Sutton
Author Photograph, Helen Cooper

ISBN: 1492119598
ISBN-13: 978-1492119593

Sir Laurence Dies has had many helpful contributors along its journey. I would like to thank the following people for their kindness, their generosity, and their perseverance. In no particular order: Rob Reddan, Clare Wadey, Andy Thompson, Wendy Bertsch, Richard Sutton and John Campbell, Sandra and all at JEA Press.

Todd, Alison and Dinger.

To Mum, Dad and Trayc. My rocks of support throughout the writing of this book.

This book is dedicated to the memory of Evelyn Parkin, who was an inspirational, fair, and generous woman, taken from us far too early. My only regret is that she never saw the book finished.

Table of Contents

ACT TWO

ACT THREE

PROLOGUE

◆

It was a hot day of the Last Summer, August 1914. The grounds of the Smythe estate were impeccable in their intricate horticultural design. The staff went about their duties without giving much thought to the wider issues of life outside the estate. What did it matter to them if a great war was looming over the horizon? It was all so far away. Everybody knew about it. Everybody talked about it. There was hardly any other topic of conversation. The general population were reminded, on a daily basis, that the Kaiser was evil and would be stopped, eventually.

Troubling though this news was it was hardly as important as serving tea on time, or making ready the tennis courts for when the Smythe and Gregson families needed to use them.

◆

'Come on, Ellie.' Larry Gregson shouted up to the top of the house. The neatly cut lawn flexed underneath his rubber-soled tennis shoes. 'Rain won't hold off forever you know!'

Her smiling face came through the open window.

'Coming, darling.'

Captain Larry Gregson held himself with military bearing. He had a real Army look about him. In his early thirties, he was good looking, extremely approachable, gently firm with his subordinates, and beyond fair. He looked up and his lips curved into that famous smile as Anthony strolled into view carrying a tennis racket over each shoulder. Anthony, being around the same age, had an attractiveness about him that went beyond "good looks." It was often described by the older generation as boyishly handsome. He was the type of person that could easily turn heads in a crowd.

Anthony, like Larry, cut an athletic figure when playing any sport, especially tennis.

'I say, Larry,' Anthony said as he quickly made it to his tennis partner's side. 'I think it's going to be a splendid day after all.'

Larry, nodding in agreement, asked:

'You've set the court up, old boy?'

'Certainly have. Nets are all ready, need the players now!'

Ellie Gregson and Agatha Smythe finally appeared around the corner of the house. The twin girls were both wearing light summer dresses and tennis shoes. They were also carrying tennis rackets. Ellie's dress was pastel white-blue; Agatha's bright pink with yellow flowers.

'You boys better be ready, we're in very good form today!' Agatha and Ellie shared a wicked look as they slowly approached. Anthony laughed and handed Larry a racket. They waited as the girls sauntered past, and followed them to the court.

Ellie caught Larry's eye from over her shoulder and winked. A fleeting gesture, but enough to make him smile.

The court was set up pristinely. Along to one side, away from the court itself, a parasol, upright and open, in the centre of a large white summer table surrounded by matching chairs, was being attended to by a handsome young footman with a bleary eye. He busied himself preparing refreshments for the inevitable break in their game. Although he took his duties very seriously, he was a footman for General Smythe after all. He looked as though at any given moment he might simply fall asleep. Hearing the approaching party, he stood, straightened out his already immaculate uniform, and made himself ready beside the table.

As each of them passed, they acknowledged him. He made no movement at all, like a palace sentry, but on seeing Anthony, his professional manner broke somewhat and he smirked slightly. Eye contact was made for the briefest moment and Anthony simply raised an eyebrow. The footman quickly returned his eyes to where they should have been, looking out at nothing. Larry, noticing that Anthony had fallen behind, looked back. His quick eye took in the exchange and he frowned.

'You coming, old boy?'

With a wave, Anthony jogged towards the party. Larry was still frowning as he caught up.

Larry turned to Agatha. 'Where's David, Aggi?'

Agatha scoffed at him. 'Oh, he's far too busy talking to my wretched father to come out and play with us.'

Not that David ever played any games, other than lowdown ones, Larry thought. To Aggi he simply said. 'Never mind.'

'Now, now, Aggi darling.' Ellie purred. She put a well-manicured hand on her sister's arm. It was a light, fleeting touch, but enough to soften her sister's mood. 'He's keeping father indoors and not out here annoying us.'

'Well, that's certainly worth a degree of forgiveness then, I suppose,' Agatha admitted, grudgingly, but she wasn't smiling.

When they reached the court, Agatha gravitated towards Anthony. Larry shook his head.

'Not this time, Aggi.'

She looked down her nose at him. 'I'm certainly not pairing with you!'

Larry laughed. 'No, that's not what I meant. Why don't we break with tradition? Let's do boys versus girls.'

Larry handed a ball to Agatha. 'You said you were both in good form...shall we?'

Ellie and Agatha looked at each other and then smiled at exactly the same time.

Larry then flipped a coin, called, and the girls won the toss.

'I'll serve, then,' decided Aggi, and Larry and Anthony moved into position. With a wicked grin, she served the ball with force. Anthony had to move quickly but managed to return it hard. Ellie backhanded it straight to Larry. They played for thirty minutes and then stopped for a break.

'Two to us I believe,' Ellie said breathlessly. 'You're off your game, darling.'

'You beat us fair and square in that last game,' Larry replied, wiping sweat from his angular bronze-skinned face.

'You keep hold of that one,' Agatha said downing a glass of freshly squeezed orange juice.

'I will. He's my peach!' Ellie smiled a big smile at Larry and then a thought occurred to her. 'Anthony, did you get that paperwork sorted?' She refilled her glass.

'Yes thank you, Ellie. The General organised everything, he even swung me a commission! The age thing wasn't even an issue apparently. General Smythe made all the necessary calls, so that's that!'

'That's great news, Anthony. Didn't I tell you it would be fine? Anyway, it'll be good to have you alongside me.' Larry said this with great affection. 'We'll show these Germans what the British are made of!'

Anthony laughed as Ellie rolled her eyes. Agatha simply coughed to hide a laugh.

'Boys, boys!' Ellie mocked them with good humour, 'You need to learn to beat us girls at tennis first!'

'True enough,' Larry chuckled and turned back to Anthony. 'Time to show these girls, don't you think?'

'Lead on, sir!'

The game lasted almost an hour and then they broke for tea.

◆

The sun was slowly setting over the family house as Larry and Ellie Gregson walked out into the garden. When they were far enough away, Ellie turned and put a hand on Larry's chest.

'Do look after him, darling, he's only a boy.'

'I will, Ellie. I won't let him out of my sight.'

She smiled at him. 'You'd better not, Larry Gregson!'

'And how is Dawson taking the news?'

'As he always does, my darling, with dignity and quiet grace.'

'Meaning he hates the idea?'

She laughed. 'He hates the idea, yes.'

'Good.'

They looked at each other for the longest time. Her pretty eyes sparkled. He leaned in for a kiss.

She put a gentle hand to his lips. 'Do come back to me, Larry.'

'I will, my love.'

They embraced.

'I promise.'

They stood together for some time, hand in hand. Two pairs of eyes were fixed on the sky. The sun disappeared behind the tree line, leaving a vibrant orange-blue sky in its wake. Eventually Ellie Gregson led her husband back to the house.

◆

From a window high in the disused west wing of the house, Anthony had also been watching, unnoticed. He quietly pulled the curtain closed as the pair disappeared from his view.

ACT ONE

Chapter One

The Boat

Doctor Pieter Straay stepped out of the restaurant's cabin onto the main deck and shuddered as a biting wind penetrated his woollen overcoat. He stretched out his tall frame, placed his fedora firmly onto his head and turned his collar upward. Straay had enjoyed a light meal and some interesting conversation for the past thirty minutes, but now he wanted to stretch his legs.

The steamer was small but comfortable. Doctor Straay had enjoyed the crossing so far, because the sea had been calm. The English expression "like a millpond" had instantly come to his mind. As he reached the stern, he looked back over the horizon with a fond smile. He was leaving his native country, although it was not always his home. New adventures awaited him in England.

Doctor Straay was a people watcher. It was never boring. It was an art. He would imagine a faded photograph. The detail missing, out of focus, just out of reach. With each new person, each different encounter, he gathered that detail. Observation and study introduced him to differing facets of the subject, fuelling his hunger for arcane and often superfluous knowledge. It increased his understanding and, in the same way that a child who is given complex puzzles to solve organises the misshapen pieces to form a picture, he used that technique to bring a person into focus. It sharpened his mind. As a boy, he had always been fascinated by the actions or reactions of adults and from childhood to adulthood, the fascination never left him. It was because of this he chose to study psychology.

There were people of all classes on the boat, mainly English, which always made for an interesting study. For some reason that even he had not yet been consciously able to fathom, he found the English to be his favourite study group. They could present, on occasion, a varying degree of idiosyncratic dynamics that could leave him both amused and appalled at the same time.

He ran his eye around a mixture of women and children, all wrapped up in woollen mufflers and hats, pointing at sea birds, oblivious to anything else around them. To one side he observed an assortment of rough looking men standing in huddles smoking clay pipes. Their conversation was hushed, with the occasional loud grunt or burst of laughter. Close by were well-dressed young men, talking politics or city based business news, each standing stiffly against the wind. The overlapping conversations flooded the air around him.

Doctor Straay turned his head slightly, his interest directed towards two women who had just wandered into view. One, over-dressed and smoking a cigarette through a fancy holder, was gesticulating flamboyantly. The other was a little on the plump side. She wore a shabby hand-knitted shawl right up to her neck. Her hat, which was more suitable for a summer wedding, sat precariously askew on top of her head. She gripped the hat with one hand and held the rail with the other. Her head nodded in agreement as she answered every question her companion spoke. Both were English. Their conversation was amusing, but utterly trivial.

'Typical really,' the well-dressed one barked. 'I mean really? It's just typical isn't it?'

'Oh yes! You're so right, Dotty, it's typical.'

'Who'd have thought anything would come of it?'

'I'm sure I couldn't say, Dotty.'

'Well, I just think the whole thing is so…?' Dotty was searching for the right word.

'Typical?' suggested her friend quickly.

'Yes! That's it exactly.' They looked at each other for a few seconds nodding. 'Typical!' they said together. Dotty laughed and the other joined in.

'She'll have to tell him, you know,' said Dotty as she attached a new cigarette to her holder and lit it in a well-practiced way.

'Oh yes, Dotty, I quite agree.'

'There'll be the most awful scandal!' Dotty said the word with a smile and a twinkle in her eye. It was clear that Dotty loved a scandal.

'Well, she did bring it on herself, didn't she?' her friend replied dutifully.

'She did,' agreed Dotty happily blowing smoke from her cigarette, which drifted back towards them both.

Her friend coughed.

Dotty ignored it.

'I said to Bernard the other night, isn't it just typical, I mean, really, one just can't express it in any other way, well can one?'

'What did he say, Dotty?'

'Well he agreed with me of course. That sort of behaviour is just so…?' Dotty looked at the other and raised an eyebrow.

'Typical, Dotty,' said the other on cue.

What did this conversation tell him about these two women? One was clearly dominant the other passive. It was also evident the dominant, Dotty, held some position in society, but hadn't always. Here was a woman not born into money or position. Her husband was probably the intellect or breadwinner, possibly both. He must be a very easily pleased man, Straay thought.

Her bearing, her manner, her speech, even her posture all indicated that she was elevated middleclass. An upper-class lady would not be called Dotty; she would be called Dorothy. Her companion may possibly have been a relative, but then he remembered that old adage, *you can choose your friends, but not your family.* He shook his head slightly and dismissed his first assessment. She had to be an old friend. Dotty was quite simply a very dull and uninteresting woman.

Now her passive friend, however, was of interest. She showed the higher intelligence of the two with her quick-witted replies and her way of anticipating what should be said, and how it should be said. Her eyes shone with an underdeveloped intelligence. Here he saw potential. If only society had encouraged such a woman as she to pursue academics. The world would be a far better place for it. He interpreted her untrained abilities as foresight, precognition even. She wore the clothes that would befit someone of her class and she wasn't trying to display anything other. She was also very faithful to her now richer friend. No one could easily tolerate such a woman unless there had been a lifelong friendship, possibly as far back as childhood. The intelligence was also shown in the fact that she was on a boat out of Holland which, given her status and class, she could not have afforded on her own. A reward maybe?

He smiled to himself. He liked her, if for no other reason than her loyalty to her irritating and shallow friend.

Straay turned his attention to a man talking to a child. He was clearly a navy man. The tattooed anchor just visible under his right cuff gave that away. The child, probably around twelve years old, was nodding politely.

'Ships are the best method of travel you know, my boy. Never go wrong with a ship. Get in an aeroplane and before you know it, a wing falls off and you'd be done for. Now, on a ship, if anything unlikely ever happened, well, you'd be fine.' To emphasise his statement, he pointed to a life raft.

'See here, these rafts will keep you safe. No such thing on an aeroplane,' he said with a touch of disgust in his voice. Even the word aeroplane was distasteful, clearly a biased man.

'Wing falls off and that's it, you're done for. No getting out. Down you go! Not for me, ships for me always, safer than an aeroplane.'

Here the boy stopped nodding. Straay observed that the boy was putting a lot of thought into his answer. It occurred to him if he were to have this conversation, he might point out the fateful last journey of the Titanic as a counter to the argument. The man would of course simply reply it was *because* of the lesson of the Titanic that boats were safer. He could picture the man saying, "Every boat has the right number of life rafts in the unlikely event that a ship goes down. Freak accidents happen, but you always have time, and you always have a life raft. No such thing on an aeroplane!" He might even suggest poor judgement on behalf of the captain or some other rhetorical answer that wasn't based on any fact, just his biased view of ships and the world.

Eventually the boy said, 'I went on an aeroplane once.'

'Oh yes,' the man said with no enthusiasm at all.

'Yes, we flew to France. I liked it. Watching the world go by, the clouds looked like cotton wool. On a boat all you can see is the sea!'

'What's wrong with the sea? Full of mystery is the sea.' He turned his attention to the ocean beside him.

'Aeroplanes are exciting!' continued the boy.

The navy man turned sharply. 'Well, you wouldn't say that if a wing fell off. You'd be done for.'

The boy changed the subject.

'Are we on the port or starboard side?' he asked.

'Port,' the man said with a smile. 'You want to know a little saying that helps you to remember it?'

'Oh yes please!' the boy answered enthusiastically.

'You know what Port is, the drink I mean?'

'You have it after dinner, don't you?' the boy seemed unsure with his answer, but the seaman nodded approvingly.

'That's the stuff. Any more of that Port *left.* That's what you say.'

The boy was, again, thoughtful. 'Anymore of that Port left?' The man nodded at him. The boy was clearly still confused but eventually he got the meaning.

'Oh, Port, *Left,* I see. That makes it much easier, thanks!'

'You're welcome, my boy. So, which is safer then, hmm? Boats or aeroplanes?' He pulled out a white crumpled bag of humbugs and playfully looked inside.

'Well…,' said the boy eyeing a humbug the man had selected and slowly popped into his mouth.

'Aeroplanes do have life jackets…' the boy said hopefully.

'They're not much use to you if a wing falls off though, are they?'

The man toyed with the sweet bag.

'True—unless you land in the sea of course,' the boy replied softly, his eyes fixed hypnotically on the bag.

'If you survive the impact,' the man said matter-of-factly as he slowly closed the bag.

'Well I guess…' The man looked down and noted with a wry smile, the boy was fully entranced by the bag of sweets.

'It has to be boats then,' the boy said firmly. The logic of his argument had been betrayed! His eyes shone brightly. It seemed that all he could think about now, was the taste of the humbugs. The man smiled a winner's smile.

'There you are, see? I was right! Boats are simply the safest method of travel. Here,' he said triumphantly. 'Have a humbug!'

Doctor Straay watched the boy enthusiastically take the boiled sweet. It had been amusing to witness the discourse. Here he saw an adult who desperately wanted a boy's approval, and couldn't get it with reason, so he had resorted to bribery to achieve his goal. It was a symptom of the times. He enjoyed observing these people converse. It didn't really matter how superficial their conversations were as long as they were happening. In a way, he felt it would always give him a reason to observe and to learn.

Straay casually lit a cigarette and slowly walked around to the starboard deck where the shade gave way to the warming sun. He manoeuvred around the two talking women, lifting his hat as he did so.

'Doctor Pieter Straay?' a voice said from behind him.

Chapter Two

An Introduction

The Dutchman looked around for the source of the voice. He quickly recovered from his initial startled reaction and smiled. He hadn't known that anyone on board knew him, and he'd told only a select handful of people his plans.

'Yes it is I, Straay, Mr…?'

The man wore a formal suit in light grey with black leather shoes and a stylish grey hat. He was in his late fifties to early sixties. The first thing that struck the doctor was the overlapping mesh of scars on the neck and left side of the man's face. His jaw was crooked on one side, his lower lip twisted awkwardly downwards, and the left cheek and muscle under his eye slightly sunken. He also had no left eyebrow. This man had clearly been in some terrible accident at some point in his early life; an accident that probably made him unrecognisable to anyone who knew him before it occurred. His bearing indicated he was a military man.

Doctor Straay had a habit, especially when presented with a person who had piqued his interest, of falling into what some of his friends would categorise as "foreign mode." He used it to disarm in some cases, and to gather information in others.

The newcomer had a cheerful nature. He removed his hat and held it to his chest as he spoke.

'Gregson,' he said. 'Laurence Gregson. Well, actually, if you want to be pedantic, Lieutenant Colonel Sir Laurence Gregson.'

'You prefer Colonel, or Sir Laurence?'

'Not sure I like either these days,' admitted Gregson with a smile. 'I used to prefer Larry, but even that seems hollow.'

'Ah but to the, hmm, how do you say it…,' he made a pretence of searching for the right word. Gregson quickly offered one.

'Unacquainted?'

'Excellent, yes unacquainted, so what would you prefer I call you?'

'Sir Laurence will do.'

'Then Sir Laurence it is, pleased to meet you.'

They shook hands.

'And I you, Doctor Straay. Psychology is your field I believe, Criminal Psychology.'

Straay raised an eyebrow. 'You are exceptionally well informed, can it be that my fame has spread further than I imagined?'

'Ah, well not quite,' he chuckled and then hastily added, 'That's not to say you aren't famous of course, I'm sure you are, in your field I mean, bound to be, it's…'

'I was teasing you, Sir Laurence.' Straay smiled, Gregson nodded once.

'Right you are. Anyway, let's just say I know someone who knows some people, who tell me things when I need to know.' He laughed at the look he was getting from the tall Dutchman.

'I'm sure you get the idea, doctor.'

'Sounds incredibly complicated.' Straay flicked the butt of his cigarette into the sea.

'Yes, it certainly can be,' admitted Sir Laurence.

'You are a member, then, of the secret service?'

'Oh good lord no! No, I'm more of a… well, let's just say, an adviser to the Home Office.' He paused for a moment. 'Got the post shortly after the war.'

Straay considered this for a moment. 'It was during the war that you had the accident?'

Sir Laurence looked puzzled for a moment, but Straay pointed to his scars.

'Oh the face?' Sir Laurence chuckled. 'Yes, bomb blast, lucky to be alive really. Ancient history now. Well, except for the scars.'

'They remind you daily of your experiences?'

'Not really, they remind me how lucky I was. Others weren't so.'

Straay nodded. 'You were saying about the Home Office?'

'Yes, a cousin of mine is a Member of Parliament and my uncle served the Home Office during the war. I think you'll find if you go back even sixty or seventy years, you'll always find a Gregson in a Government post somewhere.'

'A family affair then?'

'Something like that,' Sir Laurence smiled.

'So you return to England from a holiday?'

'Partly. Had a nice weekend in Amsterdam though, you?'

'No, for me I travel to England for my health, also I will provide some assistance in my professional capacity. It has been too long since I was last there.' There was a sparkle in his eyes. Sir Laurence noticed.

'Busman's holiday eh? So, you're a big hotshot detective now, at least that's what I've been hearing?'

'Well yes and no.'

'That's an interesting, if cryptic response, Doctor Straay.'

That's what I was going for, he thought to himself. He checked his pockets for his cigarettes and when he found one, he said, 'Yes, truly I observe and perform crime detection, I spent some time assisting the police with their investigations around Europe and now, well I am content to perform my own investigations when the mood takes me, but not as a consulting detective like your Sherlock Holmes of fiction.'

Sir Laurence offered a match, which they both shared.

'I'm more a Christie fan myself.' He leant on the rail, cigarette dangling from his well-manicured hands. 'Oh yes, Holmes was a great detective and an interesting man written by a very clever author, but I prefer the complexity of a Christie novel.' He spoke with what appeared to be good authority.

Straay agreed with him. 'Yes, I myself favour Poirot over Holmes in the novels. In nearly all the cases of Holmes, there are always little clues no one can draw any inference from, unless they have his specific knowledge of crime, science, and the underworld. For example, the lime cream from the hair tells Holmes the villain goes to one of three barbers in one side of London, because only these three barber establishments use a certain type of wax lime cream.'

Sir Laurence nodded. 'Ah yes, his arcane knowledge wins against the police there.'

Straay took a long draw from his cigarette and continued.

'Naturally, Holmes can detect this complex mixture from one strand of hair. He can gauge a man's height and stature from his footprints, which isn't as farfetched as some people might believe. He can determine the state of the man's health from the silk band in his hat. He can tell what type of cigar the villain smokes, from an extensive ash catalogue; and let us not forget the man must also be wearing the special shaped studded boots he always wears.'

Gregson laughed heartily. 'It appears these villains only ever have one pair of shoes or boots!'

'Indeed! So then,' Straay was in full flow now. 'Holmes goes to these three barbers who are each given a description. "Well, that's Barnaby Wilson!" says the second barber. Simple, logical, and well followed out, but a little unrealistic in my opinion.'

'I agree with you.' They both flicked their cigarettes into the fast moving sea below.

Straay allowed his eyes to focus on the horizon.

'No, I prefer the psychological aspect of crime. With Poirot, I find he thinks and he acts within. For the reader, it was never about the ash, the hair, or even the body. It is about his clever brain working out the solutions to twisted puzzles. No disguises. How does she describe him? A walking brain. Although the trick with discovering the employment, method of travel and maladies and other ailments Holmes employs in many stories, I like these very much.'

Sir Laurence again laughed. 'Indeed, that's what makes the detective much more interesting. The simple crime becomes more complicated. Like the nanny who knows the family secrets and later dies. Then there's the newly introduced uncle at some fancy cocktail party just off Hyde Park. He turns out to be his brother-in-law's cousin, wanted for robbery by the Yard.'

Sir Laurence was clearly enjoying himself. As Straay pulled out another cigarette and lit it, he noted with mild interest that Sir Laurence really was a connoisseur of crime fiction.

'On the other hand,' continued Sir Laurence, 'someone who isn't known as a family member but later goes on to become the love interest of some girl, so he can secretly kill her father, then goes on to claim an inheritance that passed down the family line, which skipped a generation or two…'

Straay allowed him to continue uninterrupted. It gave him time to study.

'…or maybe a man goes to war then returns, different, bitter, and war fatigued. He goes on to establish himself in some big fancy country estate, but secretly isn't the same person who left it all those years previously. Wildly absurd but a damn good read, don't you think?'

Straay's head bobbed enthusiastically. 'Yes although in fairness, the crimes in these books are always a let-down for me.'

'How so?'

Doctor Straay sighed inwardly and thought, *how many times must I explain this position?* Through experience over the years he'd found if he didn't give an adequate answer, the general impression was he was simply being difficult, or worse, it was some form of professional snobbery.

'It must be very difficult for the writer because they have to keep us interested and if we discover the identity of the criminal too early, why bother to read on? What annoys me is this. The writer always keeps little secrets from us in order to be the revelation at the end. Now I have tried on several occasions to determine the criminal in many books, but always I am wrong, because later I'm told something by the detective, which wasn't in any of the evidence or presented in any fashion during the book prior to the dénouement.' Straay finished his cigarette and again deposited it into the sea.

'It has to be this way, I suppose,' he continued, 'otherwise we'd never say. "Well I thought she'd done it," or, "I always suspected him!" This is not always the case, of course.'

'How so?'

Straay shrugged. 'Other writers have been more careful to lay out clues along the way such as a sentence here, a remark or observation there, and so on.'

'Interesting perspective,' Sir Laurence thoughtfully remarked. 'So, you stopped enjoying the stories because you felt cheated by the author?'

'Partly, but also like anyone who works in the detection of crime, to read about it for amusement tends to be like taking your work home with you. I also find it very hard to imagine England has so many idiot policemen serving in the position of Inspector or Chief Inspector. In so many cases, the police fail to discover the criminal and the good detective, the brilliant detective, hunts them down; but in reality, the police work diligently to apprehend the criminal. They have the resources and the technology at their disposal.'

'Good point.'

'What does the detective need with scientific analysis, or blood samples, or fingerprints?' Straay said this with a half-smile.

'They have the little silver cigarette case left in the open safe with the initial AG, or JL and we know at least two people who were at the party were called Andrew Johnson or Ariadne Jenkins. So the police, convinced one or the other is guilty, ignore the warnings of our famous detective and go off to search the backgrounds to determine which one of these people are guilty. Now we have the red herring thrown in to make us believe the police have it right, because Arthur Jacobs or Adrian Jefferson was the only one who left his seat at dinner. Maybe he took a call that no one can corroborate. Maybe poor Arthur is also a confidence trickster or a jewel thief.'

'He possibly has some past criminal record,' Sir Laurence added. 'They generally do.'

'Again, an excellent point. It strengthens their case. So neatly, it all falls onto him. Now the police have their man. The detective says they have it wrong but the stalwart Inspector shakes his head. No, he says, we have all the evidence we need. Therefore poor Arthur Jacobs is now charged with the crime and as far as the police are concerned the case is closed.'

'Yes I see where you're going with this; the answer is far too obvious,' Sir Laurence said.

'Exactly so. The answer then must come by some revelation only our great detective is able to determine, with the use of the arcane knowledge he and only he possesses. He determines AJ is in fact not a name, but a secret society of hatpin makers or embroidery merchants dating back some thirty years or more. This society *must* be secret and linked to, or have been directly involved in, crimes of the past, which is how he knows all about it.'

He paused for a moment. Sir Laurence seemed to be hanging on his every word.

'It is ascertained most of these people are dead, except maybe twenty or so, and only one was at the party. *Voilà!* Arthur Jacobs is now saved! The Inspector shakes the detective by the hand and grudgingly thanks him…'

Sir Laurence laughed heartily and said, 'Bravo!'

Straay bowed slightly and then proceeded to pull out another cigarette. 'As I said, it is not easy to find pleasure in a story, when you over-analyse everything you read.'

'You've really thought that through! You should write your own story. I'm sure you'd give them all a run for their money.'

'This thought has occurred to me—'

'I imagine though,' Sir Laurence said, ignoring the remark, 'if you could turn off your brain and just read the story, it would become what it is, just a story.'

'It is true what you say, but how does one turn off the brain? Or should I say the little grey cells.'

'Not easily. I'm with you there. I wish I could turn off my own brain occasionally. Still, nothing one can do about it, so best not to dwell. How long will you be in England?'

'A little while. I'm performing some work for Scotland Yard. They have a division now open to using psychology and, as an expert in my field, I was honoured to be asked to assist.'

'You're too modest, I understand you're going to the Yard to organise and develop the unit, not just to assist.'

'You are, again, remarkably well informed, Sir Laurence.' Straay studied him a little more closely.

'I am.' He gave a rather steel-like look and then a thought occurred to him. It made him smile. 'I say, why don't you come and stay with us this weekend?'

'Well—' Straay hesitated.

'I have some interesting friends and they would definitely fit the bill for a good murder mystery!' Sir Laurence gave a mischievous grin.

'Oh? You do interest me, but—'

Sir Laurence again ignored him. 'Let me see. Well first off there's the enchanting Lady Agatha. Resourceful, intelligent but little or no common sense and utterly useless with money; probably the holder of a serious and disturbing deep secret she thinks no one else knows about.' He thought hard for a moment.

'Then there's the venerable Major Heskith. A good, honest, solid chap. A history of sound decisions and perfect record but, out of the war environment, has turned to drink. Who else? Yes… There is also the debonair Doctor Powell: family doctor, intelligent, cunning and handsome. Who knows how many bodies are locked away in his cupboard, eh?' Sir Laurence was counting off people with his fingers as he spoke.

'Oh and I mustn't forget the very loyal but equally money-grabbing lawyer, Desmond DuPont, whose friendship is predicated on the size of my chequebook! I suspect you'd find a weekend with all of these people thoroughly entertaining! You must come. It would be delightful. There might even be a body!'

'Oh but you must not wish for such things, Sir Laurence. You open Pandora's Box by saying such things.'

'Nonsense old boy, never been superstitious in my life. I survived the war, so nothing that lot can throw at me could affect me in the slightest, and believe me they do. Shall we say eight? Friday? I won't take no for an answer, trust me.'

'I do trust you,' he paused for a moment to reflect on the conversation. Sir Laurence's smile got wider as he waited for the inevitable answer.

'I accept your gracious invitation, Sir Laurence.'

'Invitation? Command, old boy!'

The boat was arriving at the dock when Sir Laurence handed Straay a card with the address. He made a note on the back of the name of the railway station the Dutchman should go to, at what time he should arrive and so on. He was meticulous, Straay noted, repeating the instructions twice to ensure everything was in order. Finally, he shook Straay's hand and with a slight lift of his hat, disappeared off down the deck.

◆

Doctor Pieter Straay narrowed his eyes as he watched Sir Laurence fade into the crowd. An odd sense of foreboding crept through him; one he was unable to shake. Something in the conversation had left a nagging feeling yet, as hard as he tried, he could not determine why. Yes, the invitation was unexpected, but Sir Laurence Gregson had sought him out personally with, clearly, intimate knowledge of who and what he was. This could mean only one thing. Gregson had definitely orchestrated the meeting. The preamble conversation was the hook and the invitation was the goal.

'What could he possibly want with me at the house he couldn't tell me directly on the boat?' Straay asked himself quietly.

The sound of the Steward's voice interrupted his reverie, and he thoughtfully made his way towards the disembarkation point.

Chapter Three

The House

The train finally pulled into Euston railway station at eight thirty. Doctor Straay had been frustrated by the sudden cancellation of his first train. It was raining hard. The type of rain that would soak you instantly the moment you stepped into it. He had been able to telephone the house before his train departed explaining the reason for the delay. He was pleased to see the driver waiting dutifully outside, beside the station entrance, as agreed.

He had cleared his mind of all expectations. Sir Laurence was an interesting man, but an enigma. Professionally, Straay felt Sir Laurence was a complex man, clearly authoritarian and maybe even with a superiority complex. He had noticed a deeper undertone of steel during their first conversation. Of course, one didn't rise to the rank of Lieutenant Colonel and be knighted by His Majesty the King, without it. He had also noticed something else. Sir Laurence was scared.

The journey to the house took around twenty-five minutes and dinner had finished by the time Straay finally arrived. Sir Laurence met him at the entrance and Dawson, the butler, took his bag up to his room.

Dawson was a morose man, hard to read, with a stiff posture and a shuffling walk. His clothes were of the very best quality and well-tailored. Sir Laurence watched his back as he slowly ascended the stair.

'Finally made it then!' Sir Laurence said smiling, with no hint of annoyance at his late arrival.

'Yes, truly the trains were impossible. I apologise on their behalf,' Straay said, removing his hat and coat and hanging them on the stand beside the door.

'Not a bit of it old chap, come and meet my other guests.'

Sir Laurence led the way into what Straay understood to be "the smoking room," but in reality, smoking was permitted in all rooms, so this name made little sense to him. The idiosyncratic British and their ridiculous naming conventions amused him.

The room was spacious, like the rest of the house, with large comfortable sofas in red and black, the colour scheme of the room, and small tables, both modern and old–fashioned, all finished in matching mahogany, with rather exotic ornaments. There was a well-stocked mahogany magazine rack alongside the fireplace and on the opposite wall was a large bar, which seemed to contain every possible variation of alcoholic beverage one could think of. Neatly alongside the bar stood a beautiful cabinet. Contained within, dozens of variously shaped expensive crystal cut glasses. Heavy red curtains were pulled across the windows and the soft lighting was perfectly managed by ancient-looking gas lamps, many of which had been expertly converted for electricity. Clearly, Sir Laurence liked the décor to look old, but was not averse to modernising the house where it needed to be.

Sir Laurence introduced Major John Heskith first.

'My dearest and oldest friend in the world. Jonny and I were in the war together.' Sir Laurence looked fondly at him.

'How'd you do,' said the old Major, a little gruffly.

The Major had the expected military bearing of a senior officer. He also had a weary look suggesting he was annoyed by Straay's presence. Straay held eye contact for a moment longer than was actually necessary.

'This is Lady Agatha Smythe,' Sir Laurence said with a smile.

'Charmed, I'm sure.' Lady Agatha extended her hand. She was an elegant older woman, nearing sixty, but looking more like forty. She clearly looked after herself very well. But Straay noticed that her hand shook, slightly.

'This is my dear friend Doctor Jacob Powell.'

'Delighted to meet you at last.' Doctor Powell said smoothly. 'Sir Laurence has been very mischievous and told us absolutely nothing about you, except the fact you're a detective.'

Doctor Powell shook Doctor Straay firmly by the hand. He picked up the brandy bowl from the table and put it to his rather large nose.

Powell had that faint odour of the general practitioner. He was a man with intelligence visible in his piercing eyes. He leant forward and said in hushed tones, 'He's quite the predator our Sir Laurence. Doctor, mind you don't become his next prey!' He then laughed loudly and took a large gulp of brandy. Sir Laurence made brief eye contact with

Straay and smiled. Still chuckling to himself, Powell moved towards the decanter and poured himself another full glass.

Sir Laurence turned next to the man to his right. He put an arm around his shoulder. 'And finally my loyal lawyer, Mr Desmond DuPont.'

'A pleasure, Doctor Straay.'

DuPont was a thin faced ferret of a man with close-set brown eyes. Straay had an awkward feeling about DuPont. He didn't like the man on first impression but could not determine why. He shook the feeling away and took the outstretched hand. Doctor Powell fumbled for a handkerchief and Sir Laurence dropped his arm.

'You're here on business or pleasure?' DuPont asked. His little brown eyes didn't blink once.

'Pleasure, Mr DuPont, what crimes could there be for me in such a wonderful house as this?' Straay was cheerful but spoke with precision; DuPont couldn't fail to notice the hidden meaning behind his casual reply. If he had noticed however, he gave nothing away. He simply nodded and smiled a disarming smile.

'What indeed?' Major Heskith murmured.

Straay turned to look at him and the Major simply smiled. He then looked back to DuPont and as he did so, his eyes caught Doctor Powell. He too was looking at DuPont but with much harder eyes. When he realised he was being observed he carefully looked away and softened his expression.

Sir Laurence broke the silence.

'Sadly my daughter, Milly, had to retire early. Bit of a headache, but I'll introduce her to you in the morning.'

Straay had the odd feeling he had missed something of vital importance. Again, he mentally shrugged it off. Whatever it was probably wasn't significant, at least not yet.

◆

After the introductions were completed, the Major and Lady Agatha quietly left the group and sat down to talk. Straay observed them for a moment until he was distracted by Doctor Powell, who crossed in front of him and wandered to the other side of the room for another refill of brandy.

Desmond DuPont looked at Sir Laurence and said, 'Laurence, we've got to fix this damn will of yours and no more excuses.'

Sir Laurence sighed in a playful way. 'Now?'

'Now! I have all the paperwork drawn up. Just need a couple of witnesses and we're done and dusted. Straay here is an independent professional, a doctor. Why not ask him?' Sir Laurence turned to Straay.

'What do you say, Doctor Straay? Will you be a witness to my will?'

Straay was taken aback, but only for a moment. 'Well, it is unexpected but I do not see why not.'

'Excellent, let's go into the study and get this finished with.' DuPont started to lead the way when Straay spoke.

'What about a second witness?'

'What about old Dawson?' DuPont suggested. 'He's not family or friend is he? Just a Butler.'

'Just a Butler, who has been in my service for thirty years.' Sir Laurence raised an eyebrow. The first note of annoyance crept into his well-managed voice.

'Sorry, didn't mean anything by it,' DuPont hastily retracted.

'Mind you don't, Desmond. Dawson is as much family to me as, well, family!'

'You're right of course. Very old fashioned of me, silly mistake. What about the cook? She's new this year isn't she?'

'Yes she is,' Sir Laurence agreed with a nod. 'Good call, Desmond. Go fetch her and we'll all meet in my study.'

◆

The study was, like the smoking room, neat and organised. The mahogany theme ran through all the rooms on the ground floor and possibly upstairs too. The room itself was sparse. There was a large solid desk with minimal items on it: a penholder, a blotter, some paperwork, and a large ashtray. Over the fireplace stood an ornate mantle and on this were a few framed photographs, a large clock and above it, a painting of Sir Laurence in full military regalia. Beside the desk in an alcove next to the chimneybreast was a collection of shelving, sealed behind locked glass doors, housing rare and expensive porcelain. Possibly *Ming Dynasty*, Straay thought to himself. Below the shelves sat a large well-used cast iron safe. Over by the door, almost hidden from view, an old-fashioned hat stand stood, looking suspiciously unused. Nothing in the room, however, seemed out of place.

After a short discussion, DuPont produced the will and a pen, and Straay and the cook witnessed Sir Laurence's signature. Once complete, the cook left, followed shortly by DuPont.

Sir Laurence, who had watched the back of DuPont carefully, indicated Doctor Straay should shut the door.

Chapter Four

Sir Laurence's Plea

Doctor Straay had watched the domestic and the lawyer leave the room and wondered, not for the first time, why he was there. Sir Laurence poured two generous glasses of whiskey and, handing one to him, took a gulp of his own. It seemed to steady him.

'Do you enjoy music, Doctor Straay?'

'That depends on what type.' He lifted the glass to his lips and let a little of the spirit pass onto his tongue, savouring the flavour and allowing it to almost evaporate into his mouth. It was, like everything else in the house, an expensive brand.

'Well, what are your favourites?'

Straay swallowed the whiskey in one gulp and placed the glass carefully onto the table. 'The classics are my favoured choice. Mozart, Stravinsky, Bach.'

Sir Laurence let out a sigh of relief. 'Well thank goodness for that at least. For a moment I was worried you might be a regular Philistine. Although Stravinsky is a bit modern for my taste.'

Straay watched him intently. He hoped this preamble was the build-up to something a little more interesting than simply musical taste.

'I find music to be quite a challenging but rewarding subject, psychologically speaking.' Straay folded his arms and dropped his chin to his chest. He hoped this posture would give the impression he was expecting more, much more. However, Sir Laurence ignored it.

'I'm not sure I understand what you mean.'

There was an almost imperceptible shrug of his shoulders. 'How we process music, how we react, behave, the way we separate the physical from the psychological.'

'Everything has a far deeper meaning in your field, doesn't it?'

'Everything always does, Sir Laurence.' He knew the man wanted to talk, but clearly, he wasn't in any rush to do so.

'How do you separate it?'

'I'm sorry, separate what?'

'The physical and psychological experience in music?'

'I start with the assumption that hearing a piece of sound is purely a physical experience, and listening to music is the psychological effect which this experience creates.'

The men stared at each other. There was an awkward silence in the room. Straay felt he could have elaborated on his answer, maybe even drawn Sir Laurence into a debate about it, but ultimately decided this small talk was pointless and leading nowhere. Sir Laurence finally sighed.

'Gilbert and Sullivan, now there are some composers for you!' Gregson watched for a reaction.

Straay nodded.

'Yes, they do give one a greater insight into the psychology of the English.'

An awkward silence filled the room.

'Look here, Straay, I want to be completely honest with you.'

Straay smiled inwardly. *At last,* he thought.

'You perhaps wish to tell me the true reason you invited me here tonight?'

'No fooling you I see. Good man.'

'No, it is not possible to fool me. Everyone eventually tells me everything I want to know, even if they do not believe they have done so.' Straay was silent for a moment. He could see Sir Laurence was wrestling with a heavy burden. He was uneasy in mind. There was a slightly nervous twitch in his right hand. Unconsciously he massaged it. At length Sir Laurence's indecision was gone.

'I need your advice. Well, actually, I need your help.'

'Tell all to me, I shall be happy to advise you.'

'I think I'm in danger.'

'By what means? Physical or otherwise?'

'That's the bloody problem, I don't know. It's just a feeling. Well, more than a feeling actually.' Sir Laurence sighed.

'You mean a premonition?'

'Yes. I mean, look, I'm rich. It's not a secret. Everyone wants something from me, one way or another.'

Straay considered this carefully. Sir Laurence sat down behind the desk. Straay walked over to the mantle and absentmindedly rearranged the photographs. He looked up at the picture for a moment.

'You are concerned somebody here might consider killing you for your fortune?'

'Frankly, yes.'

'What has happened to make you think this now?'

Sir Laurence frowned. 'I don't quite understand.'

'Well, you have been rich for some years, yes? Why now does it concern you more than, say, a year ago, or maybe five years ago?' Straay stepped away from the mantle.

'Oh I see.' Sir Laurence thought for a moment. 'I can't put my finger on it. I overheard a few conversations between Powell and Heskith, and there's Lady Agatha—she always wants more money! Then there were the accidents…'

'Accidents?' *Now we're getting somewhere,* he thought. 'These seem more interesting. Explain them to me; be precise in your detail.'

'Well, the first was out at a shoot. We have one every year, you know, pheasant, wood pigeons, that sort of thing. Anyway the Major, Jonny, accidentally fired a shot. Nearly got me. If I'd been a minute faster in walking, it would have killed me. We laughed it off, but something he said worried me.'

'What did he say, exactly?'

"Sorry old boy, bit trigger happy there! Agatha will probably be disappointed I missed!" or something near to it. I just couldn't, can't believe he'd be out to kill me—not after what we went through together in the war—so I never thought any more about it. Then there was the time we all went fishing on the lake. My boat was fine the day before, but not long after I launched her, the damn thing fell apart. I nearly drowned that day. If it hadn't been for Powell, I might well be dead. Two accidents in such a short space of time. Can't be coincidence…'

'Well as isolated incidents go, these could be simple accidents.' He paused before saying, 'They could also be attempts on your life.'

Sir Laurence nodded.

Straay continued: 'If they are accidents you have nothing to fear, but...' Again a pause. 'I believe you are right to be cautious.'

'I also overheard a brief conversation between DuPont and Jonny. Pretty heated, I can tell you. I don't know what it was about, but I heard DuPont say: *"It's going to happen soon enough so you two had best get used to the idea."* To which Jonny replied, *"Over my dead body. You stop prying into other people's affairs or something might happen you won't like."* The last thing I heard was Jonny saying something like, *"Take your cut, or step aside."* When I came into view, they both shut up like oysters. Tried to pry it out of Jonny but he just laughed and said it was nothing serious.'

Straay considered this conversation together with the accidents, weighed up the possibilities, and finally came to a conclusion.

'Then I have an answer for you; simply make it obvious you intend to leave no one anything in your will, yes? Have a new one drawn up.'

'What use would that be?' he asked, puzzled.

'Well, I suggest if someone here is considering killing you for what they might receive upon your death, you simply make it that no one benefits at all. This may dissuade them from taking action, if these actions are real and not figments of the mind, you understand.'

'I see…' Sir Laurence was thoughtful for a moment.

'It's a little more complicated than that, though. I can't very well cut my daughter out, now, can I? Then there's Agatha. With her it's impossible. You see, she is the sister of my late wife. A legacy went to her from my wife's estate. One I currently manage. When I die, if she is still alive, she inherits the entire estate.'

'Your wife's estate includes this house?'

'Yes and practically everything in it.' He said quickly, 'The money goes to Milly along with my estate, and my business. Frankly, it isn't as much as I'd hoped to leave her. Still, it is considerable.'

Straay had taken out a notebook and pencil. 'When did your wife die?'

'Fifteen years ago exactly, to the day.'

'Oh, so this is, forgive the way I word this, the anniversary?'

'Yes.' Voice as firm as flint. Straay filed this for reference later.

'So then, Milly is how old?'

'Thirty-two,' he said fondly.

'So she was seventeen when her mother died.'

'That's correct.'

'What will Milly inherit upon your death?'

'Around sixty thousand pounds in cash, the contents of my house, cars, boats, any other little collectable knick-knacks. She'll also inherit the sixty-eight percentage stake in my business. That alone is worth around another thirty thousand a year.'

Straay whistled, 'Such an inheritance a person might well kill for.'

'Not Milly! Never! She's been my rock ever since her mother died.'

'People have died for significantly less, Sir Laurence.'

Straay was silent. Eventually he asked: 'If Lady Agatha died before you, where would her inheritance go?'

'Split up amongst the surviving members of her family. The house is ultimately left to Milly. Agatha can't sell it.'

'It is strange your wife didn't leave her estate to her daughter.'

'They didn't see eye to eye on a lot of things. She was a hard Victorian woman. Milly is modern and has a mind of her own. Her mother felt Milly wasn't deserving of her fortune. Milly has a head for business. It was at odds with my wife's upbringing. Because of this, Milly was cut out. There was no love lost between them.' For a moment, he lost his façade and Straay was able to see a darker bitter man. It lasted a moment then Sir Laurence regained his composure.

Straay considered many options and possibilities, but ultimately came back to his original idea.

'Then make it obvious you intend to leave everything to Milly. You cannot change the requirements of your wife's will, but any legacy you might have left to servants, friends, other family, you should withdraw. At least make it known you have done so. No one saw the contents of the will. Only you and DuPont know what it truly contains. If you do this, I think you may well avert the kind of disaster you foresee happening. It is of course entirely up to you, but I think it a wise precaution.' There was something else.

'Sir Laurence, I suggest you find yourself a new lawyer, too.'

'What? You think DuPont might be in on it?' He seemed genuinely shocked for a moment, and then sniffed. 'Money grabbing lawyers, eh?'

'I do not know for sure I believe there is an "it" as you say,' Straay remarked, 'but surely if you consider what you already know, DuPont is an interested party.' *And there's something odd about the man I don't yet understand.*

Sir Laurence looked out of the window for a moment and rubbed his chin. He was deep in thought.

'Does he inherit?' Straay narrowed his eyes as he awaited the answer.

'Yes.' He turned back and looked Straay straight in the eyes. What was going on behind them, Straay couldn't ascertain. He felt he was missing something. 'Five thousand pounds.'

'Anyone else?'

'Powell and Jonny both benefit from my will, everyone you met today has a good reason to want me dead.'

'Then by now it must be obvious to you what you need to do.'

'Yes, you're right, although I hope I'm wrong. I'm worried though. It's enough to drive a man crazy enough to put a bullet through his own head!'

'Forgive me for saying this, Sir Laurence, but you do not seem to me the type of man who considers such an option.'

'We can't always be right about people all the time, Straay,' Sir Laurence said sadly.

'No,' he agreed. 'Tell me something. How did you know about me, before the boat I mean?'

Sir Laurence smiled. 'You remember George Halloway, don't you?'

At the use of Halloway's name, Straay stiffened slightly. 'Yes, the last case I worked in England, he was involved.'

'Chandrix, right?'

'Indeed.'

'Well he told me about you, that's how I knew.'

Straay nodded thoughtfully.

◆

The night had been long and since Straay had missed dinner, he was grateful that Sir Laurence's butler had made up a cold platter for him.

The kitchen was like the rest of the house. Tidy. He sat at the kitchen table to eat the meal, much to the annoyance of the domestic staff. *Guests don't usually sit and eat with servants, but here is where I want to be.*

'Sit and tell me a little about this house, Mr Dawson,' Straay said between mouthfuls. Dawson looked oddly uncomfortable for a moment, but eventually took a seat at the table.

'Just Dawson, Sir.'

'Ah, sorry. Dawson, then. Please to continue.'

Straay observed the hesitation. It was evident Dawson was agitated. He appeared to be upset at the intrusion, the interruption of his schedule. His strict adherence to service demanded he must answer the question eventually. His loyalty to his master meant he didn't have to answer any questions honestly, but Straay knew that already.

'It's an old house sir, with a long history. Been here a generation or two. I'm sure there's a book or two in the library about the history of it.'

'In Sir Laurence's family?'

Dawson was shocked. 'Oh no, sir. This house belonged to his wife, Lady Elizabeth. Of course, she was originally Lady Elizabeth Smythe before she married. This is a Smythe house, sir, *not* a Gregson house.' Straay nodded. It was as he had already been told. Still, it didn't hurt to corroborate information. He had gained something new, however. Dawson's loyalty. Not to his master but his long dead mistress. *Interesting.*

'Forgive me but it appears to be a Gregson house now, does it not?'

Dawson did not answer.

'Her death must have been a tragedy.'

'To some, I suppose that would be true,' Dawson remarked unguardedly. He had been rattled by the last question, Straay inwardly smiled. Without looking up from his plate, he asked:

'But not to others?'

'I'm not one for idle gossip, sir.' Dawson's answer was firm. There was a steely look in his suspicious eyes.

'I apologise if I offended you,' Straay finished his meal and took a drink of water.

'You have not offended me, sir.' *A lie.*

'What I meant was, there were others in the family who were not saddened by her loss? Possibly others not in the family? She was a hard Victorian woman, so I'm told. Hard on the staff. You understand what I'm saying?'

'I understand perfectly, sir. Lady Gregson was mistress in this house, and she is remembered fondly by those who knew her well but not by some of the staff, particularly the younger men, who were treated very harshly. They are gone now. My Lady dismissed the men, kept the women. Until her death, I was the only man she allowed to work in this house.' Dawson tried to be conversational.

'Interesting. Do you know why Lady Elizabeth dismissed the male staff?'

'I'm sure I couldn't say, sir.'

Couldn't or won't? Straay wondered.

'How many staff work here now?'

'Myself, Cook, the Scullery Maid (she gets everything ready, peeling potatoes, opening tins, that sort of thing.) There's Mary, of course, Lady Agatha's maid, and two girls clean the rooms during the week and serve breakfast and dinner. At weekends, there are only three of us; five during the week and depending on whether we have guests, maybe six, but no more.'

'So this evening, there are just the four of you?'

'Yes, sir.' He stood. 'If you're finished, the cook and I would like to clean the kitchen.'

A dismissal. Politely given but a dismissal it was.

'Yes I am finished. Please, tell the cook I enjoyed the food. I will go and join the others in the smoking room.' Straay smiled and left the kitchen. The door was about to close when he caught it quickly and re-entered as a sudden thought occurred to him. He observed Dawson's narrowed eyes on what would have been his back, and the sour look on the face of the cook in the butler's pantry doorway. Both of them quickly became expressionless. The cook did a little curtsy as she entered and cleared his plate from the table.

'Was there something further, sir?'

'No, thank you,' he said, maintaining eye contact. 'I think I got what I needed.'

◆

Straay passed the clock in the hallway and checked it against his own pocket-watch. It was an old habit. The time was exactly nine fifty. He left the hall and entered the smoking room. There were three people in the room. Sir Laurence and Major Heskith were playing cards at a table by the window. Desmond DuPont, behind Sir Laurence, was watching, a large brandy in one hand, a cigar in the other. They were so heavily absorbed in their game they hadn't noticed he had entered the room. He picked up a glass, poured himself a whiskey, and added a little water. He quietly walked over to the card table and stood behind the Major. Sir Laurence smiled at him.

'Had some food now? Bet you feel better for it, eh?'

'Oh yes indeed, the food was very good. I am well fed now!'

'Your go Larry,' Major Heskith said stiffly.

'Right you are Jonny, two hearts.'

'Three diamonds!'

'Four no trumps!' Sir Laurence smiled at his hand.

'Hmm,' Major Heskith said slowly, 'Six clubs.'

Straay wandered over to the fireplace and warmed himself, as the game went on. He lit a cigarette and looked up as DuPont joined him.

'Silly, really,' DuPont said looking into the flames.

'Pardon?' Straay blew the smoke away from DuPont's face.

'Those two, playing this made-up bridge game night after night. It's all a bit mad really, just the two of them.'

'Ah well, sometimes the games we make up are far more exciting than the ones laid out for us by others, don't you agree?'

'No, not really. Established games have rules and you can play with others.' There was a tinge of bitterness in his voice.

'You never played make believe as a child? Never made up your own games with a good friend? A special friend?'

'Well, yes, as a child.'

'You think their game is childish?'

'Frankly, yes, it's made up nonsense.' He took a sip of his brandy.

'And yet, if they wrote the rules down and explained them to you, it would not be childish would it? It would become a real game, a game others could play, that perhaps you could play too?'

'They wouldn't write down the rules, they probably make them up as they go along.'

'But if they did,' Straay persisted, 'the game would be like any other, would it not?'

'I suppose so,' DuPont said reluctantly.

'You are fond of Sir Laurence. He is a good friend, yes?'

'Yes…' His eyes were fixed on a flame in the fireplace. The dancing orange light flickered across the reflective surface of his unfocused eyes. 'A good friend…'

Straay watched him for a moment. 'You have been friends for how long?'

DuPont shifted his focus from the hypnotic flames.

'I don't know, now...' He took a sip of his drink. 'Probably about three years. I knew him before then, but only in passing.'

'Ah, and how did you become friends?'

'Through Jacob Powell. I came to a dinner party and Jacob introduced me to Larry. As it turned out, he needed a lawyer so I jumped at the chance. We've been friends ever since.' DuPont smiled as he spoke. Straay turned back to the fire and flicked his spent cigarette into the flames. The contact created a shower of sparks. When he finally spoke, it was with such softness DuPont had trouble hearing him.

'Friends are our lifeline in this world. Cut them off and we sink. Keep them close and we prosper.'

'That was very profound,' DuPont said with a slightly puzzled expression.

'Just a little advice, Mr DuPont,' Straay said, finishing his drink.

'I'm not jealous you know,' DuPont said, hastily adding, 'of Heskith, I mean.'

'No?'

'Not at all.' He smiled an unconvincing smile.

'And now,' Straay said, before DuPont could utter a further response, 'it is time for bed.'

◆

Straay said goodnight to them and retired to his room. It had been a very interesting night. *There is certainly a lot going on in this house,* he thought to himself. *Dark corners and secrets.* He pondered on a few things that had struck him.

Was Sir Laurence in real danger? Clearly, he thought so. Sir Laurence was not as tough as he made out. He was frightened. Could this fear have manifested in such a way as to produce a *paranoiac* effect, causing him to foresee non-existent possibilities? Was he simply misinterpreting innocent actions or activities? Considering the accidents he mentioned, it was certainly a sound analysis, but something didn't seem right. Ignoring the possibility that Sir Laurence may have been lying about everything, if he was paranoid, the half-heard conversations would significantly heighten this fear, in an already suspicious mind. Straay wasn't convinced. The man had been through the war. He'd probably been closer to death on more than one occasion. He didn't fit the paranoid type. His character was too strong.

This man is not paranoid.

This man is king of his castle and everyone has reason to envy him for being so.

He moved on to Sir Laurence's reaction to DuPont regarding Dawson the butler, which gave him pause. *What history is there between these three people?*

His emotional response or rather non-response when talking about his late wife was also significant, he was sure about that. The lack of any pictures of her or any evidence that she had existed at all, bothered him.

Then there was the Major.

What exactly is his relationship to Lady Agatha?

No one could fail to spot the softness with which he spoke to her, or the way in which he patted her hand when they sat together. Yet it seemed contrived somehow. All for his benefit. Why, also, did he make the comment about possible crimes, only to shrug them off?

Why was Doctor Powell staring angrily at DuPont, only to avert his gaze when caught in the act? The question was not easy to answer, although perhaps it had something to do with the doctor's introduction of DuPont to Sir Laurence, and the friendship that had blossomed from it. Without a detailed profile on each, it wasn't easy to tell. It was possible that at some point in Powell's past, DuPont had crossed him professionally. Reasonable, but then he frowned. *Why would Powell introduce DuPont to Sir Laurence if he didn't trust him?* It would have to be something else. Something that happened after the introduction, perhaps?

Straay yawned and slipped into bed.

'What is it you would say, Sherlock? I cannot build bricks without clay. Truly I have some bricks to build here and the clay exists in these people I share this house with.'

With this thought in mind he sighed, closed off the light, and sank into a dreamless sleep.

Chapter Five

Sir Laurence Dies

A deep hammering from somewhere close by woke Straay suddenly. He blinked a few times and held his breath, staring at an object in the room, focusing on it, not moving a muscle. His heart raced and he could hear the beating of it. Feel it throughout his body. A few beads of sweat trickled down his neck.

It was a throwback to the war. As a child, he and his family were frequently in hiding. From his earliest memory, he remembered his mother's soothing voice, willing him to wake, urging him to remain still and quiet. He could recall the steel arm of his father holding him down, shaking in anticipation and fear. Although his eyes had been as strong as flint, deep down he knew his father had always been scared, scared for his family, scared at what he might have to do to save them, to save himself. How many times had he woken and seen spiders crawling along the floorboards centimetres away from his face?

'Doctor Straay!' It was an urgent voice, accompanied by banging on the thick oak door.

He shook the fear away and jumped out of bed, grabbed a dressing gown and opened the door. There, standing in the doorway, was Desmond DuPont in the most awful state.

'What has happened?' Straay asked, fearing the answer.

'Larry has shot himself,' DuPont said, white faced. 'Shot himself…'

The first thought that struck him was simply why hadn't he heard a shot? For now, that question would have to remain unanswered. He exited his room and descended the stairs quickly, DuPont following. He heard the voices down the hall and there, beside the study door, the group of guests and domestic staff had all assembled. He read as much as he could from their expressions. Guilt, anger, frustration, sadness, misery and, he thought, joy. They parted for him. Lady Agatha was comforting a very distressed girl who must be Milly, Straay thought. Her eyes were red with tears. Dawson and the Major both stood in the doorway. As Straay went to enter, Dawson stopped him.

'We should wait for the police.' Dawson looked haggard and thoroughly destroyed within, but it was clear he was trying to maintain the appearance of the same calm, emotionless butler he'd spoken to just hours before. Major Heskith shrugged.

'Seems little point, man shot himself, didn't he? What a shame. What a shame.'

Straay turned to the Major, a man of authority and a man used to following orders. He spoke sharply and with precision.

'Major, please take everyone into the smoking room.'

Heskith paused for a moment and then nodded, tacitly accepting Straay's taking control of the situation. 'Come along everyone...I'll get us all some brandy. I know I could use some!'

They slowly made their way back down the hall and entered the smoking room. Dawson remained.

'You have telephoned the police?' Straay ran an eye over the room from the doorway.

'Yes sir, I spoke with them about five minutes ago. They are coming and should be here fairly soon.' Dawson hesitated for a moment. 'Should I go to the smoking room too, sir?' he asked, tears forming in his otherwise hard eyes.

'Not yet. Did you find the key?'

'No, sir. I had to open it with mine.' Straay took the key from him and locked the door.

'See to it that no one enters this room until the police arrive. I will get dressed.'

It took Straay little time to change from his sleepwear. As he made it back down the stairs, he heard several cars pulling up outside the house. Dawson opened the door to a man who entered, followed by three uniformed Police Constables. The lead officer was tall, well dressed in civilian clothes, with keen grey eyes. He swiftly appraised the foyer and the butler with well-practiced observation before speaking.

'Chief Inspector Drake,' he said politely, 'and you are?'

'Dawson, sir. Sir Laurence's butler. I'm the person who called this tragedy in.'

'Right, we'll try to be as prompt as we can. Take us to Sir Laurence's body."

Dawson stepped sideways and indicated the direction with his hand. It was then that Drake caught sight of a familiar face. Straay smiled as he approached, his hand outstretched.

'You know me, I think, Chief Inspector.'

Drake and Straay met in a handshake.

'Goodness me, Doctor Straay, it's been what, three years? What the devil are you doing here?'

'Three years? Seems like just the other day. As to why I'm here,' he smiled, 'well it's, as they say, a long story, my dear Drake.'

'I look forward to hearing it,' he returned the smile and turned to the butler. With sympathy he said, 'You'd better show us the body now.'

They all fell in behind the butler who led them to the locked door of the study. Straay took the key from his pocket and handed it to Drake.

'I thought it better to lock the door so the room was not disturbed.'

'Good,' said Drake. He turned to Dawson and asked: 'The rest of the household?'

'In the smoking room, sir. Doctor Straay suggested they all gather there.'

'Thought of everything, haven't you?' Drake appreciated the attention to detail.

'I try my best to please.'

Chief Inspector Drake turned to the uniformed officers and gave them instructions. They left, and Straay and Drake entered the room.

'The room is almost exactly the same way it was earlier,' Straay said as Drake scanned the room from left to right.

'Nothing different?'

Drake turned and examined the lock.

Straay shrugged slightly.

'Sir Laurence was not lying dead across the table.'

'Other than that?'

'No, it all looks very much as it was.'

Straay watched as Drake finished his examination of the lock, and carefully checked Sir Laurence's pockets. He found the key.

'Locked door you said. Key was in his pocket.'

The first thing that struck Doctor Straay as he entered further into the study was the smell. Pungent cigar smoke. Sir Laurence's body was slumped forward onto the writing desk. His right arm outstretched in front of him, his left arm hung downwards. They both saw the gun loosely clasped in Sir Laurence's left hand. He was still seated in the chair. To the left of this, a cigar had burnt a deep hole into the carpet.

Chief Inspector Drake wandered around the body for a moment and made a few notes in his notepad. He was careful not to disarrange anything. He left the body and moved towards the fireplace.

Straay examined the body in a little more detail.

'Head wound on the left temple,' he said aloud.

'Well, it's consistent with a shot from that side,' Drake said without turning. He was examining the hearthstone.

The table had practically nothing on it, aside from the ashtray and set of pens in their fancy holder he'd observed earlier in the evening, and Sir Laurence. Straay leaned forward and pulled out a letter partly concealed by the body. He read:

> *'My Dearest Girl,*
>
> *Nothing I write will help you understand why this was necessary. I'm sure at some point, when you are much older than you are now, you will look back at this day and think more kindly of me.*
>
> *Know that I will always love you…'*

Straay moved over to the fireplace and handed the letter to Drake. He scanned it.

'Unusual paper this,' he remarked. 'It's not a full sheet either. Looks like it was torn from a notebook.'

'Or a diary perhaps? You notice the printed lines?' They both looked. 'They are typical of a diary.'

'I wouldn't rule out a notebook though.' Drake looked back towards the body. 'Is there a diary on the desk?'

Straay re-examined it. Finding nothing, he opened each drawer in turn.

'I cannot see one, nor do I see a notebook. There are full sheets of writing paper.'

'Do they match the note?'

'No,' Straay said slightly puzzled. 'They do not…'

'Odd but not significant at this stage.' Drake had moved to the safe. He tried the handle. It was locked. 'It's possibly just a discarded scrap of paper he had at hand.'

'It's possible,' Straay said frowning. He felt Drake was just going through the motions. There was no spark to his work. It wasn't like him at all.

Drake folded the note into a large envelope. On this, he wrote "Suicide note." He then pointed to the clock on the mantle. It was broken.

'Time of death easy to fix from this,' Drake said, removing a bullet from the glass front. 'Eleven Fifteen. Bullet stopped it. Handy. See here,' he knelt down, 'glass shards on the base of the hearthstone. Must have been blown out when the bullet struck the clock.'

Drake placed the bullet into a small white envelope and wrote "clock" on it. Straay was still concerned, but he had to smile inwardly at his police friend's orderly method. Drake stood and Straay went back to the body. He examined the gun closely from a kneeling position. Leaning forward, he smelt the barrel. It had definitely been fired. He moved to the cigar and frowned. The cigar was an enigma.

A series of thoughts and questions rapidly flowed through his mind. *What is it that bothers me here? It is the right kind of cigar. The kind Sir Laurence would smoke. It is fancy, expensive. How had it burnt a hole so deeply into the carpet?*

Cigars tended to go out very quickly. This one had not.

Eventually their survey of the room had to stop. Even though both had formed their own opinions, any further discussion would have to wait. The police surgeon, Doctor Carmichael, had arrived to examine the body.

'Good to see you, Chief Inspector.' he said shaking him warmly by the hand.

Drake introduced him to Doctor Straay.

'Ah yes, the Criminal Psychologist, I've heard of you. You caught the famous Paris mimic if I remember correctly. Wasn't he the one who killed his victims and, dressed up as them, casually walked away from a crime scene in front of all the witnesses?'

'I helped the police to find him, yes,' Straay evaded.

'I followed that case. I'm a bit of an amateur sleuth myself.'

'Everyone I've met since my arrival appears to be,' Straay said with good humour.

'Well, I tend to restrict my sleuthing for the medical examination. It's very sad to have to meet under these circumstances.'

'Yes indeed, doctor, a pleasure all the same.'

Carmichael held Straay's hand firmly and then released it and turned to the body.

'Dear me, this poor fellow has been in the wars!' He twisted the head a little to get a better view of the scar tissue. Once his curiosity had been satisfied, he turned his attention to the fresh bullet wound. After a few minutes of work, he turned back to them.

'Death occurred within an hour to an hour and a half. It's not possible to be completely accurate on the time of death. I know you'll want me to skip the technical details now, so I'll save it for the post-mortem. If you're done with the body, Chief Inspector, I'll have it removed to the morgue.' Drake agreed and the body was removed.

'One moment, doctor, I have a question.' Carmichael finished packing his bag and turned to Straay.

'Of course.'

'In your opinion, how quickly would death have occurred?'

'Instantaneously, given the wound.'

'He could not have been alive for any time, after he had been shot?'

'Oh, very doubtful. Seconds, if at all.' Carmichael clipped his bag together.

'Thank you, doctor.'

'You're most welcome. Incidentally,' Carmichael asked, 'what ever happened to him?'

Straay was puzzled for a moment. 'To Sir Laurence?'

'No, the Paris mimic. Did he get the death penalty in the end?'

'No, he killed his lawyer and hid his body in a cupboard. Disguised as him, he casually took his place in the court. Once the alarm was raised, he walked out of the courthouse in front of the jury, police, and the judge.'

'Really? That's the most brazen thing I've ever heard!'

'I warned them but they knew better,' Straay shrugged.

'We'll I'd better get on with my work.' He turned to Drake and nodded. 'Chief Inspector.'

After the room was cleared, Drake turned to Straay, who forced a smile and thrust his hands deep into his overcoat pockets.

Chapter Six

Suicide

Straay had observed the silent way Chief Inspector Drake took in the scene. It was clear, from his body language, that he wasn't at all thrilled to have been called in to investigate this death.

'It is fortunate that you are here,' Straay said, encouraging Drake back into conversation.

'Yes,' he said with a false smile, 'very fortunate.'

'You don't sound very happy about it?'

Drake shot him a look. 'You're right I'm not. But,' he sighed, 'it just happens I was down here clearing up a fraud case when the call came through to the station.' This time, Drake's smile was genuine. He continued:

'Superintendent George Baker is quite a formidable man and I owe him. George and I have been friends for years. He calls me in, on occasion, to get my expertise on some of his more interesting cases.'

'So he personally drafted you?'

'George has competent men at his station,' he replied nodding, 'but if the situation requires a more delicate hand…'

'I comprehend.'

'Anyway, it's largely thanks to George that I was promoted beyond Inspector. So yes, I owe George a lot.' He swallowed the sigh in his throat. 'So, what were you doing here then?'

'I had an appointment with Sir Laurence. We met on my voyage over. We had a brief discussion related to our professions. He was very interested in crime—an enthusiast, you might say. Specifically crime fiction. After we talked for maybe twenty minutes, he invited me to dinner. I was impressed by him but I was also convinced he had orchestrated the meeting.'

'Oh, how so?'

'Well for one thing, he knew far more about me than he could possibly have learnt from anyone on the boat. The reason why he sought me out in the way he did eluded me at the time. But I was interested, oh yes, very interested.'

'You hadn't met him before?'

'No. I hardly knew the man at all.'

'Does that happen to you a lot, Straay? Invited to dinner by complete strangers?'

'Not often, Chief Inspector. I think Sir Laurence liked to have foreign friends. I also think he wanted to put the cat amongst the pigeons, so to speak. I came as instructed and later discovered my initial theory was correct, he wanted me for some other purpose. Once I got here, he took me aside and proceeded to tell me he felt his life was in danger.'

'Did he now?'

Nodding, Straay said: 'Yes, I shall go over it in greater detail later. Why he couldn't or wouldn't tell me this on the boat remains a mystery; one that possibly will never be solved.

'So, does Superintendent Baker think your experience and position qualifies you better to attend a suicide, than a regular Inspector?'

'Clever, Straay. This man, Sir Laurence, was very well connected.'

'I know. He had some unofficial government position; his cousin is also in the Home Office so he told me.'

'Well,' Drake rubbed his chin. 'I can tell you a little bit more than that. Sir Laurence Gregson sat on four different non-government committees. He also advised, as a sort of silent director, on three military contract committees. He's very well connected with heads of services and is a member of a few top-notch clubs, but politically, he's an unknown. Superintendent Baker was concerned there might be more to it. He knew Gregson well, he said, had played bridge with him and so on. They were friends, so naturally he wanted an experienced hand on this one. I was happy to oblige him.'

'Happy?' Straay noticed his posture and raised an eyebrow.

Drake offered him a tight smile, which seemed to say, 'Let's move on.'

'Well, now you're here, we should get to work.'

Drake scratched his eyebrow. 'Well from what I can see, it's a clear case I'm afraid. Not much work needed here.'

'You think so?'

'It's suicide, no question. All the markers are here. Suicide note, doors and windows locked, weapon in the dead man's hand, key in his pocket and a bullet in the clock for good measure, fixing the time of death. Suicide.'

'But there are still many questions, I think.'

'With your type there always are,' Drake quipped with good humour.

Straay simply said, 'This man, why would he kill himself?'

'Money problems, maybe. Big estate probably caused a lot of financial stress.'

'But here we have a rich man, yes?'

'Well…' Drake thought for a moment, 'okay, maybe he was ill, depressed?'

'We need to know what type of man this was. We have need of his motive I think. There is certain nostalgia around us here. What am I seeing? We have a man nearing sixty years of age who has taste. Expensive furniture, silver tipped walking canes. Hats braided with silk, gold cigarette cases. Order I think. Method. Tidiness.' Straay walked around the room as he spoke. 'He is also a rich man and a hard man. A hard-working businessman, who runs the many business deals as well as the Government work. He is still in full control of his company and household. He never takes no for an answer. He thought he might be in danger because of his wealth; aside from that, from what I saw of the man, he had in my opinion everything to live for. Why then, I ask you, would he kill himself? You understand?'

'Yes, I do understand what you're saying but whatever his motive, the circumstantial evidence clearly points towards suicide.'

'Unless the psychology strongly suggests it wasn't. Then maybe we have to lift our eyes off the ground a bit.' Straay looked directly at Drake, raising his eyebrows slightly.

'Now look, I don't have all the answers. What I do have is a body in a locked room, the smoking gun, and a suicide note. I think I know what stones I'm turning over here.'

'Ah. You see the locked door as circumstantial evidence of suicide, whereas it might be evidence of murder. The psychological view of this evidence suggests it might not be what you assume it is. Your assumption is that a man about to commit suicide would always lock himself in? No, I fundamentally challenge that assumption. Why, for instance, did he not kill himself at one end of his considerable estate?'

Drake considered this for a moment. 'I can't debate the psychological viewpoint with you Straay, you're the expert there. What

I can tell you is, statistically speaking, a high proportion of suicides are done behind locked doors. I can also draw on a lot of experience to support that fact.'

'So, you are turning this probability into a certainty?'

'As opposed to your psychological certainties?'

'Psychological certainties are few, so I do not assume them. Do you not entertain the possibility he was murdered?'

'I'll be happy to entertain it, if you have proofs. As it stands, until such time as I see real hard evidence to the contrary, it's suicide.'

Straay was thoughtful. 'Well, the post-mortem could clear this up, but that will take time.'

'Yes,' agreed Drake. 'It is standard procedure in apparent cases of suicide, but you're right, we won't get many answers for a while from Carmichael.' Drake softened his stance a little. 'I'm not saying there isn't a good possibility of a murder. As you said earlier, rich man… someone is clearly going to be very wealthy… Then, and you rightly pointed out a moment ago, there's his position in the Government to consider, but I can't start a murder investigation on your hunch.'

Straay sighed. 'Truly it is the hunch I have, intuition maybe but then maybe more. I am convinced there are many things wrong here.'

'Okay I'll bite,' Drake flipped his notebook over. 'For example?'

'The cigar for one thing.'

Drake shook his head. 'What the blazes has the cigar got to do with anything? The man smoked one then shot himself; I don't see anything in that.' Drake was beginning to get frustrated now, Straay could see, but he persisted.

'A last request perhaps? I do not know. Then we have the pen.'

'The pen? What's the pen got to do with any of this?'

'I simply commend it to you as a fact worth investigating.'

Drake studied Straay closely for a moment.

'Okay Straay, you're clearly holding something back from me, something you know, or something you found out. I can't help if you don't talk to me. Spit it out man.'

Straay rubbed the bridge of his nose.

'You are right I am holding things back. Feelings, conversations, looks, unspoken things, spoken things. I need to arrange my thoughts because they are jumbled up at this time. I can tell you this. Sir Laurence was fearful someone would kill him. He wanted me here, I think, to prevent it. I believe now whatever the motive was in killing him, it was probably accelerated by my arrival. I am probably the reason why Sir Laurence is dead right now.'

Drake began to understand things a little more clearly now.

'You can't blame yourself for that, Straay.'

'But I do blame myself. I suggested a course of action that would alleviate his fears. I suggested he change the contents of his will so no one benefited from it, you see?'

'Well no, frankly, I don't see but—'

'What if someone overheard the conversation?'

'And decided he needed to die sooner rather than later? Yes, I do see what you're driving at now. Look, the Superintendent isn't interested in theories. He'll want hard evidence to support a murder investigation, so we'd better get him some. He does share your suspicions regarding the nature of the death. In fact he said himself Sir Laurence wasn't a man to take his own life.'

Straay suddenly comprehended. 'Ah, so this is the reason you stick with suicide? You want to be sure you're not already biased?'

'Yes, well, it's important to prove a case, not run on assumptions. I didn't know Sir Laurence, so I have to go with my own observations. Now, I'm still not sure I agree it is murder, but I'll go with your hunch for the moment and we'll investigate this as a suspicious death, acceptable?'

Straay nodded.

'What facts have you so far got to prove your theory?'

'I have already mentioned these facts to you.'

'Okay, let's have them in a logical order this time.'

'I will tell you two of the facts again that give me concern. The cigar smoke and the writing pen and ink.'

'Okay. We found the cigar under the desk, burnt right through the carpet until it went out.'

'Would a dropped cigar usually burn so deep a hole?' Straay asked.

'Actually you'd be surprised how hot the end of a cigar is. Although it does seem odd, it explains the smoke, doesn't it?'

'Yes, indeed it does.' Straay sat behind the desk, 'But let us consider something for a moment. Our man who decided to finish it all, smokes a cigar, then during this he raises the gun in one hand, whilst still smoking a cigar with the other? Engaged in this two-handed affair he pulls the trigger, kills himself and drops the cigar on the floor?'

'Well, it could have been in this ashtray and when he fell against the desk, it dislodged and rolled onto the floor?' Drake walked over to the desk.

'Then where is the ash?'

Drake grimaced. 'I see your point. The desk is clean. If it had happened as I just said, there would be residue on the table. But let me just try this.'

Drake reached into his pocket and pulled out a cigar. He placed it on the table and it slowly rolled forward, away from Straay. Drake knelt on the floor and saw at once, the table had a slight camber.

'Well that answers that. Even if the cigar had been dislodged, it couldn't have rolled backwards towards the body, only forwards.'

Pleased, Straay continued.

'So we get back to the idea he was holding a cigar and a gun in different hands and shot himself. No. It cannot have happened that way, I refuse to believe this; therefore it must have happened some other way. The fact is now curious is it not?'

Drake couldn't formulate a better theory and acquiesced.

'So, what you're saying is, either he was smoking at the time and was shot in the head by an unknown person who caused him to drop the cigar or an unknown person came in and dropped one after he committed the crime?'

'That would mean a boldness do you not think?' Straay shook his head. 'To enter smoking and then to commit a murder? No, in my mind this also is wrong. It can only be Sir Laurence was smoking and an unknown person shot him.'

'Well it does seem the most plausible explanation,' agreed Drake.

'The psychology is all wrong! To end your life in such a way… a man can be said to be mad, but in my experience once the decision is made it is usually cold reason that decides the resulting actions, not madness. A man does not write a note, light a cigar and then in the process of smoking it, shoot himself in the head. He might smoke one first and then shoot himself, but the smoking whilst doing so is all wrong.'

'The pen? The ink?' Drake wanted to move on.

'There is one more problem with the cigar that we have not addressed,' said Straay.

'Okay what's that?'

'What do you smell in this room?'

'Cigar smoke of course,' Drake replied quickly.
'No gunpowder…?'

Chapter Seven

Murder!

There was a moment of sudden clarity and Chief Inspector Drake's eyes went wide.

'You're right! I only smelt the cigar. We should have smelt gunpowder—enclosed space like this, the room should have reeked of it. It's inconceivable I didn't pick up on it.' Drake made a note in his writing pad and Straay felt a little happier because of it. Convincing Drake was always going to be an uphill battle, not because he was stupid, far from it, but he wasn't called Bulldog for nothing. Once he'd formed a theory he usually wanted to stick with it until every thread had been thoroughly and meticulously checked, sometimes double-checked. Straay decided to hasten the thread checking because, in his opinion, they didn't have the time to waste.

'Let us move onto the pen now, I tried writing with it, you saw?'

'Yes I did, why?'

'To test a theory. The fountain pen moulds itself to the hand of the writer. The very nib becomes set in the way a person writes. I noticed two problems with this pen. First, the pen had no ink in it. Curious, that. He had just written a suicide note, but not with this pen.'

'That's interesting,' Drake agreed. 'What was the other point?'

'Let us look at the first point. If he did not write the note with this pen, then where is the pen he used?'

'There were no pens on the body.' Drake began searching the desk drawers. 'There are two other pens in the top drawer, although I'll grant you, they don't look like they've ever been used.' Drake became grimly aware that the little inconsistencies Straay was drawing his attention to, were adding up. He was beginning to see where this was leading. It wasn't pleasant.

'It's true he carried a pen, I saw him use it.' Straay said. 'The pens in the drawer look more like relics, artefacts. Maybe when he is away from his desk, he uses another pen, but this is his writing pen.'

Straay picked up the pen from the table, examining it closely.

'It is well worn and it is often used. This man, he has his little things as we have already established. He has his expensive ink, his old-fashioned pen. You see here, it has no little plunger inside. No storage for ink. It needs to be fed ink to write.'

Doctor Straay held the pen close to his eye and Drake leaned forward so that they were almost touching. 'This is the type of pen a man like Sir Laurence used. It goes very nicely with this old-fashioned writing desk. Not a new pen, an old pen. He likes old things. This is in keeping with the psychological character, the profile we have built, yes?' Straay replaced the pen in the desk holder and the men moved apart.

'Yes, that fits with what we know about the man,' Drake agreed. 'So we have missing gunpowder, and now a missing pen. These two facts alone are suspicious in themselves. Individually they may be overlooked in favour of the other evidence, but together…' He trailed off in thought. Shaking his head slightly he asked, 'What's your second point?'

'Ah! The most interesting point of all. I say to you that the pen moulds itself to the person. This point confirms to me Sir Laurence was killed. I am left-handed, as is Sir Laurence.' Straay dipped the nib of the pen in the inkbottle and proceeded, with a little difficulty, to write on a scrap of paper.

'The pen, it is of the very best quality, yet it splutters and does not glide on the paper.'

He changed it to his right hand.

'Now you see it becomes more cooperative. You comprehend?'

'I agree it's odd, but I'm not sure….' Drake didn't fully understand where this new direction was leading them.

'And this also.' Straay cut him off, standing.

'Sit at the desk a moment, just so. Now reach for the pen and take it. Yes, good. Now replace it and stand here. Now I sit and do the same. What do you see?'

'I see that you have to make an awkward reach for the pen. As a right-handed man, I reach for it without a problem.'

'The pen on the desk was that of a right-handed man.' Straay said finally.

'Well that's an interesting theory, but from what I am told about Sir Laurence, he was left-handed. He wore a wristwatch on his right wrist.

You said he smoked with his left hand, drank from glasses in his left hand. Why then has he suddenly changed to a right-handed man?'

'When we were on the boat, and when we were in this room signing the will, I watched him write with his right hand, but the penholder, it is fastened down. It cannot move.'

'So… so he *was* right-handed then?' Drake was slightly confused.

'Yes, a puzzle eh?' Straay said with a smile. Straay liked puzzles. Drake sighed. He didn't like puzzles at all.

'Well, it's hardly conclusive.' The investigations of all the threads were still not fully exhausted yet. At length Drake said, 'I do agree, though, that right-handed men don't tend to shoot themselves with their left hand.'

'Well one thing is clear,' Straay said resolutely. 'He couldn't have been smoking and shooting himself with the same hand, could he?'

'No… The cigar could only have been in his left hand because if he had dropped it from his right, it would have either fallen to the right of the chair or across the table.'

'Correct, ignoring all other facts for a moment. Can you see any other explanation for the position of the gun and cigar?'

'No I can't'

'Neither can I.' Straay's brow furrowed.

'Drake, he did not shoot himself. Someone else did.'

'It's all pointing that way isn't it? Is it possible that someone could have moved the penholder? I noticed here on the table there is a mark that could indicate that it had been in this alternative place before today.'

'No one entered this room after he died. Only the door was opened. Dawson and Major Heskith stopped anyone entering. I had the door locked as soon as I got to the room. So really, only a person who was with him when he died could have moved it, but why would anyone bother?'

'It just occurred to me,' Drake turned his attention to the desk again. 'There's always the possibility that this was a suicide dressed up as a murder. There is one fact against this, though. You've just proved Sir Laurence was right-handed. Naturally he wouldn't have shot himself with his left hand.'

'Unless he was trying, for some unknown reason, to keep up the pretence that he was left-handed…' Straay said slowly.

'What? Hold on a moment, what are you saying? Didn't you just spend the last twenty minutes persuading me this wasn't suicide?' Drake said angrily.

'Sorry, you are right. I do not believe that this was anything but murder. I said my thoughts were jumbled, you see.' Straay rubbed his temple.

Drake said finally, 'Well we're still going to need to find some evidence to persuade the Superintendent to open a murder investigation. Granted we have the missing pen and the lack of gunpowder smell in the room, and the position of the gun and the cigar, but a good lawyer could turn that to rags in the courtroom. We need something that cannot be disputed.'

Straay agreed. As much as these facts were worth noting, without hard evidence to back them up, they were circumstantial at best.

'There is one thing that still bothers me more than anything else.' Drake said, pulling out the suicide note from its envelope. 'If I'm to agree with you about your profile of the man, why would he write what he did? It's in his handwriting; there's no getting around it.'

'Yes, that is as you say the one big flaw in my profile.'

Straay took the note from him and read it again.

'This note doesn't sit correctly with a murder. If this were a suicide then the note would work, but we would have a different profile entirely, one more complex, determined by the interaction between various factors such as biological contribution, personal history, family history and other circumstantial and direct events leading up to the act.' Straay handed Drake the note back and continued, 'So we work on this case as a murder, and now our profile fits… except for this note.' Straay shook his head.

'Another puzzle?'

'Well if we agree this was a murder, then it is obvious that someone wanted us to believe otherwise. The note therefore was a necessary prop. It could have been forged. Whatever the reason, we have to dig deeper. We have built up our profile by simply looking at his room, the things Sir Laurence has, et cetera. What we must now do is add to the profile and unlock the missing idiosyncrasies of his social and family environment. There we will find the answers.'

Drake put the note away.

'Perhaps the daughter can enlighten us on the point; it was surely written to her?'

'That is as good a place to start as any,' agreed Straay.

Drake studied the clock on the mantle for a moment.

'Now that I'm thinking more about the possibility of a murder, there's something that doesn't add up.'

'Yes, that clock, it has been weighing heavily on my mind too.' Straay moved beside him at the fireplace.

'This evidence, along with the alarm being raised, clearly established the time line. With the bullet embedded in it, we knew beyond doubt that the death occurred at eleven fifteen.' Drake held the clock for a moment longer and then replaced it on the mantle. 'We have to assume that the bullet in the clock was staged, yes?'

Straay nodded.

'Right, so we're now investigating the possibility someone else was in this room. That person put the clock forward, smashed it, and pushed the bullet into the hole. How did they leave the room before the door was opened? Was anyone missing when you got to the door?'

'No one was missing. A few minutes, if anything, passed before my arrival. Certainly not enough time for someone to get out of the room unseen. Even if someone had been in the room when it was opened, one of the others would have definitely seen them come out. It's possible that someone may conceal the truth, but I think unlikely.'

Drake was thoughtful.

Straay then said: 'Considering your own logic, it must occur to you if this person put the clock forward, then it would mean the clock was not already at eleven fifteen.'

'That makes sense,' Drake agreed. 'Why bother putting the clock forward at all in that case? Are we now saying that this murder occurred earlier and its discovery was meant to be at eleven fifteen?'

Straay considered something else. He left the fireplace and knelt down beside the desk. Drake followed him and saw what he was looking at.

'How long would it take for a cigar to burn through this carpet?'

'I'm not entirely sure, but I imagine it would take some time.' Drake allowed his fingers to probe deep into the burnt mesh hole.

'Ten minutes, maybe?' It was a suggestion, more than a question.

'Possibly longer,' Drake said standing. 'It's not easy to give an accurate timeline because we don't fully know the conditions at the time.'

'This then must answer your initial question regarding material evidence.'

'I'm not sure I follow you.'

'Well, we have an anomalous cigar burn. It throws our timeline out completely, doesn't it? At the very least it indicates that death occurred no less than ten minutes earlier.'

A smile slowly spread across Chief Inspector Drake's face. 'It does. With this, we can tie in all the circumstantial evidence as well as the physical findings. There's no question now—it's murder.'

Straay was running many scenarios around in his head, and he could tell by the expression on Drake's face, he too was formulating ideas. Straay watched as Drake ran a hand through his thick hair. He'd convinced him by his persistence. Now it was time to work together to get the events clear for the inevitable discussion with the Superintendent. At length, Drake said:

'Let me walk through the logic of this with you, just so we're on the same page.'

'Good idea.'

'Sir Laurence sat here and maybe he heard a noise or someone called his name and he turned.' Drake acted out the conversation for his own benefit. Straay found it useful to see physically the positions and the movement for himself.

Drake continued:

'The shot entered the left side of his head and exited through the right, but goes where?'

'Not into the clock,' Straay said smiling.

Drake looked over at the clock and then back at Straay.

'No...,' Drake said slowly. 'Okay, so we know his cigar dropped from his left side to the floor just beside him. We know he smoked with his left hand, so this is consistent with our profile.'

Again, Straay agreed.

'This, we surmise, happened when he was shot and as we know, it apparently burnt through the carpet. So based on this evidence, we can now say with some certainty the shot occurred earlier than we originally thought.'

'So far we are in agreement.'

Drake paused for a moment. 'My men will only have done a cursory check of the room, based on the standard procedures for suicide. Now that we believe, well, know it's a murder, we'll need to have every part of this room searched.'

Drake thought for a moment and then chuckled.

Straay looked puzzled at him and he waved a hand.

'Sorry, just amused me for a moment that a murder or suicide all hinged on a cigar.'

'Hinge? Hinge? Waarom? Het raam! Ik wil naar het raam kijken!' Straay said in sudden excitement.

'What is it, Straay?' Drake jumped out of the chair.

'The window! I must check the window!'

'What about it?' Drake said examining it closely.

'Ha,' Straay said, 'I have it. It's possible... yes, it's certainly possible, but no, it can only be this way.' Straay was muttering to himself in Dutch. Drake stepped aside and watched as his friend examined the lock. Finally, he turned and said apologetically, 'This window is older than the one on the other side. You see here that this is an older clasp. The window to the left is newer and has a snip lock.'

'I don't follow your logic.' Drake said, examining the window for himself.

'Forget that for a moment. If I'm right, then the shot did not occur in the room.'

'You think the shot came from outside this window?' Drake was wide eyed.

'There are a few indications that suggest it. If it was so, Sir Laurence was side on with this window when he was shot.'

'I'm following you,' Drake said moving swiftly to the doorway.

'So the bullet would have hit,' he ran his hand around the doorframe and said triumphantly, 'here!'

'Bravo Chief Inspector, now you see, we make headway.' They both returned to the window. Straay opened it and said: 'It was not closed at the time Sir Laurence was killed.'

'That also explains the lack of gunpowder, but that doesn't explain how the window was locked when the body was found.'

'I will show you how someone could close and lock this window from the outside.' Straay opened the window, lifted the latch lock carefully, so that it rested against the window frame, and then pulled a reel of black cotton from his pocket. He tied one end of it loosely to the lock, careful not to disturb it, and stepped back. He then gave a sharp pull on the cotton and when the window closed, the latch flipped down and locked itself. Drake was amazed.

Straay removed the cotton and re-opened the window. He ran a hand along the hinge and rubbed his fingers and thumbs near to his nose.

'Oil,' he said answering the look Drake was giving him.

Drake then went to the newer window and tried to open it. 'This window hasn't been opened in the last few days, possibly not in the last few months. Just a moment. An open window also explains how a cigar could continue to burn, long after it was dropped, the draft must have kept it ignited.'

Straay said nothing. He was lost in thought. His gaze was fixed on the darkness beyond the window.

◆

'Very good, sir, yes, I'll get on it right away. No... Everyone is still here sir; we'll not let anyone leave until we've interviewed them all. I'll do that sir. Very good. Thank you, sir. Goodnight.' Drake replaced the receiver and looked up at Straay.

'Superintendent Baker agrees. It's now an official murder investigation. Well done, Straay.'

The doctor took the praise modestly.

'Now we interview the guests and find our murderer.'

'I've asked a constable to get Doctor Powell back here. Although he did leave early in the evening, I'd still like to interview him.'

'You realise that any number of people could have stood outside that window and killed Sir Laurence; it doesn't have to be a member of this household.'

'Yes it had occurred to me.' Drake rubbed his neck. 'What's your gut feeling though?'

Straay thought back to the introductions made earlier that evening.

'Honestly, I think the murderer is someone in this house.'

Drake sniffed. 'I agree. Someone in this house had to make a shot-like sound at exactly eleven fifteen. Nobody heard an earlier shot, so it's highly probable that the first shot was silenced.'

Straay was in deep thought as Drake continued.

'I'll ask my team to do a fingerprint search of the room and windows. I'll also check the outside for footprints and so on. Most of this will have to wait until morning though. I'll also have a section of carpet and an identical cigar taken back to the laboratory. Let's see if we can establish just how long it would take to burn a hole into that carpet. We have a new timeline to establish. I suggest we interview the household and then let them sleep. It's already nearly two in the morning, if we leave it any later we'll get nothing useful from any of them.'

Straay agreed. Things were moving positively forward and his thoughts now turned to what was needed next to apprehend the culprit.

'We're dealing with a clever and resourceful murderer, Drake. We don't know the full picture behind this, and there are some questions I need answers to. I've made a list. Is it possible to get me this information?'

Drake took the paper and read the questions.

'Yes I should think so; some interesting questions here… I'll ask Sergeant Hawkins to look at this for you. He works in the records office at the station. He's been in the force here for over forty years. I should imagine he would be able to get you whatever you need, or at the very least, know who to ask to get it. Scotland Yard should be able to assist with the military information.'

◆

Chief Inspector Drake had arranged for each person to be interviewed in the lounge, adjacent to the smoking room. The chairs were arranged so that Straay and Drake sat opposite the person being interviewed. Because it was late, they agreed not to mention murder until the morning. They wanted the facts leading up to the death. Harder questions would be asked once the preliminary questions were out of the way. The first person to be interviewed was Major John Heskith.

Chapter Eight

Major John Heskith, OBE

Heskith was an old soldier of impeccable dress. His dark blue suit was cut well and his shoes gleamed under the glow of the lights. His left hand was permanently in his jacket pocket, unless he was seated. He had an upright, stiff posture when standing.

Drake indicated a chair.

With military precision and fluidity of movement, he undid his jacket button, sat—pulling out both jacket-tails as he did—crossed his legs, interlocked his fingers and angled a highly polished shoe at them both.

'Can you please tell us a little about last night?' Drake asked pleasantly—his way of disarming suspects. He felt it was better to be polite and agreeable when starting this process, then to go in heavy. People tended to respond more positively to politeness.

'Where'd you want me to start, old boy?'

'From the dinner, if you would be so kind.'

'Right. Dinner at eight. We were waiting for Doctor Straay but old Dawson came in with a message saying he was late due to the trains or something, so Larry said he'd have something cold prepared for him when he arrived. Powell had given Larry a medical checkup, and they came into the dining room as we were all seating. Milly sat next to Agatha. We had roast lamb with all the trimmings. Dinner lasted about thirty minutes, give or take. After port and cheese, we went into the smoking room. Girls drank sherry, the boys drank brandy, and we all smoked for a bit. Milly left first, went to her room, said she had a headache. Larry and DuPont were away for, oh, about ten minutes then Doctor Straay arrived. After introductions, DuPont, Straay, and Larry went off discussing something or other and then DuPont came back. Straay and Larry came back about ten minutes or so later. We had some more brandy and Straay went off for food. Agatha went up to bed at around nine forty-five and Powell left about the same time or just before. Not long after that, Straay came back. Larry and I were playing cards. Straay went to bed at about ten, followed by DuPont. Larry and I played for twenty minutes or so and then he looked up at the clock at twenty-five minutes past ten, said he was feeling tired and needed to finish some work, then went to his study. I read my book. I was absorbed by it and didn't realise how long I'd been reading. I heard a shot at eleven fifteen and left the room immediately. The smoking room door was open so I was quickly out. I couldn't quite make out where it came from at first, but it was close. Tried to open the study door but it was locked. I banged and shouted for Larry but got no answer. Old Dawson came down the hall on hearing all the noise. He opened the door with his key. On seeing the situation, I told him to phone the police. The rest you know.'

'What cards did you play?'

'Hmm? Bridge.'

'With just two?'

'What? Well. A form of bridge we'd devised together.'

'If I may say so, you do not seem surprised by Sir Laurence's death?'

'Surprised? No.'

'You expected it?'

'Was rich wasn't he? Obvious motive, that.'

'Agreed, an obvious motive, as you say. You don't seem moved by his death at all.'

'I was in the War.' The remark was directed at Doctor Straay with, he thought, a little sneer. 'You probably don't understand that, doctor, being Dutch.'

Straay smiled at him. 'I was living in Belgium with my family when the Germans invaded, Major. I assure you, Dutch or not, I saw my share of it.'

This didn't seem to change the Major's opinion of him, but it did help Straay to understand that earlier feeling he had, as to why the Major was not happy with him being there. Simple prejudice at Dutch neutrality during the war perhaps, or was it something else?

Drake asked: 'Being "in the war," is that a way of saying you become desensitised to the deaths of others?'

'Something like that.... Watched a chap blow his brains out once, damnable thing.'

'This affected you?'

'Not in the least.'

'You liked Sir Laurence?'

'Yes we were best friends Larry and I. Solid chap. A bit queer in his ways.'

'Was he an emotional man?'

'Not really.'

'Did he have any enemies that you know of?'

'Made his money breaking a lot of people. Probably had many enemies. Hundreds maybe. Was a hard man, old Larry, fact!'

'Any that you know of?' Drake persisted.

'Well, no one springs to mind.'

'He lived in comfort, I see.'

'Well he would, wouldn't he?'

'You think he was depressed at all?'

'No, never! Man was solid. Fact! Anyway if he was, well, a bit out of sorts, not the sort of thing a solid chap says, know what I mean?'

'Until he kills himself in a locked room, perhaps?'

'Why on earth should a chap of standing lock himself in? Something's wrong there, old boy. What... have his dearly beloveds battering down the door? Don't think you have that quite right. Going down the wrong track there, I fancy. I mean... ex-military officer like Larry? He'd have unlocked the door. Have to think about how you get the bodies off the battlefield, what! It simply doesn't make any sense, that.'

'But it does appear, if you'll excuse me, that he did shoot himself.'

'Look here, Larry was a dependable sort of chap. Suicide? Never. Fact. Murdered he was, and there's an end to it.'

'But the evidence looks like suicide. Why do you say it looks like murder?'

'The locked door man! Who has the key but the murderer?'

'It was in the pocket of Sir Laurence, Major.'

'Oh. Well, it's damn fishy still. Fact!'

'I shall tell you some facts, Major. The room was locked. The windows were locked. The gun was in his hand, with one bullet fired. The key to the door was in his pocket, there was a suicide note on the table and the clock had been smashed by the bullet, establishing the time of death. These are facts.' Drake watched the Major's reaction carefully.

'Not ones that would have fooled Conan Doyle. Thought you were a detective! Door could have been locked with a duplicate key, man! Then the murderer ran off just before I came down the corridor.'

'I do see your logic but there is one flaw.'

'Oh? Seems a solid theory to me.'

'I apologise, Major. Let me explain. The bullet hit the clock and stopped it. That makes the time of death easy to establish you see. Eleven fifteen and thirty two seconds.'

'Well?'

'You said you left your room as soon as the shot was heard. At eleven fifteen, you said. It takes thirty seconds to go from that room to this. If your door was open, twenty seconds at the most and there is only one exit and entry. It was the sound of the shot that brought you to the door—you said—as soon as you heard it. You had no reason to pause; your door, you said, was open.'

'Fact!'

'Then if I may rely upon your fact. Let me then ask you. Did you see anyone else in the corridor? Hear anyone running away?'

'Well, no…'

'Surely they would have passed the room you were in, wouldn't they?'

The Major shrugged his shoulders. 'Possibly. Anyway, none of this disproves murder. It doesn't prove it either.'

'That is true but it still cannot have been the way you described. Therein lies the problem.'

'As you say.'

'So what explanation is left?'

The Major shifted a little in his chair. He uncrossed his legs and planted his feet firmly on the floor. He leaned in as he spoke: 'Look, Chief Inspector, if you're convinced that old Larry shot himself, I hope you have a bloody good reason why!'

Drake met his gaze, each of them firm as flint. Drake eventually smiled.

'Thank you, Major, we will talk more in the morning.'

The Major sat for a moment longer. He looked from one to the other, annoyed. The Major was not used to be dismissed so.

'Thank you, Major,' Drake repeated, this time raising a hand towards the door.

Sir Laurence Dies

◆

Straay had said nothing during the entire interview after the Major's comment about the war. When the Major, grumbling, finally left, Drake turned to him.

'You all right?'

'Yes I am. I was just pondering a question.'

'Who the culprit is eh? Or how our stiff Major doesn't like being kicked out?'

'No, why was Major Heskith so insistent that Sir Laurence was murdered when all the facts and evidence, in so far as we've allowed it known, clearly point to suicide?'

'Yes he did seem stubbornly fixed on murder. Fact!'

Straay laughed. He put his little notebook into his pocket and pulled out a fresh packet of cigarettes.

'He has an intransigent and bigoted attitude, I fear. It's the kind of attitude that gives the British a bad name abroad, I'm sad to say.'

'What does intransigent mean exactly?'

'His refusal to compromise, his inability to abandon any extreme position or attitude. I see him as a superficial character, we don't get any sense of the man beneath; he is just… flat, two-dimensional even.'

'That does sum him up perfectly then, stiff upper lip. Still, you can't deny the man survived the War. That must have affected him,' Drake said with more compassion than he actually felt.

'One shouldn't forget that,' Straay acknowledged. 'The Major reminds me of a patient I once had to help in a hospital in Holland. He was a war veteran too.' He lit the cigarette, took that important first pull, and slowly exhaled before continuing.

'In every respect he seemed perfectly sound, except once a day we would find him in the cleaning cupboard with the lights off, smoking. He would say it was because he preferred the solitude of a cubicle, where he could have a cigarette in peace. I decided early on that he liked these small dark places because they reminded him of the trenches; it was his shelter against whatever enemy he perceived was after him. I believe that I was that enemy. He wouldn't admit it. He would often awaken in the middle of the night in tears, afraid to go back to sleep, and always be drawn into the same horrific nightmares where he would relive the experiences of the war. His biggest fear was he would end up in some institute for the rest of his life. He created a fictitious world around him, where odd behaviour was transformed into normal behaviour. He was also intransigent. I never gained his trust. I was convinced that he would do himself harm, but I was a junior doctor at the time. My superior was an incompetent man who was not interested in my inexperienced observations.' Straay shook his head.

'What happened to him?'

'When they released him, he found a dark place and cried one last time. They found him dead. He'd pushed a bayonet through his eye, into his brain.'

'That's awful!' Drake was seriously shocked.

'What I'm trying to say here is this; the Major is showing similar signs. He has an almost two-dimensional view of the world around him. It's possibly a symptom of war fatigue. We aren't going to learn much from him because he's shut the real world out; only what he sees now and what he thinks now are relevant to him. That is how I see this man.'

Drake understood. 'How do we reach the real man?'

'Well, that will be a challenge. One I shall relish. Breaking into the "psyche" of a man like Major Heskith is something I am extremely good at, if I do say so myself.' He smiled slightly.

'You okay about that war reference?'

Straay waved a hand. 'It's an attitude I'm used to, we Dutch are made of far sterner stuff.'

Drake wasn't going to argue. He didn't know that many Dutchmen, but he thought Straay had been rattled by the Major, just a little.

'I think it's time we interviewed the next person.' Drake turned to the constable at the door.

'Go and get Lady Agatha, Jennings.'

Chapter Nine

Lady Agatha Smythe

When Lady Agatha was shown into the lounge, she looked at both men and waited. She did not want to be invited to sit. Her head held high, she had the regal air of someone who definitely expected others to stand when she entered a room and, to their credit, both Chief Inspector Drake and Doctor Straay did so. With a pleased expression she glided forward and sat, indicating the two of them should do likewise.

Lady Agatha very much liked old habits.

Lady Agatha had a Victorian view of the world. She believed most assuredly that she was of a higher class than ordinary people. Ordinary people like the Chief Inspector, and foreign doctors, had to understand their place in the world. She had been born into a privileged position and she was definitely not, in any sense of the word, ordinary.

'Thank you for your time, Lady Agatha.' Drake smiled at her.

'You are both most welcome.' She looked regal in her chair, Straay thought, but she also had a keen eye. It darted back and forth between them both. Her eyes seemed to be saying, *"serve me an impertinent question, and I'll bat it right back at you."* She reminded him of a stern schoolmistress, no, an aristocrat. Straay never liked being dared to do anything. He also didn't like stern schoolmistresses or pompous English aristocrats, so he decided to do what was not expected. He asked her an impertinent question.

'You are Lady Agatha, are you not?' Straay asked.

'Of course I am. You know I am. What a silly question!'

'Forgive me,' Straay sat back into his chair. Drake looked at him puzzled for a moment and Straay simply smiled and indicated that Drake should continue with his questions.

'You have had a great shock, I'm sorry to have to prolong this for you, but I have to ask you some questions.'

'Must you?' She asked a little sharply. 'I don't know anything at all.'

Straay seriously disbelieved that, but preferred to say nothing.

'Yes, I fear I must.' Drake replied with an edge in his voice. A subtle edge, which said, "Don't play games with me." Lady Agatha did not miss the tone, or the underlying threat that came with it. She lowered her head slightly. Drake softened his voice and said: 'You may have seen or heard things that might help us, even without knowing their importance at the time. Anything you tell us will help our investigation, you see?'

'Well if you must,' she paused and then smiled. 'Yes, of course I'll help in any way I can.' She straightened out her already immaculate dress.

'You were on good terms with Sir Laurence?'

She looked sharply at him. 'Hardly. The man was a brute.'

Drake raised an eyebrow and glanced briefly at Straay. 'I see. Tell me something about him please.'

'Well, he was rich.'

'From his business ventures?'

'Oh, well, some of it, but not all. His wife, my dear sister, she was rich too, in her own right. When she died…'

'Yes. She died some years back I understand, just after the war ended. What? Thirteen or fourteen years ago?'

'Fifteen,' she corrected him. 'Fifteen years to this day, today is the anniversary of her death. It's why we were all here.' Lady Agatha scratched her left ear.

'I didn't know that. Thank you.' Drake made a note. 'Your sister had a weak heart, I understand?'

'If you say so,' Lady Agatha scratched the back of her left hand.

'You say something different?'

'Oh no. She died of a weak heart all right.' She paused a moment and looked straight into Drake's eyes. 'Bullied she was. Bullied to death. He profited greatly by her death you know, brute. Simple thing to do isn't it. Bully a woman until her heart stops and then bank all her money. This house was hers, you know.' Again, she scratched her left ear. Straay studied her as minutely as he could, without distressing her. She didn't notice his gaze. Were these actions out of nervousness or were they stress related?

'You see, you're really helping here. Again, we didn't know that. Please continue, Lady Agatha.' Drake tactfully kept up the pressure, but was careful not to annoy her.

'Well… I'm not one to gossip,' she said slowly. She was conscious that Straay hadn't spoken and began focusing on him more.

'It's not gossip we want, Lady Agatha,' Straay reiterated. 'We need to get a better understanding or picture of Sir Laurence.'

Drake waited for Straay to finish, then he continued his questions. 'Sir Laurence's wife, your dear sister, she died fifteen years ago. She left her money to Sir Laurence. He became wealthier. His daughter…'

'Oh poor Milly! Poor, poor Milly.'

Drake had found his opening and Straay inwardly smiled. It was a real pleasure to see him interviewing suspects, putting them at ease, always guiding them down the path he had laid out in his mind. Gently nudging them back, when they strayed. Straay knew very few people who could match Drake's interviewing techniques.

Chief Inspector Drake then asked, 'Was she fond of her father?'

'Oh devilishly so. They were inseparable. It's cut her deep, poor little thing, but she's strong. As strong as her father, that one. A little bit shy around men, but she has a good business head. Her father was too stubborn to let her get involved in the business until she showed him where he could save boatloads of money. After that, he gave her an important job, very high up. She loved it.'

'Milly has a good working relationship with her father, as well as the good personal relationship?'

'Oh my, yes. He doted on her, and she on him.'

'Milly loved her mother?'

'Her mother?' Lady Agatha looked down and Straay noted again, she scratched the back of her hand. 'Well of course she did… I mean… well, girls always love their mothers, don't they?' Now he felt more and more that this was stress related. Whatever the reason, she wasn't telling the truth and she unconsciously let everyone know it.

'No, Lady Agatha, they do not always love their mothers,' said Drake, who hadn't noticed the scratch repetition, but was experienced enough to know when someone wasn't being completely honest with him. 'How did Milly take it when her mother died?'

She looked up. 'Well really Inspector—'

'Chief Inspector,' Drake corrected.

'Well Chief Inspector,' she said flippantly, 'You should speak to her about this.'

'I will, but I want to hear this from you as well, if you'd be so kind.'

'It's difficult for me, she was my sister.' Agatha sighed and her shoulders dropped, 'I don't think Milly liked her mother very much, I think she felt that her mother was weak and that she deserved the treatment her father gave her. She didn't. You know, deserve the treatment I mean.'

Straay leaned forward. 'Is that a feeling you got from conversation with her, or did she tell you directly?'

'Well…perhaps a little of both. Milly often said things about her mother, usually when they had had cross words, which became more and more frequent nearer to her death. I sometimes got impressions of it from the way she would look and so on. I think Milly was a little annoyed by her mother. She thought she should simply stand up to him. Milly is a modern child, her mother was a Victorian woman and she knew her place. It's difficult for a modern girl to understand and I think Milly despised her because of it.'

Straay couldn't help feeling this behaviour was strange, and he voiced as much. 'Usually it is the man who is despised in such cases as you describe, not the poor woman who is bullied.'

'Well, yes, I suppose so. Under normal circumstances, I mean. If this were a normal situation, you would be right. This family is far from normal.' She stared forward, her eyes a little unfocused.

'I understand, from Sir Laurence, when your sister died, there was no legacy for Milly.'

'None,' Lady Agatha spat, her attention firmly on Drake. 'All her money and estate went to him, except the pittance I am supposed to live by, and that too is managed by him, the brute. At least I'll get my own money now.' She rubbed her throat and coughed a little. Straay poured her a glass of water from the jug beside him and she took it. He thought he noticed a look of disappointment on her face, but it quickly passed.

Drake asked, 'What can you tell me about last night?'

'Not much, to be honest. Let me see. Well… we went down to dinner at eight...yes, that's right. It was supposed to be seven thirty but we were waiting for you, Doctor Straay. But you didn't arrive on time.' She said this disapprovingly. 'Well… the Major, myself, Milly, Desmond—he's Sir Laurence's lawyer you know. I might say Desmond has taken quite a fancy to young Milly.'

'That is interesting,' Straay said nodding.

'Oh, it's not public knowledge, you understand, but a woman knows these things, Doctor Straay.' She tapped her nose in an "I know a secret" way.

'Go on, Lady Agatha,' Drake said, trying to keep her focused.

'Let me see now…oh, yes. Sir Laurence was a little late to the table because Doctor Powell was giving him a physical checkup. Anyway, they arrived at eight fifteen, I think… We sat and had dinner. I sat next to Milly. It lasted, oh…about forty-five minutes—maybe a bit longer. Then we retired to the smoking room and had sherry; the men drank brandy of course. Can't stand brandy, myself.' She paused again to gather her thoughts. 'What happened next? Oh yes, Milly had a headache and went to bed early. Doctor Straay arrived not long after and had a discussion with Sir Laurence in his study, something about his will if I remember correctly. The doctor left at about nine thirty, I think, and then there was a meeting in the study between you, Doctor Straay and Desmond and Sir Laurence...or was that before he left? I can't quite remember now. The Major was reading a magazine by the window, if I recall—or was it a book?—my memory isn't what it once was.' She laughed dryly. 'Not long after that I went to bed.'

'Did Sir Laurence know that Desmond had taken a fancy to his daughter?' Drake asked.

'I can't say that I know for sure,' she said unconvincingly. Quickly she added: 'You have to understand, Milly didn't say anything directly; it was more a feeling, you know? Desmond and Sir Laurence always spent a lot of time together. He practically lives here. Some mornings they'd go out early, riding; sometimes in the evenings, go out to the summerhouse for hours on end. Sir Laurence treated Desmond more like a son. They did practically everything together, so that is why I think if there was a love interest between Desmond and Milly, he'd certainly be all for it.'

Straay pondered this information for a moment.

Drake made a note in his book and said: 'Your room is above the study I believe?'

'Yes but the floor and walls are very thick. I didn't hear anything, really. Except…'

'Except? Lady Agatha, every detail is essential.'

'Well... I thought I might have heard a sort of popping sound.'

'Popping sound? Where did this sound come from and at what time did you hear it?'

'It's very hard to pinpoint really.' She thought hard for a moment. 'I distinctly remember hearing a popping sound. It wasn't very loud. Outside in the garden, I believe. Close enough to my window to hear, at any rate. It was at twenty past ten, I remember because I had left the window open and got out of bed to close it. Yes… I glanced at the clock. I heard a rustling then a popping sound and that was it. I looked out at the lawn but it was quite dark. I closed the window and went back to bed.'

'Did you see anyone in the garden?' Straay asked.

'No I'm quite sure I didn't. Well, I did see a flicker of movement, like something passing in front of a light.'

'A shadow?' Drake said leaning forward.

'Well it could have been, or it might have been a bird or a bat. My eyes aren't very good in the light, practically useless in the dark.'

'Where did this flicker come from?'

'It seemed to me to be either at or near the summerhouse.' She said confidently.

Drake then asked, 'Did you hear the shot?'

'No I didn't, but then I sleep heavily. Did you hear the shot, Doctor Straay?'

Straay shook his head. 'No, my Lady, I heard only Mr DuPont shouting for help.'

Drake asked, 'You were awakened by whom?'

'The butler shouting help…help… It was very distressing. We all rushed down to the study. Dawson had opened the door and the Major stopped us from going in. He took charge, as an officer would. I think I fainted once by the door; Milly was comforting me. No, wait...she fainted and I comforted her. Oh I don't remember. I do remember going to the smoking room and drinking brandy. I like brandy. Not much else, I'm afraid.'

'Thank you Lady Agatha, we'll talk more in the morning,' Drake said, and she stood, straightened out her dress again, and left. Straay was lost in thought for a moment.

◆

'What did you make of her?' Drake asked.

'She is a liar, but I don't know if she deliberately lies.'

Drake was shocked. 'I thought she was scatty, but I only got the sense that she wasn't telling the truth when there was information that might hurt someone like Milly Gregson.' Drake looked thoughtfully at him. 'What did you pick up on?'

'She habitually scratches herself when she is under stress. Her eyes, however, told me a little more. When she was visually remembering an image or a conversation, her eyes would move up and to the right. However, when she was visually constructing an image or conversation her eyes would move up and to the left.'

'How does that work exactly?'

'Let's say your child asks you for a cake and you ask, "Well, what did your mother say?" As they reply, "Mum said... yes." they look to the left. This would indicate a made up answer as their eyes are showing a constructed image or sound. Looking to the right would indicate a remembered voice or image, and thus would indicate the truth.'

'You learn something new every day.'

Drake was quite impressed.

'It's not a precise science and shouldn't be used in isolation.'

Drake smiled, 'So you use a question you know would be answered honestly to get a baseline. I wondered why you asked her to confirm her name. Clever.'

'It seemed a logical thing to do.' Straay smiled. 'More often than not, when you asked Lady Agatha a question, she constructed an answer rather than remembering one. It could be her memory is fragmented by drinking and it's why she is unable to remember.'

'You think she's an alcoholic?' Drake asked. He hadn't had any real time to observe this fact.

'I think it's very possible,' Straay replied, thinking back to the smoking room. There he had observed she added to her drinks with a concealed flask. 'It might explain the memory lapses and the nervous scratching and other little tics.'

'Delirium tremens?'

'Possibly the onset.' Straay extinguished his cigarette. 'At the very least, it could be some form of alcoholic dementia. You noticed that at one point she said, "I can't stand brandy," but later on she said, "I like brandy," and so on.'

'So what you're saying is her testimony is basically unreliable?' Drake sighed.

'I'm afraid if she were in the court, we'd have a problem, yes.' Straay pulled out another cigarette and lit it.

'What about the popping sound and the shadows in the garden, you believe all that?'

'She *may* have heard something,' Straay shrugged, 'She may have *seen* something.'

'But nothing we can rely on.' Drake was grim faced.

Straay shrugged. 'No, but it's something we can add to our investigation. At the very least, it's new information.'

'Fair point.' Drake read over his notes. 'Okay, moving on to Sir Laurence. Do you believe that bit about him being a bully?'

'I'm not sure. There may be some truth in it, but I think again Lady Agatha's hatred of Sir Laurence clouds her judgement.'

'What do you mean?'

'Well the legacy from her sister's will for a start. Sir Laurence said she was quite resentful that he was charged with managing it for her.'

'I see.' Drake thought for a moment longer. Eventually he closed his book.

'It's a good motive for murder.'

'Probably the best we've got so far,' agreed Straay.

Chapter Ten

Mr Desmond DuPont

Desmond DuPont was nervous. He was also white faced and red eyed. His hands shook and he was perspiring heavily. His close-set brown eyes hardly ever blinked and his boyish face made him seem far younger than his twenty-eight years. Straay poured him some water and offered it to him. DuPont thanked him, and then drank it. Chief Inspector Drake leaned forward a little and smiled. DuPont smiled nervously back.

'Just some routine questions, Mr DuPont, nothing to worry about.'

'I'm not worried, Chief Inspector, I'm distraught.' DuPont's words were sharp.

'I understand, sir, but we need to strike while the iron is hot. You're a lawyer I believe, so you should be pretty familiar with all this.'

'I'm not a criminal lawyer, Chief Inspector, I'm a corporate lawyer.'

'Procedurally I meant.' Drake smiled.

'Oh,' DuPont cheek's reddened. 'I see what you mean.'

'You're a business lawyer. Company mergers, paperwork trails, that sort of thing?'

'Yes, *that* sort of thing.' He was being rude in a mean-spirited and surly way, Straay mused, and it wouldn't end well.

'My clients are made up of extremely important businessmen. I look after the legal aspects of commercial takeovers, financial trading, you know, *that* sort of thing.' He stared, unblinking. Drake maintained silence. An old trick, but it did its job. DuPont, unable to take the silence any longer, broke it first.

'This is all new to me you know, I've never been interviewed in this way before.' He was shaking. Drake smiled inwardly. Got you, he thought. You're scared of something.

'I don't know what I can tell you, but I will try to answer your questions as best as I can.' DuPont's nervousness was clearly moving to a brand new level.

'Do your hands often shake when you're distraught Mr DuPont?' asked Drake carefully.

'Really, Chief Inspector, my employer and friend, best friend, shot himself. I can hardly be expected to be at my best, regardless of my occupation.' DuPont's reply was spiked with just a little venom.

'Point taken. So can you tell me a little about last night? Especially the timeframe of the evening. When people arrived and left, where people were, where you were.'

'I can, but what is the relevance?'

'Just answer the question please, sir,' said Drake forcefully.

'Very well.' He sighed dramatically. 'I'd been up to London for the morning on business for Sir Laurence. I then met up with some friends for lunch. I arrived here at about five. Jacob got here at six-thirty, after his rounds. Lady Agatha, Milly, Major Heskith, and Sir Laurence were here.' Drake looked up when DuPont had stopped talking.

'Go on.'

'Really...this is pointless. I'm sure you know all this already. What can my version of the same events matter?'

Drake leaned forward, his face unreadable. 'Go on, Mr DuPont.'

With another dramatic sigh, he continued. 'Dinner was postponed until eight, but as Doctor Straay was held up by the appalling train service, we finally went on and had it without him. Roast lamb, vegetables, wine, and so on. We then went into the smoking room about nine...that's when Doctor Straay arrived. Sir Laurence introduced us all. I suggested Doctor Straay be a witness to Sir Laurence's new will and when it was completed...' he looked directly at Straay, '...they continued their conversation alone for about fifteen minutes. I went back into the smoking room and chatted with Major Heskith and Jacob until they returned. Doctor Straay then went off for a cold dinner and Sir Laurence and Major Heskith played their silly card game for the rest of the evening. I had a brief conversation with Doctor Straay. He retired to bed, at about ten, and I followed shortly after. I awoke at around fifteen past eleven to a commotion. Dawson told me that Sir Laurence…' He faltered and his eyes began to water. He choked back the tears and cleared his throat. 'I woke Doctor Straay and followed him down to the study. We were then herded like cattle into the smoking room and forced to wait for the inevitable interview at god-awful o'clock in the morning. Did I miss anything?'

'Thank you, Mr DuPont. Nice and concise. I want to ask you a few other questions now regarding your relationship with Sir Laurence.'

DuPont sat bolt upright. 'My relationship with Sir Laurence was purely professional, Chief Inspector.' The angry way he had said those words made both Straay and Drake look at one another.

'No one was suggesting any other kind, Mr DuPont,' Straay countered soothingly.

'I'm sorry... I'm just... well I'm bloody well shot to pieces by all this. It's put me on edge. Forgive me, I'm tired.' He rubbed a hand over his eyes.

Straay looked away and frowned. He again had the same feeling he was missing something vital. He'd had it before, when he was being introduced to them all. Twice now, so it wasn't coincidence. Something someone had said then, and something he had heard or read afterwards had triggered it.

'How well did you know Sir Laurence?' Drake asked.

'Very well—intimately you might say. I handled all his daily legal work and correspondence, both for him personally, and for his company.'

Drake made a note and then continued: 'You were introduced by Doctor Powell I understand?'

'Yes. Jacob introduced us.'

'When was that?'

DuPont thought for a moment. 'It was about three years ago. We met at a business function. Jacob told Sir Laurence about me and he sought me out. He hadn't been invited, if I recall but, well, he was so well known no one ever questioned why he was there. A lot of directors of other firms often had Sir Laurence in their confidence.'

Again, Drake made a note. 'I understand you also have a relationship with Sir Laurence's daughter?'

'Who said that?' DuPont asked wide-eyed.

'Are you in a relationship with Milly Gregson?' Drake asked more directly.

'I refuse to answer the question as I do not see its relevance.' DuPont answered.

'Well either you are in a relationship with his daughter or you aren't.' Drake leaned forward again. He could be an intimidating man when he chose to be. When no reply came, he sat back in his chair. 'It's a relevant question when you consider the man shot himself, don't you think?'

'You mean it could have been the reason he took his own life?' DuPont asked carefully.

'Well, I put it to you that it could have some bearing on it, yes. Can you think of any reason why Sir Laurence may have wanted to shoot himself?' Drake asked.

'No I can think of no reason, he was in his prime.'

'You still refuse to answer my question?'

'Yes. It's impertinent.'

'But again, I stress, relevant. We are trying to conduct an investigation into the reason for his suicide. This information could assist us. You're not obliged to answer it, but don't you want to assist us in determining why he took his own life?'

Straay had been watching DuPont carefully. Desmond DuPont was flustered. He knew it and Drake certainly knew it. Like a dog with a bone, he wasn't going to give up without a fight.

'Of course I want to assist you,' DuPont said unconvincingly. 'I've already indicated I can think of no reason why Sir Laurence would kill himself. My personal relationship with Sir Laurence's daughter is therefore irrelevant.' DuPont crossed his arms defiantly.

'It's more than just a friendship then?' persisted Drake.

'Why would you say that?'

'You're protecting her, Mr DuPont. If you weren't in a relationship of any kind with her, you'd have no reason to get so angry at the question, or withhold your answer. In fact, I'd go so far as to say you'd be quick to deny it. You're not doing either.'

'Guesswork,' DuPont said shaking his head.

'Logic,' Drake fired back. 'You've given yourself away by your obstinacy. Again, I put it to you that you *are* in a relationship with Milly Gregson in some degree or another, and having established it, I want to know if Sir Laurence knew about it.'

DuPont refused to speak. They locked eyes for what seemed a very long time to Straay.

'Eventually I will find out, Mr DuPont.' Drake maintained eye contact unblinkingly. 'Why not simply tell me now?'

'I refuse to be interrogated further by you. I remain here in deference to your investigation and will assist in any way I can regarding Sir Laurence's professional activities, but I will not answer any further questions of a personal nature unless arrested and charged.' DuPont stood and Drake smiled.

'Sleep on it Mr DuPont. We'll talk again in the morning.'

DuPont, red faced, exited the room, and slammed the door shut behind him.

◆

Drake sat for a moment in thought before turning to Straay.

'I'm greatly interested in Mr DuPont...oh yes, greatly.' Drake thought back over the conversation. 'He's defensive, emotional, nervous and a liar. You'd think his father had died by the way he's acting. He's hiding something, I'm sure of that.'

'I agree. A lot more than his relationship with Milly Gregson. And there's something about the man I can't place. Something is just not right. The same feeling I got when I first met him. His familiarity with Sir Laurence, for example, strikes me as odd. He's a young man, twenty-eight. He holds a legal position far above his experience, in my opinion. He works for Sir Laurence but he is not treated as an employee. You appraised him as a liar; I agree with you. He lied about how he met him, either to you or to me. When I asked him the same question, he said it was at a party, not a business function. Whichever is the case, we should endeavour to find out.'

'Well, he's a more likely suspect than Lady Agatha. You think he had some hold over Sir Laurence or Sir Laurence over him?' Drake asked making another note in his little book.

'I think if that were true,' Straay considered for a moment, 'it would have to be the former rather than the latter because if the latter were true, well, I doubt he would have been moved as emotionally as he clearly has been by his employer's death.'

Drake sighed. 'Are we getting anywhere at all or just raising more questions?'

'A little of both, I think.' Straay smiled to himself. His answer was cryptic and he knew it, but he wasn't sure how he could easily answer the question—certainly not in the way Drake would like it answered.

'We must know more about this DuPont, Drake. There's more to this relationship than his simply being an employee. I'm sure of it.'

Drake smiled. 'Illegitimate son perhaps? Who knows? I'll get my man to start digging.'

'Why does the word familiarity keep forming in my mind? What is it I am missing here?' Straay went over the conversation in his mind again.

'I honestly can't answer you.' Drake began reading over his notes again. He continued speaking without looking up. 'I don't see anything here that gives me a clue about his relationship with other people, but a background check should answer these questions for us.'

Exasperated, Straay shook the thoughts away. 'My mind is a curse sometimes. Always working and never sleeping.' He shook his head again, 'Sorry, I over analyse.'

'Your mind is not a subject I'd be able to or even want to analyse in a million years.' Drake chuckled at the thought and closed his book.

Straay couldn't stop his mind throwing up the word *familiarity* repeatedly.

'He constantly used titles when discussing people.' Straay said quietly. 'Lady Agatha, Major Heskith, Sir Laurence, but not "Doctor Powell." He is referred to as Jacob.'

'They were friends, so you said, old friends even. Natural enough.'

'He was friends, good friends, with Sir Laurence, yet he doesn't refer to him as Larry in the same way the Major does. It's…odd.'

'Like I said, I couldn't begin to fathom the way your mind works.'

'There's an old phrase, isn't there, with the word *familiarity* in. What is the phrase?' Straay tried to remember it.

'What, familiarity breeds contempt?'

'Yes,' Straay nodded happily. 'The answer is somewhere in that phrase. I'd bet my coat on it.'

'I'm not sure I understand.' Drake began to feel his headache returning. He rubbed at his neck.

'How do I express it?' Straay thought for a moment. 'Here's a hypothetical scenario. I have a friend who is a well-known celebrity. People will come up to him and say, "Oh! You're so and so from so and so aren't you!" but to me, he's just James. This illustrates a positive application of that principle, because if I were in awe of James, it would be hard to remain his friend, you see?'

Drake shook his head. 'No, not really.'

'The lesson is the fear of something, fascination and awe, is reduced through getting to know it better. Let's take spiders. People are afraid of spiders. I am afraid of spiders. However, the more I see them and the more I interact with them, pick them up maybe and even examine them, the less I fear them. Eventually that fear has left me and I will always think of spiders in a different way, but other people will still fear them. This is how I see the relationship between DuPont and Sir Laurence.'

Drake still didn't fully understand, but that was acceptable. So long as Straay understood what he meant, Drake knew he didn't have to.

Chapter Eleven

Milly Gregson

When Milly Gregson entered the room, it was clear to both of them that she was a beautiful woman. Her auburn hair sat very neatly on her shoulders. Her emerald green eyes shone with fierce intelligence. The only blight on her fair skin was the puffy redness of her eyes. In every respect, she was a model of beauty.

'My father,' Milly began, 'was an extraordinary man. He served his country during and after the war with distinction and honour. I loved him and will miss him more than I can express.' She wiped a tear from her eye. Straay and Drake both offered their condolences on her loss.

'I'm deeply sorry to have to ask you some rather personal questions regarding the death of your father, but I have a procedure to follow.' Drake soothed her with a touch of fatherly concern in his voice. He had a daughter much younger than her. Seeing Milly now with her strength and confidence made him think seriously about how his own daughter might react under similar circumstances.

'It's perfectly alright, Chief Inspector. My father spent his entire life a slave to the procedures he'd laid out for himself. Frankly a structure at this time is most welcome.'

Straay couldn't help but admire her character. Here was a girl, no, a woman who had suffered a significant loss, yet she wasn't overcome with emotion and unable to articulate her thoughts. Straay thought the emotional responses of DuPont, Sir Laurence, and Milly were all tied together. He also believed Drake had definitely hit the nail on the head when he doggedly pursued a connection between them. His psychological view was that Milly should have reacted as DuPont had, and he as she had.

Drake leant forward and asked: 'Can you tell me about last night, up to the discovery of your father's death, please?'

'Of course. I had dinner with the others and shortly afterwards I went to bed. I came over extremely tired, which was odd because I hadn't done anything to warrant it.'

'Can you elaborate on that?' Drake made a note of this in his book. Straay also paid particular attention.

Milly thought for a moment.

'It's the kind of tiredness you get after a lot of exercise.'

'I see.' Drake made more notes. He stopped to look up when she didn't carry on speaking.

'Please continue,' he said kindly.

'Well, I feigned a headache and went to bed. I must have gone out like a light and only woke when Agatha told me the news.'

'Had you felt this kind of tiredness before?' Straay asked.

'Yes but, like I said, only after exercise.'

'You misunderstand me.' Straay rephrased the question. 'This tiredness you said, did it come to you suddenly? Or did it come to you gradually, over some time?'

'I'd have to say suddenly. I felt as right as ninepins before dinner.'

'So I ask you again, have you felt this kind of sudden tiredness before?'

'No.' She paused for a moment and then a thought occurred to her. 'Well actually, yes, now I think about it, once before. It was after I'd had my tonsils out at the hospital, I felt the same kind of tiredness after the operation. It's the best way I can describe it to you.'

'You aren't able to tell us any more about the dinner?' Drake asked.

'I wish I could, it was roast lamb. I ate a little but all I could think about was bed. Father was concerned and told me to get some sleep.' She put a hand to her breast and did her best to hold back the tears. 'If only I'd known his goodnight kiss would be his last. Why did he kill himself? I just can't fathom it at all. It's completely out of character, not him at all. I asked myself, who is this dead man in my father's study because it can't be my father. He wouldn't do this to me...to us.'

Drake took out a clean handkerchief. 'Here,' he offered. She gratefully accepted it.

'You're very kind, thank you.' She wiped her eyes and clutched at it tightly.

'Your father wrote a note, I wonder if you could read it and perhaps tell us what he might have meant by it.' Drake handed it to her. Milly read it.

'I'm sorry but I don't know what he means at all. Perhaps his sorrow at committing suicide? I wish I could tell you more, but I can't.'

'Do you recognise the handwriting?'

'Of course, it is my father's. May I keep it?' She asked hopefully.

'Sadly no, it's evidence. Once we're finished with our investigation I'll speak to the Superintendent and see if he'll release it to you.'

Straay asked her: 'Can you tell me about your father? His habits, his concerns, his general health, and wellbeing?'

Milly comprehended and cleared her throat.

'My father was a very strong man, a hard man. He was also a loving, kind man. I knew him better than anyone did. Trust me when I say you shouldn't believe everything you might hear about him. The people he was harshest with never had a good word to say about him. I saw him broker huge deals that cost men their fortunes and he never blinked, but if you saw him in the garden moving spiders or beetles from harm's way so they wouldn't be squashed, you'd think he was a different man. He didn't have many concerns I can recall, at least not personal ones. Businesswise, he did have daily concerns: financial news, legal paperwork, you know the sort of thing, but these were business issues and quite the norm. His health was good as far as I can recall. He did have a little bit of chest pain recently. Desmond asked Doctor Powell to look him over. Other than that he was well.'

'What was your relationship like with your father before the war?' asked Straay.

'Ordinary. He paid me little interest back then. As far as I can remember, he always wanted a boy. I was a disappointment, I'm afraid.'

'And after the war?'

'Completely different. The war was tough and he had fought through it hard. He came back a changed man. He was almost the opposite of how he was before he went away. My mother and father's relationship quickly failed when he returned home. They argued frequently and hardly spoke at all after just a few weeks. I, on the other hand, enjoyed a brand new relationship with my father. My mother and I had drifted apart while father was away. Sadly, we weren't on good terms right up to her death. I'm sure Agatha has been spreading her gossip about how father bullied her and so on, but really, mother was ruthless with him from the moment he returned. They occupied separate bedrooms after he came back. Before the war, they shared a room. She used to call him "my peach."' A fleeting smile, it soon passed.

'Did you know my mother dismissed the men in service and just kept the women? Father had to do all the work around the estate because of it, including the gardening. I don't think he really cared that much, to be honest; he enjoyed working for hours in the garden, or in the summerhouse. I didn't fully understand what had happened to mother back then, but now with older and experienced eyes, I see the same thing happening to Agatha. Mother drank secretly but like most alcoholics after a while, they stop their pretence and start to drink anywhere. My mother would start drinking at eight o'clock in the morning. Agatha is the same. She thinks no one notices.' Milly sighed and then thinking quickly she added, 'Don't get me wrong though, I do love my aunt.'

Straay liked Milly Gregson. The more she spoke the more she impressed him. She had realised a fatal flaw in her mother's abuse of alcohol and it had led her to reason that which he himself had deduced earlier about Lady Agatha.

'Can you tell me about your relationship with Desmond DuPont?' Drake passed her a glass of water. She gratefully accepted it.

'Darling Desmond? He's like a brother to me. He and father were great friends but as to a relationship...I like him a lot, though I'm not sure he feels the same. I think he's a bit shy of women, especially someone like me who knows what they want. I keep expecting to walk around the corner and find him down on one knee. Silly really. I used to think he spent so much time with father just to be close, but he has never made any advances.'

'I don't think it's silly at all, he might be shy around women as you say.' Drake decided it was time Milly rested.

'Why don't you run off and get some sleep; we'll talk more in the morning.'

'Thank you both.' She handed back the handkerchief and the suicide note, then left the room.

◆

'What a remarkable woman,' Drake voiced his thoughts.

'Remarkable is the right word. And intelligent.' Straay leaned back in his chair as he spoke. 'I understand now why Gregson gave her full run of the business. Mr DuPont is a lucky man. She is logical and imaginative. I expect her to achieve great things, Drake; she'll go very far indeed.'

'If she murdered her father, she'll go straight to the gallows,' Drake said sadly. 'I do hope she didn't.'

'Time will tell,' Straay said softly.

Chapter Twelve

Doctor Jacob Powell, MD.

Doctor Powell knocked once. Hard. He entered the room smoking a cherrywood pipe. It was old fashioned, but then so was the doctor. He was a tall debonair man of six feet who looked remarkably good for his sixty-seven years of age. His neatly cut silver hair showed oddly metallic blue under the soft light of the room. His suit was well worn but not ill fitting. There was a boyish charm to his face and his mouth was permanently etched into a Cheshire cat grin. Straay was reminded of Alice who had remarked that she'd often seen a cat without a grin but never a grin without a cat.

Doctor Powell had been awakened by a police constable and driven back to the house. Although if he had truly been asleep, Straay thought to himself, he had put on the same suit he'd worn for dinner. Powell smiled at both men as he closed the door. He took a seat and tapped out his pipe into the ashtray. He began to refill it as Drake quickly brought him up to date.

'What an evening!' He lit his pipe and puffed furiously to get it going.

'Larry did away with himself eh? I wish I could say I was surprised by it; sadly I can't.' Drake offered him a glass of water.

'Oh, thank you.' He drank it down quickly.

'I think we can dispense with the usual questions about dinner and so on,' Drake stated cordially. 'Can you tell us about Sir Laurence and why you weren't surprised by his death?'

Doctor Powell nodded. 'Yes indeed.' He switched his pipe to his right hand. 'Larry was a strong man with a very high opinion of himself. Medically he was as fit as a fiddle. Aside from some aches and pains typical of his age, I really couldn't fault him. He had a good diet and he exercised well. He did not drink to excess and smoked infrequently. He had the fitness of a man ten years his junior. His mental health, however, was my primary concern.'

Drake asked:

'How so?'

'Well he showed signs, on occasion, of extreme paranoia. He expressed on more than one occasion that people were out to get him. I think he had some hang-up about the war, too.' Straay watched as he rubbed his pipe against his lips.

'His reaction, or rather lack of reaction, to his wife's death was deeply concerning. I assume you both know Major Heskith almost shot him on one occasion. We were shooting grouse. Larry stepped out in front of Heskith's stand and nearly bought it right there and then. Luckily, the Major saw him and adjusted his aim. Then there was the boating accident...well, had *I* not been there he'd have most certainly drowned. He said he'd checked the boat that morning, but the boy who runs the boathouse swears Larry hadn't been near the place, and the boat he took out had been condemned the week before. Little things all pointed to some form of mental breakdown. He'd jump out of bushes and accuse friends and family of plotting things. Even me. I prescribed him a sedative but he refused to take it.'

Straay moved forward in his chair. 'You've been his physician for how many years, doctor?'

'I'd say forty years, give or take. I've looked after most of this household, in my time, along with the surrounding neighbourhood. I looked after his wife too, poor Ellie.'

Straay nodded at Drake and sat back into his chair.

Drake continued:

'Tell me about Ellie Gregson, if you would be so kind.'

'Of course. I'd known Ellie for at least twenty-five years, ever since she was a teen. Ellie was an old school Victorian Lady. She was wealthy and had status. Like many people of her class she didn't allow herself to become ill or, in any event, let it been known. She positively refused the services of a doctor, unless the situation was almost life threatening.'

'Which, in her case, it ultimately was,' Drake mused. 'Go on.'

Frowning slightly Doctor Powell said:

'I first noticed her circulation was poor one summer's evening when I had been invited over for dinner. I casually mentioned it and she nearly threw me out of the house. Was a sticky moment, I can tell you. I left but she had a car sent around for me an hour later and fell apart in apology. From then on, I saw her intermittently.'

'How frequently?'

'Once a month, if that.' Drake noted this down.

Doctor Powell continued:

'It became pretty obvious she didn't want to be seen by anyone and she hid her condition well, pretty much up until the end.'

'Your initial diagnosis was?'

'A weakened heart and possibly liver disease.'

'Which one of these was she most in danger of, in your medical opinion?'

'Seems academic now but actually I didn't think she was in any real danger of either, clinically at least—not initially. I felt a change of diet and her routines would do her more good than drugs. She was a heavy drinker and took hardly any exercise.'

'You prescribed her the tonics?' Straay asked.

'Yes, but they were mere placebos to be frank. Her main problem was stress.'

Drake sat back to let Straay continue the interview.

'Psychological or biological?' Straay asked.

'Both, actually,' Doctor Powell stated confidently. 'Ellie Gregson exhibited cognitive and behavioural as well as emotional and physical signs. She intermittently showed poor judgement when it came to the wellbeing of herself and her daughter Milly. She worried excessively and her mood would swing rapidly. When I first started noticing these symptoms, I also catalogued intervals of irritability, agitation and an inability to relax. Clearly, she was suffering from the anxiety of her husband being away at war. Feelings of isolation, depression, and loneliness were common complaints from many of my patients at the time. Biologically, her symptoms worried me more.'

Straay inwardly smiled. 'The psychological gave way to the biological, this is your opinion?'

'It is. Once she was able to put her trust in me, she described her symptoms in more detail. Ellie suffered frequent nausea, dizziness, chest pains, and diarrhoea. She put it down to a bug one month and poor quality food from rationing the next. Every time I questioned her, I got the same old stories. They were just, you know, turned over a bit and added to each time. I began to suspect an underlying problem. She was neglecting herself and her daughter and it was becoming more and more noticeable as time went on. Her dependency on alcohol increased as her symptoms worsened and not long after that, I suspected she had a weak heart, although again I was unable to examine her thoroughly enough to form any real diagnosis.'

'Was this just intuition then?'

'No, Doctor Straay, not intuition. Through experience and knowledge— through observation.' Doctor Powell was clearly irritated by the question. Straay had chipped his armour a little, Drake thought. *Good.*

'I apologise.' After a pause he asked, 'So, as you say, these symptoms were not uncommon given her personal circumstances?'

'No, and yet they bothered me.'

'How so?'

'Ellie Gregson was actually Elizabeth Shurbury Geraldine Smythe, daughter of the late General Sir George Albert "Freddy" Smythe. She was from hard stock and not someone I would have considered a candidate for any form of stress. I was briefly his doctor as well. Still, I always suspected the scandal associated with her Grandfather was probably a major factor, not that she believed or showed it in any way.' At this revelation, Doctor Powell relit his pipe.

Drake leaned forward, his note-taking interrupted. 'Excuse me? Her Grandfather?'

'Yes, didn't you know? Now let me see. The scandal broke just about a year before the end of the war. Turns out old "Freddy" Smythe had kept a big secret. Grandpa Albert was in fact Baron Adelbert Schmidt, who'd left Germany under a big cloud well before the war started, settled in France initially, and moved to England under a false name, so I read. Was a huge scandal at the time, apparently, but all hushed up. Ellie said she never knew her Grandfather and the old General, her father, kept his mouth shut about it. Seems *he'd* been educated in England and spent most of his youth in military school here anyway, so no one really knew anything about it, or his natural heritage. Ellie herself was indifferent to all of it, as she said to me at the time. *"Most of the noble families of England were descendants from French or German ancestry anyway, so what was the problem?"* Her father had died a few years before the story broke, so apart from an article in the Times, it was never really mentioned again, but we were at *war* with Germany. It got a few backs up. Locals don't forget or forgive. '

'But this secret,' Straay asked with new light in his eyes, 'it could have had a devastating effect on Sir Laurence, could it not?'

'Well if it did, I never knew about it.' Doctor Powell was careful with his reply. 'He was still working for the Government until his death as far as I knew.'

'What was the cause of death for Ellie Gregson?'

'Officially recorded as peripartum cardiomyopathy, PPCM we call it, also called pregnancy associated cardiomyopathy. It's a rare cause of heart failure. Affects women late in pregnancy or in the early puerperium.'

Drake and Straay looked at each other.

'She was pregnant?' They commented in unison.

'Oh yes, hid it well. No one knew, not even her sister.'

'Did Sir Laurence know?' Straay asked.

'I can't be sure if he knew before her death. It seems unlikely. From what I understand, the moment he got back from the war, they occupied separate rooms. He treated her harshly from the moment he got back, I'm led to believe. He certainly knew at the time of her death because we tried everything we could to save the child. A boy, you know, at least two months premature. Saddest thing I'd dealt with in a long while. Mother died, baby died. It turned out to be another scandal.'

'How so?'

'Well because there was no possible way Sir Laurence could have been the father, what with his being away at war. He expressly forbade any mention of it, you know, and whilst we couldn't hush up the reason, the events recorded on the death certificate go into little or no detail. The child was buried in an unmarked grave. He refused to give him a name.'

'Was the father of the child ever discovered?' Drake asked.

'Not that I'm aware of. Of course, it could be just a coincidence. Shortly after Sir Laurence returned from the war, the men, with the exception of Dawson, were all dismissed. Another mystery eh?'

'No, doctor,' said Straay with precision. 'I'm beginning to suspect it is all part of the same mystery.'

'Then you've both definitely got your work cut out for you.' Doctor Powell smiled a mischievous a smile.

Drake nodded. 'Thank you, Doctor Powell.'

◆

With the doctor now gone, both men sat in silence for a while. Drake sifted through his notes, while Straay pondered the nature of what they had learnt.

Was there a connection between the General, his German heritage and Sir Laurence's death? Straay considered it for a moment. The information could have been offensive to Sir Laurence. It could equally have pushed him to the brink of some form of breakdown, as Powell had suggested, but only if he already *had* a fragile mind. He dismissed the idea almost as soon as he'd thought it. From what he had learnt about the man, the revelation wasn't likely to have bothered or affected him at all. Based on his initial observations and on those of the suspects he had talked with, he was quite comfortable believing Sir Laurence's character would stand a far greater burden than a simple family secret, even though this one was far darker than most. As they had uncovered more data, he had been able to build on that profile and it had increased in depth. Sir Laurence's profile *was* full of holes *and* it didn't make any real sense, specifically where it needed to. Psychology was complex. It wasn't always simple or even entirely explainable. Even Freud had trouble.

Straay's mind was full of unanswered questions. Out of the fog, one came to the forefront. Who was the real victim here?

What was the doctor's reason for spoon-feeding them this information? Was it even useful? The German ancestry may have been a key factor if they were talking about Ellie Gregson. The revelation that her Grandfather was German just didn't seem to be of any value at all when applied to Sir Laurence, and he couldn't see how knowing it would have affected him. Straay decided it was just plausible Doctor Powell's motive had been purely one of misdirection. The details about Ellie Gregson's death, however, were significant.

Chief Inspector Drake rubbed his eyes and yawned.

'I don't think my brain can absorb any further information tonight.'

'This morning,' Straay corrected, through an involuntary yawn of his own.

'Maybe I'm just tired, but we seem to be left with even more questions than when we started.'

Straay nodded. 'I agree.'

'So Ellie Gregson died in childbirth, eh?'

'So it would seem.' Straay was still deep in thought. *So it would seem...*

'Well,' another yawn, this time longer. 'I don't see any significant advantage in knowing it.' Drake stood and stretched. 'What are your feelings?'

'I think that the good doctor is a very clever man.'

'As a medical practitioner you mean?'

Straay chuckled softly. 'No, I meant clever in a much more devious and dangerous way.'

Drake was intrigued. 'Dangerous...how so?'

'He has the hypnotic power of suggestion, Drake. He has charm and cunning and he knows how to use it; he knows just what to say and how to say it. This makes him dangerous.'

'It's too late for riddles, Straay.'

'You're right it is. I'm sorry.' He looked up at Drake. 'So what will your next move be?'

'I think I'll look into the ancestry of General Smythe a bit. Dig out Ellie Gregson's medical records. See if I can get all the medical files and so on. Might be a link there somewhere. I mean, now that we know about it, we should follow it up, don't you think? Tie up all the threads.' Drake opened the door. 'I'll see you in the morning, Straay.' He left shortly afterwards, taking one of the constables with him.

Doctor Straay smiled as the door closed.

It wasn't a happy smile.

He slowly shook his head.

Chapter Thirteen

Breakfast

The morning had come around far quicker than Pieter Straay would have liked. He rose from his slumber with a yawn and put on his dressing gown. It was a glorious morning. Through the open window facing south into a beautiful garden, he watched as the sunlight danced across the hedgerows. It was quiet and calm outside. Birds flew to and from the trees out near the summerhouse. From his vantage point, he could now clearly see the path that led out through the rear of the house and past a well-manicured rose garden. It looked picturesque. There was only one thing that gave any indication a murder had occurred the previous evening—the lines of police constables pacing the garden under the direction of Chief Inspector Drake.

Straay left his room with his wash bag and made use of the very modern toilet. Once he had performed his morning routine, he returned to his room, dressed in a modest suit of grey, checked himself in the full-length mirror, and went down to the dining room.

Breakfast had been laid out along the wall on a set of trolleys. Highly polished silver dishes containing scrambled eggs, kedgeree, toast and butter, were piping hot and well stocked. Tea, coffee and orange juice sat in equally polished containers. Two young maidservants stood at either end of the wall, waiting patiently to assist the guests and clear away dishes. Seated at the table was Lady Agatha in a lilac dress with a white shawl. Next to her, reading the local paper, sat Major Heskith. Opposite them was Desmond DuPont who had a very full breakfast plate. Doctor Powell was smoking his pipe and reading a medical journal at the other end of the table. Milly Gregson was missing. Everyone looked up as Straay entered. He made a slight bow to them all, then helped himself to eggs and coffee. The mood in the room was sombre.

'Beautiful morning,' Doctor Powell broke the silence. He was watching the police sweep as it passed the windows.

'Wonder what half the constabulary are doing here. Seems like overkill, doesn't it? For a suicide I mean.' The question didn't seem to be addressed to anyone in particular, so Straay decided not to answer it. He sat next to Mr DuPont to eat his breakfast. Straay believed breakfast was the most important meal of the day. In his line of work, it was not always likely he would get lunch, so breakfast was never missed. In this case, he felt lunch would probably be possible, but he could not assume he would have time to eat it. It was a perfect time to assess the players. Observing them as he ate was easy because not one of them was prepared to make eye contact with him. Naturally, he thought, if one of them is guilty of murder, they wouldn't want to make that known. It must have occurred to them all by now something far greater had occurred. As he approached the dining room Straay noted the constables stationed at practically every exit. Their presence must have given each of the suspects cause for concern.

Drake hadn't stayed at the house the previous night. He had instead opted to return to the station and start the background checks, laboratory work, and other important aspects a murder case of this prominence would need. Straay thought, knowing Drake, he'd probably left notes for the medical examiner, too. He wondered if Drake had actually had any time for sleep. It didn't seem very likely.

Lady Agatha sipped her tea and ate lightly buttered toast. She was well made up, but in the light of the morning, it didn't appear that she'd had a lot of sleep either. Her face was pale and her eyes were tired. Her hand shook slightly as she lifted the toast to her mouth. She nibbled at it, in the same way a bird pecks at crumbs. Straay wondered just how long it would be before that first drink would calm her.

In contrast, Major Heskith looked well rested. He wore a lighter blue suit than the one he had on the previous evening. The dark blue and turquoise cravat contrasted well against his white shirt. Here was a man who took great care of his appearance. He had now turned to the crossword page at the back of the paper and had taken out a pen. The pen looked remarkably similar to the one Sir Laurence had used on the boat to write directions to the house. It was a silver and gold Parker pen. A very expensive pen.

Straay turned his attention to Doctor Powell who was still inspecting the garden through the window. The doctor was wearing a sports blazer with a motif sewn onto the pocket. It was possibly a club membership jacket. He wore a dark reddish brown bowtie that matched his shoes. Straay observed the methodical and practiced way he tapped out and refilled his pipe. Lifting his cup and finding it empty, he looked over at one of the maidservants. The cup was instantly refilled, the girl lingering a little longer than was necessary. Doctor Powell salaciously eyed the back of the girl as she provocatively walked back to the sideboard. Here was a man who knew how to get, and take, what he wanted from others. 'Pretty little thing,' he murmured, unconsciously running the tip of his pipe along his bottom lip.

Lastly, and with a little difficulty, he observed Desmond DuPont. Here, again, was an oddly nervous young man. White faced, red eyed. Clearly emotionally disturbed. His shirt was buttoned haphazardly as if he'd rushed to dress, and his trousers and jacket did not match. Straay shook his head slightly. It was not easy to make out just what DuPont's problem was. He was obviously deeply affected by the death of his employer, yes, but to this extent seemed just a little over the top.

Desmond DuPont had now finished his breakfast, and wiping his mouth on his napkin, he finally broke the silence.

'What is going on here?'

Everyone except Powell looked at him. Doctor Powell, who did not look up from the magazine he was reading, said:

'Breakfast, dear boy, the most important meal of the day.'

'Don't be silly, Jacob. That's not what I meant, and you know it.' DuPont snapped back.

'Of course I knew what you meant, silly boy!' Powell looked sharply at him briefly. He quickly and rather noisily flicked a page over and then went back to reading.

DuPont looked down for a moment. 'Sorry,' he said, chastened.

Lady Agatha sighed dramatically. It was a childish sigh. She had been out of the conversation far too much, Straay thought. Quite coldly she said:

'Is this really necessary? Larry is dead. What can the Chief Inspector mean by locking us all up in this house? In my house! It's all frightfully undignified.'

The Major looked over at Straay. He pulled at his moustache in thought and then, with the precision of a man blessed with very simple ideas, asked. 'What's the big story, Straay?

Doctor Straay finished chewing, put down his napkin and reached for his coffee. 'I'm sure we'll all be told soon enough,' he offered pleasantly.

'Stalling tactics!' Doctor Powell was cheerful again. 'You're not a very good liar, Doctor Straay,' he chuckled at his own observation.

Straay smiled and non-confrontationally, he said, 'I assure you, if I were lying, you wouldn't know it.'

'This really is intolerable,' Lady Agatha again complained loudly.

Major Heskith patted her hand. 'I know, but we'll get an answer before long. Probably just procedure. You know what it's like in a service—rules to follow, paperwork to tie up. All takes a bit of time, but it'll all work out.' She smiled at him fleetingly but caught Straay watching and instantly turned away withdrawing her hand from his.

'Yes, well, I'm not going to be treated like this, not in my own home. You, girl,' she called to one of the maidservants. 'Girl, ask Mary to bring me my bag; I've run out of cigarettes. And go and get that awful policeman at once. Bring him to me.' The maidservant curtsied and turned to leave but stopped suddenly. Chief Inspector Drake was standing in the doorway. No one had heard him enter and he had evidently been there for a minute or two.

'That won't be necessary.' Drake made brief eye contact with the maidservant before turning to Lady Agatha.

'The awful policeman is here already.'

She had the good grace to look at least a little embarrassed. Drake came over to Straay.

'Morning, Straay, a word if you don't mind.' Straay stood and followed Drake to the door, pausing only when Drake turned around.

'Please, all remain in this room until Doctor Straay and I return.' It wasn't a suggestion.

'I want my maid, Mary, here please.' Lady Agatha was stern. Drake conceded and Mary was called for.

◆

Drake led Straay outside into the warm morning air. The garden was even more beautiful close up. It was clear that Sir Laurence had what they call a green thumb. They followed a path around the side of the house. The old building was well looked after and the small flowerbeds along each side of the path were full of mixed flowers. The mixture seemed perfectly balanced. Each window had its own flowerbed. The back of each plot, nearest the building, was attractively made up of perennial green shrubbery and lines of coloured flowers made up the front. The soil was damp and there wasn't a weed to be seen between the plants. Straay liked the fact that each bed had its own distinct colour scheme. They continued around the house to the study window. As they reach their destination, Drake pointed at the ground.

'There, you see?'

'Yes, footprints, fresh. Every flowerbed is meticulous except this one.'

Drake knelt beside the wall.

'There's a hose that runs around the wall here, keeping these little flowerbeds watered. It's quite a nice idea actually, saves a lot of back and forth with watering cans and so on. I've had it turned off for now to preserve the scene. This hose here,' he said, stepping to one side and pointing, 'had a leak. It kept this particular bed wet. However, since we didn't notice any muddy footprints inside the room, I'm going to assume our murderer took his or her shoes off and left them here,' he indicated the footprints nearest the window, 'and then went in shoeless.'

'I told you we were dealing with a clever individual.' Straay leant forward to examine the prints and as he did so, he reached up to support himself against the window and stopped. 'It's okay to touch?'

Drake nodded, 'Oh quite okay. All dusted for prints now. Oh... talking about prints, we have the results back from the study. Four sets of prints found on the table, the mantle, and the windows. Sir Laurence's, naturally, then Dawson, Lady Agatha, and Doctor Powell.'

'You know this already?' Straay was impressed.

'Yes, I got a reference sample first thing this morning.'

'What about on the inner doorframe?'

'Nothing. Not around the frame or near the bullet hole.' Drake replied.

'It was worth a little hope, don't you think?'

Drake simply inclined his head.

Straay stood up and measured the height from the ground to the window.

'Well, our murderer wouldn't need to be much above five feet to reach the window from this position, so that doesn't help us much.' He crouched again and re-examined the prints. 'They are uniform. A person definitely stood here. You notice the impressions are much deeper than the prints nearest the path?'

'Yes, I did notice that, and if you look closely enough, you can see the tread patterns on each print are different, they slightly overlap. I think whomever it was, slipped off their shoes by the window, did the deed, and then carefully placed their feet back into them when they exited, walking backwards just as carefully into their original prints. You can see only one set leading to the window.'

Straay continued his study of the footprints as Drake continued.

'We did have a little breakthrough of sorts. Follow me.' He left the small flowerbed and walked along the pathway a little.

Straay stood and followed. The Chief Inspector picked up a pair of muddied shoes and handed them to him.

'These shoes match the prints by this window.' He said. Straay was again impressed.

'You've been very diligent and busy whilst I slept, I feel ashamed.' He turned the shoes over and examined the tread. They matched the pattern of the prints exactly.

'Nonsense.' Drake was in good humour this morning. 'You need to rest your brain, no use to me if you can't think! Anyway, these won't help us much.'

'How so?' Straay said with a tinge of disappointment.

'We found them in the summerhouse. It's unlocked. They're Sir Laurence's gardening shoes.'

'How can you tell?'

Drake took them back and turned them right side up.

'He wrote his name on the tongue, see?'

'Makes sense I suppose, although it's possible somebody may have written that afterwards.'

'Yes, I suppose that's true,' Drake said with no enthusiasm. He then placed them back into the paper bag they had originally come from. The bag was marked, "Study window shoes / prints—Summer-house."

'Still, they are evidence so we'll catalogue them appropriately. I think it's time we showed our hand to the others.'

They walked in the direction of the smoking room patio.

Straay asked:

'Was there anything of note in the garden?'

Drake shook his head. 'No, nothing really. Well, we did find a few wheelbarrow tracks that led to the summerhouse. Oddly, the barrows are kept on the other side of the garden in a potting shed. I say shed—it's bigger than my lounge!'

Straay was thoughtful but said nothing.

They walked side by side. Drake cast a quick look at his companion and said:

'I want you to remain in the house as a suspect.' They stopped outside the patio doors and Drake put a hand on Straay's shoulder.

Straay looked quizzically at Drake for a moment who smiled a particularly ruthless smile.

'Pretence, if you like.'

Chief Inspector Drake, it seems, had a plan.

'I want you in close proximity to the others. I need your thoughts and observations. You'll have everything you need from me, but it will help me to have you close to them. You'll be one of them. Someone is bound to say something unguarded. If that happens, I need someone I trust.'

'Someone who might interpret an unguarded comment for you?'

'Yes, I'm not going to lie to you, Straay, it could be dangerous.'

'Meaning that you're putting me in the cage with the lion?'

'Yes, is that okay?'

Straay shrugged. 'Danger is part of my trade.'

'Well,' Drake smiled at the reference. 'Let's hope this isn't your "final problem", then.'

'Agreed,' Straay solemnly nodded.

'I'll explain to them it is procedure, because actually it is, but before we do that, there are a few things I need to tell you.'

Chapter Fourteen

Drake's Plan

Chief Inspector Drake was conscious they might be overheard, so he led Straay out into the garden near a large hedge, which was dense enough to mask any conversation.

'The laboratory tested that section of carpet against the cigar last night. The lab boy's said it took twenty to twenty-five minutes to burn a hole through it. They made every effort to match the size of the one in the study. They can't be completely accurate, of course, but it's a good start, it means we can now assume Sir Laurence was killed at around ten-forty-five. There were no pens found in his clothing and no gunpowder on his hands. The ballistics report says that the revolver, a Webley Mk VI, matched up with the bullet, so it's definitely the weapon used to kill him. We know that the shot was silenced somehow, but this particular revolver hasn't that capacity. We're searching the area for anything that might resemble a metal tube that could have been slotted over the weapon, it's a long shot, and we're not hopeful.'

'Is it at all possible to trace the owner from the serial number?'

Drake shook his head. 'No, they don't keep accurate enough records and since the war, many veterans came back with a Webley or two. Souvenirs mainly. There aren't any real lists of owners. No solid information of who has them at all. It's possible that it was Sir Laurence's own weapon. Then again, it could have been the Major's...or anyone else's.'

Straay nodded. 'I see your point.'

'Well, like I said, we're searching the grounds. Doctor Carmichael is going to start the autopsy today. When I spoke to him this morning, I asked him to be very thorough and he reminded me that he always is. He did say one thing that I thought might interest you.'

'Which was?'

Drake pulled out a note from his inside pocket. 'He said there was a significant lack of blood in the wound tract and on the body. His initial observation was that a wound of that proportion should have secreted more. A lot more.' He handed the note to Straay, who thought for a moment.

'What was his explanation?'

'He hasn't formed an opinion yet. You know what doctors are like, they won't tell you anything until they've done all their tests.'

'But, Chief Inspector, I also know you,' Straay raised an eyebrow, 'so what did you get him to tell you?'

Drake laughed.

'Okay, well, he said one possible reason was that Sir Laurence's blood pressure was so low, when he was shot, there wasn't enough pressure to pump out the blood. Without a full autopsy, though, he simply wouldn't commit to anything else. Took everything I had to get him to tell me that much. I'm not sure that it gives us much, but it's interesting.'

'Very interesting indeed. It suggests to me that Sir Laurence may have been sedated, possibly with something that lowered his blood pressure. Was he on any medication that we know of?'

'Not that we know of, at least according to the testimony of both Doctor Powell and Milly Gregson. We made a search of his room and his bathroom but there's nothing there. We're also going to check all the chemists to be thorough, of course. Doctor Powell wrote me the name of someone I should talk to at his practice in order to have Sir Laurence's medical files released. Actually, with his help on that, we'll be able to get the information far quicker than if we'd applied through the courts. I have a man there now.' Drake thought for a while on what Straay had just said about the low blood pressure.

'Why sedate him if you intend to shoot him? That doesn't make any sense to me.'

'It's not easy to answer that. A theory that has just formed in my mind suggests a few reasons, but nothing tangible. We'll have to wait for the autopsy to be sure, but it's quite suggestive. As to the pen I saw Sir Laurence use on the boat and for the signing of the will, I think Major Heskith might have it. I saw him using an identical one in the dining room.'

'It might be one of a pair, they were friends.' Drake suggested.

'Possibly, but if that is so, we have another pen to find.'

'True. Well, we know how it was done. Now we have to understand why and by whom.' Drake's face was set firm.

Straay was pleased.

'Agreed, we must now set our sights on the background information of our main suspects.'

'Yes, I've got my men at the station and also back at the Yard working on that. It's going to take a little time. I suspect the Yard will come up quicker with the military information you requested than the local station will. That's beside the point though; we will get what we need. I'm just hoping it tells us something.'

'Well I suspect that any information will be better than none. What about Doctor Powell's alibi?'

'Oh yes. He was home all evening. His neighbour remembers seeing him in the house. He actually spoke to him, he said, through the window. Asked him the time and mentioned something about a book he'd borrowed. He told the constable both of them are usually up late so it's quite usual they might converse a few times during the evening. The constable who picked him up from his home also reported that the neighbour came out when he heard a car pull up. Doctor Powell had mentioned he needed to grab something and rushed back in. He came back out with a book and handed it the neighbour. Made comments about how it was a good read, nice twist at the end etc.'

'How long is a car ride to the house?'

'It's about twenty-five minutes, give or take.'

'Well it's possibly enough time to get back, kill Sir Laurence, and then drive home again.'

'Except that the neighbour was up most of the night writing. He's a journalist for the Daily Herald. His writing desk is in front of a window that faces out to the road. He swears that Doctor Powell didn't leave his house until he was collected by us, and his car remained where it had been parked when he returned home that evening. The alibi is cast iron.'

'Yes, it does seem pretty solid,' Straay agreed.

'One down, four to go, eh?'

'Five,' Straay corrected him.

'Five? Four, surely. Lady Agatha, Major Heskith, Milly Gregson and Desmond DuPont, who am I missing then?'

'Dawson, the butler.'

'I hadn't really thought of him as a suspect.' Drake considered this for a moment. 'Well not in the list of main suspects, if you know what I mean. Everyone in the house is a suspect of course, except you. I've interviewed Dawson, the cook and the assistant cook already, they had nothing of worth to say. Dawson just reiterated his long service and the cook had only been there about three months. I'll have my notes typed up for you so you can read them.'

'If you don't mind,' Straay asked, 'could you have the interview notes typed up for me so that I can read through them all? I'm still having that feeling that someone has told us something important and I missed it.'

'Of course, you'll have them today.'

They made their way back to the smoking room patio doors.

◆

When Straay and Drake got back to the dining room everyone, including Milly Gregson, was assembled. Drake had asked a constable to have all household members who were present the previous evening brought into the dining room, including the kitchen staff. Now that they were gathered, he stepped forward and looked at each person in turn. They all noticed his pleasant cheerful face had now become much harder.

'Ladies and gentlemen,' he said sternly, 'it is my duty to inform you that we now believe Sir Laurence Gregson did not, in fact, kill himself.' Straay watched the faces of everyone for the slightest response.

'He was murdered. Murdered, we strongly believe, by one of you.' He waited until that information had sunk in. No one spoke, initially; a state of shock filled the room. Eventually Milly Gregson said:

'Thank you Chief Inspector. In an odd way I'm relieved to hear it because the thought that father took his own life was just unbearable.'

Major Heskith's face was set in stone. 'One of us you say?'

'Yes Major, one of six possible people. Yourself...'

'Preposterous, he was my oldest friends!'

'Milly Gregson...'

'No! I loved my father, I'd never harm him!'

'Lady Agatha...'

'The very idea is insulting. How dare you!'

'Doctor Powell...'

'Hardly, I'm a doctor, not a murderer!'

'Dawson...'

'I've served this family for years, never!'

'And Mr DuPont.'

'Nonsense. None of us had any motive whatsoever!'

'One of you did.' Straay stepped forward. 'One of you killed Sir Laurence and dressed it up as a suicide.'

'Why isn't he a suspect too?' Lady Agatha snapped, pointing an aged hand at Straay.

'Doctor Straay is a consultant specialist attached to Scotland Yard who was invited by Sir Laurence to visit the house.' Drake's determination and firm voice was authoritative. 'He had no prior knowledge of him and his integrity is beyond doubt.' He was stern. Lady Agatha sniffed at him. He continued. 'It just happens that a murder occurred that evening. However, he, like the rest of you, is now confined to the house until this investigation is completed.' He turned to Straay. 'That is procedure, Doctor Straay.'

'Of course, Chief Inspector.'

Drake turned back to the others.

'No one may go anywhere outside of these walls.'

'What about the garden?' Milly asked.

'The rear of the house has an enclosed garden only accessible via the conservatory,' Dawson suggested. Drake nodded in agreement.

'Yes, that's acceptable. There are constables posted around the perimeter and on every exit. This house has everything you need to be comfortable, whilst Doctor Straay, my staff and I finish the investigation. Anyone attempting to leave this house will be arrested and taken to the police station. Do you understand?'

'I don't like your tone, Chief Inspector!' It was clear that Lady Agatha didn't much like being told to do anything.

'I'll afford you every courtesy, my Lady, but in the end, I always get my man.' Drake was careful with his answer.

'Then you hardly need detain me.' Lady Agatha spat back obstinately. She pulled a fur around her shoulders and looked down her nose at him.

'It was a figure of speech.' He held her gaze for a moment and then turned to leave.

'I'm sure this isn't legal,' remarked DuPont. 'You can't lock us in here you know.'

Drake paused and then turned.

'It's perfectly legal, Mr DuPont. You're all under house arrest. You're welcome to try to leave, but I'd recommend you think hard about it. Oh, and incidentally,' he stepped towards him. 'When I return, I'll be conducting more interviews. I'll be starting with you first, Mr DuPont, so I'd suggest you prepare yourself very carefully. This time,' he said leaning slightly towards DuPont's face, 'I won't take any refusals to answer.' They both stared at each other for a moment. Eventually DuPont looked down. Drake put on his hat and left the house.

Chapter Fifteen

The Work Begins

Doctor Straay and Major Heskith were sitting in the smoking room together. Heskith had been quiet for a while reading the newspaper. Every now and then, he looked over the top of the paper at the foreign detective. It was clear to him that Straay wanted to talk so he folded up his paper and forced a smile.

'You don't like me do you, Major?'

The Major considered his answer.

'Actually,' he finally said, staring darkly at him, 'you're wrong there, doctor. I dislike your nationality.'

'A brutal but honest answer...it makes it easier to talk to you. You dislike the fact that my nation did not partake in the war, even if some of us were forced into it?'

Major Heskith crossed his legs, interlaced his fingers, and tilted his head slightly. He was a very stern looking man, a man you certainly wouldn't want to face on any battlefield.

'You can forgive a German,' he remarked coldly. 'They were just following orders, doing what they thought was right, but your lot…'

'My lot were on the fence, isn't that it? My lot were…?'

'Cowards.' He was a hard man. 'In my book anyway. Didn't pick one side or the other; left the rest of us in the lurch. Don't pretend that isn't so, doctor.' The Major wasn't angry, he was very calm, but his eyes were like flint and said so much more. Straay met those eyes with steel of his own.

'You think it was easy for me, growing up with this attitude?'

'Probably not. That is why I don't dislike you personally,' the Major answered evenly. 'If your lot *had* taken a stand against the Germans, what might the outcome have been, hmm?'

Straay thought hard for a moment. 'There are many possibilities.'

'Go on,' the Major pulled out a cigar case from his jacket pocket. He carefully pulled the band off it, clipped it, and took the match offered. 'What in your opinion might have occurred?'

'I suspect had the Netherlands entered the war, it is very likely that the Germans would have invaded. It may have been enough to split the German forces and even possibly halt or slow down their advance into France. However, I believe the outcome would have been much the same.'

'Agreed, to a point. I doubt very much the advance into France would have been any different. The Germans had planned to invade the Netherlands well before the war actually started.'

Major Heskith couldn't be faulted on his knowledge. His mind was sharp. He looked down his nose at Straay just as if he were a schoolmaster. *He's allowing me to make my own mistakes,* Straay thought.

'If this had happened,' continued Straay, 'then it's possible that the diplomatic efforts my people were involved in might never have been started. In that event, the war may well have continued on far longer, causing a far greater loss of life.'

'What you say is true, I can't deny the logic of it, but…' the Major wrestled with his emotions for a minute or two. Eventually he sighed. 'The truth is, the man who caused the death of millions, the man who should be taken out and shot, is alive and well and still living like an Emperor in…' again he met Straay's eyes. 'Where, exactly?'

For the first time since they had met, Straay was starting to see the real man behind the façade. He had reached him.

'In the Netherlands.'

'Exactly, so forgive me if I don't have any love for your people. They spent the war eating well and staying neutral, whilst millions of people were slaughtered, and when it ended, they took the one man who started it all and hid him away. It's abhorrent and utterly unforgiveable.'

'You're right,' Straay said carefully. 'I agree with you.'

'Really,' he said sarcastically.

'Oh yes, really. I am Dutch. I am a liberal if you like. I also firmly believe in the law.'

A look of doubt creased the Major's brow. It was only for a moment, but it was enough for Straay to notice.

'You think he should be taken out and shot?'

'I think he should be tried by an international tribunal and if found guilty, he should face the consequences.'

'Wilhelm doesn't deserve the civility of a trial,' the Major snarled.

'You think he should be simply hanged, then?'

'Yes, the entire world knows what he did.'

'There we move onto a philosophical debate about jurisprudence, Major. Besides, it is unlikely that Kaiser Wilhelm will ever face a trial. His influence on world politics has ended. He will grow old in his castle. Imperial Germany has died.'

The Major snorted. 'They'll rearm,' he said softly. 'You mark my words...they'll come at us again.'

'I very much hope you are wrong, Major.'

'So do I, doctor, so do I.' the Major smiled slightly and his posture relaxed a little.

◆

The conversation had been very useful. It had given Straay an insight into the mind of the man. Here was an old soldier with the simplistic view that the law was an ass. He would have no compunction in arbitrating an injustice and issuing his own form of punishment. He would become, in essence, judge, jury, and executioner. It was an understandable if somewhat worrying state of mind. The man had lived through the trenches and seen a multitude of horrors. The fact remained, though, that somewhere in this house was a killer and right now, Straay had reason to consider Major Heskith above everyone else. If Sir Laurence had done something so heinous that Heskith felt he needed to intervene, it was highly possible that, without thought to the consequences, he would hand out a death sentence and then act on it. However, because his character was essentially black and white, and because he had not attempted to conceal his thoughts in any way, Straay felt that covering it up and going through the charade of suicide just didn't fit him at all. Every instinct he had suggested that Major Heskith might have simply shot Sir Laurence and calmly dialled the Police. He needed to dig deeper.

'Anyway, enough about the past.' Heskith stood, walked over to the drinks cabinet, and poured two large whiskey and sodas. He then handed one to Straay and sat again. It was a peace offering of sorts and Straay accepted it.

'I imagine you want to ask me some questions about Larry?' The Major took a large gulp of whiskey.

'Yes, do you mind?'

'Not at all, fire away.'

'What can you tell me about Sir Laurence?'

'Not sure what you mean old boy.' The Major had a look in his eye that said, I know exactly what you mean, but I'm not going to make it easy for you.

'Well, his personality, his habits, his time in the Army. That sort of thing.'

'Oh, I see...building a profile.'

'Yes that is it exactly, the profile of the man.'

The Major settled into his chair.

'Well, I first met Larry, that's what we called him back then, in the war. He was Captain Larry Gregson. A heroic hard-nosed officer who treated his men hard, but looked after them, know what I mean? First rate shot as well. Mind you, he was one for the women, too. He had this very odd compulsion, if that's the right word, about cleanliness. Almost mad about it. It's rather a difficult business, being a clean boy in a world full of mud and death. Anyway, he rose through the ranks quickly, more quickly than I did. Made it to Major in less than a year, and then got a post in some quirky outfit. Not that he was a desk jockey, no, far from it. He went deep into combat zones, ended up in all sorts of operations. All very hush-hush. Larry and I were very close for many years, talked about what we'd do once the war was over. He was a little, how shall I put it, edgy. Like a cat on hot bricks. Even his own commanders were a little intimidated by him. His father was an MP and he had an uncle in the War Office, Colonel Douglas Gregson. About a year before the war ended, Larry had made Lieutenant Colonel and was running half the allied forces in provinces all around the north of France. I hooked up with him there and spent my last few years under his command. He treated me well.

'"Jonny," he'd say, "when this war is over, you come live with me." So, when we were all back in Blighty, I looked him up at the address he'd given me and here I've been ever since.'

'Were you intimidated by him, Major?

'Not in the least.'

'When was he made Sir Laurence?'

'Knighted you mean? Shortly after the war. Seems his covert stuff was all part of a bigger plan to help the allies end the war. Not much was said about it, but he was whisked up to London and got the sword from HRH. I was there, you know, picked up my OBE at the same time. Very proud I was too.' The Major crossed his legs and picked at some imaginary fluff on his trouser leg.

'You knew his wife Ellie?'

'I didn't know her too well, really. He'd met her before the war. Thing is, she was a bit of a weak girl health-wise, from all accounts. Father was a General you know, good stock, but she could be hard on the servants and on others too. Well, she would be, wouldn't she, being a General's daughter? Oh he loved her well enough, as well as a man loves a woman, but after the war…' The Major stopped himself.

'He had changed?'

'The war changed him. She changed too, became reclusive, irritable and difficult.'

'It happens more frequently than we'd like to believe. I daresay it changed you in some way.'

Heskith shrugged a little. 'Possibly. I won't deny I saw some pretty awful stuff. Dodging the bullets one day with the friends you'd made in the mess, then burying those same men the very next if you can, or just leaving them broken on the ground. It hardens you. Makes you, how do I put it, less inclined to make friends. That stays with you. It's very hard to turn that off, even now. Thing is, during the time I spent with him, he hardly talked about Ellie.'

'Interesting. He had also the war wounds?'

'Oh yes, very early on in the war, before I knew him, he caught a blast in the face, horribly burnt he was. No one expected him to live through it, but he was too strong for that.'

'He was disfigured...I saw the scars.'

'Yes, people who knew him before the war could hardly recognise him afterwards, took months to recover. Luckily, he had his tags on when they found him. Three other officers bought it, so I hear. Larry was the lucky one. After recovery, he was offered some job back here but he wouldn't hear of it. As soon as he was able, back he went. Remarkable man really, I shall miss him.'

'Did the war have any other effects on him?' Straay asked.

The Major shook his head.

'No, honestly, he seemed fine. He never lost his nerve. Never lost his edge and never ever lost his belief that we'd kick Fritz back to sausage country. That was until he got home. Once he'd retired to this old house he became a bit moody. He told me, on occasion, that he didn't know how to behave in the peaceful world he'd helped create.

Honestly, if a war broke out, he would have been in the queue to fight in a heartbeat, if he'd had half a chance.'

'What about you, Major?'

'No, I'd done my time, seen my share of horrors. I had some lucky scrapes I probably ought not to have. The life I have now may be dull to many people's standards, but I'm happier this way.'

'Do you know much about his business?'

'No, not really. I believe it was something to do with textiles or Asian rugs—not my cup of tea, old man. I think he did work for the Government here and there, all very hush-hush stuff. There were times he'd go off for a few days without a word and when he'd returned, he'd be fine for a while, then very quickly he'd fall back into a brown study.'

'Getting back to his wife for a moment...she could not reach him, the man he was after the war?'

'She said once that her Larry must have died in the war.'

'Meaning that the war changed him from the person he was?'

'I think so. I doubt anyone who came back from the war really was the same person that went in. She didn't understand. Well, how could she? Sitting here dreaming of the day he'd return, and when he did, she didn't like the man that came back. Natural enough really.' The Major had such a simplistic and typically British view of women.

'Not long after that, she died?'

'Six months or so, but she was a weak woman. I mean that in the physical sense, not in any other way.'

'I understand, so when she died, Sir Laurence was upset?'

'Not really. I think it was just another death to him.'

'That is sad.' Straay was genuinely emotional.

The Major agreed. His eyes seemed sad. 'The war desensitised him.'

'Yet he loved her once?'

'No doubt about it. She was a lovely woman. It's just well,' he paused for a moment to find the right words. 'Women, you see, simply can't understand what a man goes through in war...it's beyond them. Ellie expected Larry to come back, sweep her up into his arms and whisper sweet nothings into her ear like the day he left. It was never going to happen. I didn't know the Larry she knew. The man I knew would have been embarrassed by a woman like that.'

Straay understood what the Major was driving at.

'Sir Laurence was a wealthy man before the war?'

'I'm not sure about that. When I first met him, he used to cadge spare cash from me, old boy. Ellie was the rich one. This house and the estate all belonged to her. Of course by the end of the war, Larry had a considerable income from his pension and did a lot of hush-hush work that earned him a mint, so he said.'

Straay pulled out a packet of cigarettes and offered the Major one. They shared a match.

'And the estate all went to Sir Laurence when she died?'

The Major looked thoughtful for a moment. 'Well, yes and no. She left the estate to Agatha but Sir Laurence was to manage it, effectively meaning she left the estate to him. In a way it was spiteful, he could manage it but not own it; she could own it, but neither draw income from it nor have much of a say on how it was run. I think it was Ellie's way of keeping some control over both of them. Larry and Agatha didn't like each other much, but when Ellie died, he couldn't kick Agatha out of what was effectively her own home and she couldn't kick him out because he was legally charged with managing it. Agatha is a bit frivolous with money, according to Larry. She denies this and believes that Larry forced Ellie to write that clause into her will. She says it's because he wanted the money. Ellie could be very vindictive, though, and from what I know of her, she couldn't easily be persuaded to do anything financially she didn't want to do. I don't get too involved in that side of things—easier that way.' The Major flicked the end of his cigarette into the ashtray.

Straay thought about this relationship among the three of them: Ellie, Laurence and Agatha. It was shrewd of Ellie Gregson to maintain control of her husband and her sister even after her death.

'What can you tell me about the dismissal of the male staff?'

'Not much. Larry had a few drivers, a couple of gardeners and some other handymen—well, boys really. Most of them were young; you know, twenty or so in age. He used to have them all lined up in the mornings, issuing orders and giving them their daily schedules. His little army she called it. As I said before, she could be vindictive. It wasn't beneath her to remind him whose house and estate it was. Sacking the men was probably her way of making a point.' Straay nodded. That made a lot of sense.

'What about Milly? Were she and her father on good terms?'

'Yes. Milly was a proper tomboy. Real head for figures, good at making economies, all that financial and business stuff—it is way beyond me.' He laughed. 'Give me a gun and a good body of men and I'll get a job done, that's all I can do. She was a cut above most of her age and class to be frank. He was very hard on her for a while, but she just took it and gave back as good as she got. Larry liked that about her. Secretly he had always wanted a son, but once Milly started pointing out various ways he could better his investments, cut expenditure and so on, well, he basically let her run his entire operation. Effectively, she managed his entire estate. She wasn't on speaking terms with her mother when I arrived, never had much to do with her right up to her death.'

'Did he pay her well?'

'You'd have to ask her about that.' The Major was shocked by the question.

'Now I must ask you a question about Sir Laurence's murder.'

The Major smiled, 'Ah, wondered when this was coming. Did I do it? That's what you want to ask me?'

'Well, not initially, but now you have asked the question yourself, how would you answer it?'

'Did I kill my oldest and most personal friend, a man who has made my life rich and full since leaving the service?'

'Yes.'

'I think I just gave you my answer.'

◆

An hour or two later Straay entered the enclosed garden outside the conservatory. It was a quiet area with a neat lawn. Sitting in a recliner with an umbrella was Lady Agatha. Next to her sat her maid, Mary, reading a book. He approached them and asked if he could sit. Lady Agatha waved nonchalantly at the vacant chair.

'Thank you.' He angled his chair so that the sun was not directly in his eyes. Mary looked up and stood to leave but Lady Agatha pointed to her seat, so she sat.

'It is a beautiful morning, is it not?' he remarked conversationally.

'If you say so,' she scoffed. 'Mary,' she said turning her back on him, 'fetch my morning tonic will you.' Straay smiled inwardly. He wondered how many morning tonics had already been made up. Mary got up and placed her book on the chair. She straightened her skirt and curtseyed before she left. Lady Agatha looked sideways at Straay for a moment, then sighed.

'What do you want?' she asked frowning at him.

'To ask you some questions,' he replied simply.

'I'm not in the mood to answer any.' She looked at him sternly. When he did not apologise and leave, she said:

'Why are you still sitting there?'

'Because I haven't asked you any questions.'

'English isn't your first language is it?' She was being sarcastic. He understood her meaning but decided to play it innocent.

'No, Dutch is my first language.'

'Oh, you are an irritating man, aren't you?'

'It has been said to me on a few occasions, yes,' Straay replied nodding.

She stared at him for a minute or two and he simply stared back.

'You're still here,' she finally said, her irritation reaching a new level.

'Evidently, my Lady, if you wish me to go, perhaps you'll answer a few questions for me. Then I can leave you in peace.' He was nothing if not persistent.

'I don't want to be bothered by you...go away. That should be English enough for even you to understand.' Her bluntness was alarming, but it didn't faze him.

'Why are you angry at me?' Straay asked with a frown. 'Is it because I'm a foreigner?'

'Don't be absurd! It's because you don't do what I ask. Go away!'

'You seem, if I may say, very agitated this morning. You're upset, I can see, from the death of your brother-in-law. I do not wish to increase that agitation.' He reached into his pocket and pulled out a hip flask. 'I do not know if your maid will return very quickly, but maybe I can offer you a little something, to help? To ease your agitation, yes?'

He had knowing eyes. She hesitated briefly and then held out her hand for the flask. He handed it to her. She looked at it for a moment then back at him, at first he thought she would open it and take a long drink, but then her reserve kicked in and she simply put the flask into her pocket.

'That's kind of you.' She softened her voice slightly. 'My weakness. You understand it, I can see. It makes me irritable.'

This was as close to an apology as he was ever likely to get.

'I won't take from it now.' She looked back at the house briefly. 'When no one is around...including you.' She smiled slightly.

'Since you've done me a kindness, I'll grant you a few minutes to answer your questions, but realise,' she looked imperiously at him, 'that I may decide not to answer them.'

Straay inclined his head. 'Can you think of anyone who might want to kill Sir Laurence?'

'Yes, plenty of people.'

'Anyone in the household I meant.'

'Oh, the suspect list? Well, actually yes—me.' She smiled at him.

'Did you kill him?'

'No. I thought about it many times, does that count? Does that make me a murderer in your eyes?'

'Certainly not, my Lady. Having the thoughts and performing the actions are two separate things. So, if not you, who else do you think would have the motive and the ability to not only kill Sir Laurence, but dress it up as a suicide?'

'I've thought about that a lot this morning. Who would not be noticed doing the deed? Well it certainly wasn't Milly or I. That I know for sure. You see I was upstairs and Milly was in bed. I checked in on her to make sure she was all right. She was very tired at dinner, and I thought she might be running a fever, so I checked her temperature. It wasn't Doctor Powell either; he wasn't even here, and I doubt the Major would raise a hand to the man who kept him alive. The French have a beautiful saying: *"Cracher dans la soupe!"*'

Straay was taken aback. 'To spit in the soup?' He frowned for a moment trying to comprehend her meaning and then he smiled. 'Oh I see, you mean to treat what's given to you or what's available to you with neglect and disdain, in other words, not to bite that hand that feeds you?'

'Yes,' she said with a wicked smile. 'Of course I could have used the literal translation of: *"Ne mordez pas la main qui vous nourrit,"* but I prefer the idiomatic expression.'

'It was a well-chosen one.' Not for the first time he was impressed by her intellect and knowledge. She did her best to hide it, to cloud it in an aura of battiness, but Straay had seen through it. She too had realised, he was sure, that her idiotic pretence did not fool him.

'I thought so.' She smiled at the sun.

'Getting back to our suspects; if it wasn't you, Milly, Doctor Powell or Major Heskith,' he paused for a moment, looking along the tree line in thought. She waited for him to finish his sentence. He looked back at her, and she at him.

'That doesn't leave very many people, does it?' He remarked to her.

'No, it doesn't.'

'In fact it leaves two. Mr Desmond DuPont and Dawson the Butler.'

'That's quite true,' she agreed, nodding.

Straay was thoughtful again. It was clear that Lady Agatha was always going to set him along whatever path she chose, and he was content to let her think that she could. Eventually he continued his questions.

'You have medical training?'

She was initially shocked by the question, but quickly recovered her composure. 'Yes.' She looked over at the tree line for an instant, then back at him.

'I was a Volunteer Auxiliary Nurse during the war. Did my bit for King and Country, you know. I rather enjoyed it. I had a service number and everything. I went to Dover and served for two years. I saw a lot of poor wounded men. Some of them didn't live long.' She sniffed. Straay wondered if that was when she started to drink. As if reading his mind she suddenly laughed.

'You're thinking, is that when the poor old dear picked up her weakness?'

'Actually I was,' he replied honestly.

'You're right. I never touched a drop before then, but when so many young men came in with bits missing, and blood, blood as far as the eye could see, I started to… you know…'

'Understandable, it must have been traumatic.'

'It certainly wasn't a picnic I can tell you.'

'May I ask you a little about your sister?'

She frowned at him. 'What do you want to know?'

'Well, I'm curious as to what happened between Sir Laurence and Ellie when he returned from the war—why they became estranged.'

'I wasn't here then. My husband had died during the war so I lived alone for a year.'

Straay felt suddenly sorry for her, she saw it in his eyes and became stern.

'I don't need your sympathy,' she scolded. He apologised. She continued. 'Once I'd paid his death duty, I had nothing left. Could barely survive. When the war ended, perhaps six months or so after, my sister insisted that I come here. Of course Laurence wasn't a bit happy about it—kicked up an awful fuss—but she got her own way in the end.'

Straay noted that she was now referring to Sir Laurence as Laurence, and not Larry. He asked, 'Were there male staff when you arrived?'

'Yes. She didn't dismiss them until I'd been here for about a month. They put me in that draughty room at the front of the house. Ellie had the room next to mine.'

'Did Ellie give you any explanation for why she would dismiss the men?'

'Ellie didn't tell me much.' She was evasive. 'She said that she'd had enough of him, referring to Laurence, and his little army of boys. She often said, "things were going to change." Most of the time, he kept out of her way by working in the garden. He used to sleep sometimes in the summerhouse you know, very common. I told him people of our class don't sleep in summerhouses, and he just told me to keep my nose out of it. He wasn't a very nice man and, well, he was common, really. He wasn't from good stock.'

'You are from good stock...you and your sister.'

'Evidently.'

'From good German stock, in fact.'

'Nothing wrong with that.' She narrowed her eyes. 'Queen Victoria herself was half German.'

'You are right. There is nothing wrong with that. I have German ancestors too. I wondered, though, if this might have caused the rift between them.'

'Rubbish,' she quipped and then paused for a moment asking, 'Why?'

'Well, he being in the war fighting the Germans and then coming home to find that your grandfather was German and not English as he'd always believed. I wondered if that may have caused him to change his view of Ellie—to fall out of love with her as he did.'

'And why he was hostile to me as well? Larry was a peach before the war. Yes it's a possibility, that. I'd not thought of it before now, but you might be right.' She looked off into the distance for a moment.

Eventually she refocused and became her usual stern self 'Anyway, it's all ancient history now...hardly of any use to you in a murder investigation, is it?'

'Possibly not, but information is as much a tool as a spade.' He replied.

'You're like a spade,' she quipped smiling. 'You like digging up information. Now leave me to my morning sun, what's left of it.' She sat back into her chair. He stood to leave and as he turned away, she called back over her shoulder.

'Wait a moment.' She fumbled in a bag beside her and he returned to her side. 'Here it is.' She handed him an old faded photograph. There were five people in it, three men and two women, one in a nurse's uniform the other in a very regal lacy dress with a matching hat. They were all smiling brightly in the photograph.

'I always keep this with me.' She looked at it fondly. 'Old memories of better times.' She looked up at Straay and, for a moment, he saw a very different woman. There was happiness in her eyes he hadn't noticed before. He held it close to her so she could point at each person, and he didn't miss how her finger gently caressed it...how she ran that finger over one man in particular.'

'The man on the left is dear David. I'm next to him.'

'It is a lovely memory...you both looked very happy. Who are the others?'

'Next to me is Anthony and next to him are dear Ellie and Larry.'

'This was taken during the war?' He asked studying the photograph.

'No, just before the boys all deployed. Things were different back then, Larry was a kinder man, and Ellie was so happy.' She took the photograph back and continued to look at it. Her happiness slowly switched to sadness and she promptly put it away.

'Anthony is a friend of the family?' Straay asked gently.

'He was, yes. Sadly, he was one of the early casualties of the war. That was the last time I saw dear Anthony. Such a bright young man, full of life. It's such a shame.' She sighed. Mary returned and Lady Agatha switched back to formal mode.

'Where have you been girl? I'm half-baked in the sun. Where's my tonic?' Mary handed the tall glass and she took a sip. 'Oh, much better.'

Straay waited a moment longer and then decided to leave. Before he did, on an impulse, he took Lady Agatha's hand, much to her initial shock, and lifted it to his lips, formally bowing his head in respect to her. She was very pleased.

'So you can be civilised, I see,' she remarked with a slight smile. He left her to her tonic. As he walked away, he heard her say, 'Lovely man; breeding, you can tell. The Dutch are so civilised.'

◆

Doctor Powell was seated quite comfortably in the games room. There was a dartboard on the far wall, with, in the middle of the room, a full size billiards table. Along the walls were comfortable red leather chairs and small mahogany tables. When Straay entered the room, Doctor Powell looked up and waved him over.

'Sit down, doctor; take the weight off your feet. Man, you look exhausted.'

Straay came forward and sat down in the chair pulling out a packet of cigarettes as he did so, and offered one to Powell.

'No thanks, I'll stick to my pipe.'

'This house is so much larger than you'd expect from the outside.' Straay took the match offered.

'From the front at least, quite deceiving, these older houses,' Powell agreed. 'I think it was an architectural decision to make them less appealing from the front, you know, to burglars.'

'Ah that makes sense, although to rob a house like this, with servants and so on...that would be a bold move, would it not?'

'Bolder moves have been made in robbery before...banks, trains. You know what these people are like better than I; they don't ever imagine they'd get caught, do they?'

'No indeed, the game for many is getting away with it. I worked on a case once where a man had robbed the same bank six times.'

'Extraordinary...six times?'

'Yes, and he was a wealthy man, even more so after the robberies. Do you know that on the last two occasions, two days after the theft, he broke back in and put all the money back? How would you classify this type of behaviour?'

'Well, that's a little out of my area of expertise,' admitted Doctor Powell honestly. 'How do you classify a thief anyway? Isn't he just a thief?'

'Well arguably there are a number of classifications for thieves. The first is your common thief. He sets out intentionally to take from you, in order to benefit himself in some way. He may overcharge you for a domestic job, or he might just rob your home, a shop, steal your car, rob a bank, or even steal a child's pocket money. He has different reasons for wanting to steal but common reasons are drug abuse and need. Whatever he steals he needs for something. Sometimes he might want it to sell. He may have a drug addiction or be in serious debt or he may just want to buy a present for his wife or child. My experience with these types of criminals is they do so out of desperation.'

'Fascinating view of the criminal mind! What others are there?'

'The most interesting type is the kleptomaniac. He will often steal from a department store or from a person's home whilst visiting. The majority of these types of thieves are doing it for the rush of taking the chance of being caught. Then there is the unintentional thief. These types of people will take something as simple as a pen or as big as a diamond necklace from a jewellery store or a friend's home. I am sure that you have done this at least once in your life; I'm sure I have also. By unintentional I mean not meaning to steal something.'

'I can't say I've ever stolen anything,' Doctor Powell frowned.

'Ah, not intentionally, but *unintentionally?* Have you never been distracted? Never picked up a pen and then accidentally slipped it into your pocket? Never taken a friend's cigarette lighter?'

'Now you put it that way, yes, I suppose I have on a few occasions.'

'You did it unintentionally. In Holland in my early days, I knew people who made mistakes in bars by forgetting to pay for a drink, or in groups, not settling their tab because they thought someone else had paid for it and left without thinking to check that the bill was settled. It's never easy to classify people, doctor. These acts are all unintentional but nonetheless stealing. So is an unintentional thief really a thief at all?'

'Good question, technically, from what you're saying, it's arguable that this type of theft is human error.'

'But taking something without paying for it, whether it is a service or an object, is still theft, is it not?'

'Yes, I suppose it is.'

'There now, you see how difficult it is for me to classify anything at all? A suicide might be a suicide or it might be a murder, and a murder could be a suicide dressed up as murder. It's never possible to make snap judgements on anything until you have all the facts in front of you. Even then those facts might not help, or in worse case, they may point you in a totally different direction.'

Doctor Powell was thoughtful for a moment. 'So, do you think Larry killed himself, or do you think someone killed him?'

'I know he was killed, doctor, the only question I have in my mind is why.'

'Really? If I were investigating this crime, the questions on my mind would be, how and by whom.'

'How, I already know. The way I look at any case is, how, why, whom. I never really examine "who" until I understand "why." You see, in nearly all the cases I've worked on, "why" leads me directly to "who."'

'Logical. How are you doing with the why?'

'In progress.' Straay put out his cigarette. 'Let me ask you some simple questions.'

'Go on.'

'Why do you think Sir Laurence was killed?'

Doctor Powell thought about the question. 'I think he was probably killed for his money.'

'Did you kill him?'

'No, I did not.'

'Do you know who killed him?'

'No, I do not.'

'Was Ellie Gregson murdered by Sir Laurence?'

'Good heavens where did this spring from? I have to say no...that is, no he can't have done it. I'm sure of that.'

'Really? But forgive me, you don't seem entirely sure.'

'The question was unexpected. I'm quite sure he didn't.'

'Let us just examine the possibility for a moment, if you would be so kind. If he had killed her, do you think it would be another motive for someone else to want to kill him?'

'Well, yes, if you put it like that, of course it would be a motive, but it's fictional. Ellie Gregson was not killed by her husband.'

'I have just one more question and then I will leave you in peace.'

'Fire away.'

'If you knew who killed Sir Laurence, would you tell me?'

Doctor Powell hesitated. Straay watched him for a moment. Eventually he laughed. 'You do like to hit me with the hard ones, don't you?'

'Would you?'

'That depends on the "why" you were talking about, I suppose.'

'It was an unfair question, but you see now how important it is for me to establish the "why" before I hunt the "who."'

'I do indeed.'

◆

Milly Gregson sat in a very large chair overlooking the garden from the warmth of the smoking room. The light played across the windows and into the room so well that there was no need to turn on any of the internal lights. It was obvious to Straay that Milly enjoyed the bright natural light of the sun. On her lap lay unfinished needlework. It seemed that she may have tired of it, or that her mind had wandered. He could tell she'd unpicked a number of stitches. She now simply looked out the window and was lost in her own thoughts. He knew she had a lot on her mind.

From his vantage point by the door, Straay was content to watch her. He had called out her name twice but she had not heard him. Eventually, he stepped further in and coughed just loud enough to bring her thoughts back into the room.

'Pardon my intrusion.' He came up beside her softly.

'No, no it's fine, come in please.' She put down her needlework and uncurled her legs from beneath her. He sat down beside her and turned in his chair so that he could face her more directly.

'I hope you will forgive my directness,' he began, 'but I would like to ask you some more questions.'

Looking directly at him, Milly Gregson said, 'I suspected it would be my turn soon enough.' She offered him a wry smile. 'You have made quite the impression since your arrival.'

'I confess that this is the usual situation for me. What is the general opinion?'

'Of you?'

'Yes, of me, what is the general opinion?'

'What an extraordinary question, I don't see the point of it.'

He thought for a moment and eventually he came up with an answer for her. 'I understand that you enjoy playing chess. Is that not so?'

'It is. I've played all my life. What of it?'

'Well, if I were to say to you, why did you make that move with the pawn, or this move with the bishop, the answer would not be a quick one, would it?'

Milly smiled warmly.

'Ah, meaning that in this game, the game of crime, you are the expert. I get it.' She thought for a moment. 'Well, Major Heskith believes you to be a capable man, but being foreign, especially Dutch, you'll probably fail to figure it all out. He believes that the Dutch are not to be entirely trusted.' She paused, but Straay just waved his hand for her to continue. 'I don't think he puts the Dutch higher up on the list than, say, the French. He's particularly wooden, is Major Heskith.'

Straay was pleased. This assessment was exactly in keeping with the profile he had built up on the Major.

'The Major and his generation have a typically British view of the world. Please continue.'

'Aunt Agatha was initially very annoyed by you, she didn't like you at all, felt you shouldn't be here and shouldn't be poking your nose in. However, I spoke to her about twenty minutes ago and she's since changed that opinion. Something you must have said to her pleased her, although she had more than her fair share of tonics this morning.'

'I think she is a very charming lady and I also think, not quite as—what was that saying someone used? Oh yes—batty; not quite as batty as she makes herself out to be.'

Milly laughed. 'Now, Doctor Powell likes you tremendously, he says that you're quite the brain box.'

'Interesting, I didn't expect that. What about the others?'

'Desmond isn't saying much to anyone. We had a long talk with him last night—told him we'd look after him and so on—but he's frightfully upset still. I don't think he has much of an opinion on anyone at the moment.' She looked a little sad. 'So who does that leave?'

'Dawson, and you.' Straay pulled out a cigarette. 'Do you mind?'

'No, be my guest, may I have one?' She took the offered cigarette and Straay lit it for her.

'Now then, old Dawson doesn't seem to have opinions. He's been very loyal to my father. Mother wanted to get rid of him after father came back from the war, but he wouldn't hear of it. Dawson has probably been the most loyal of my father's servants, you know.'

'That leaves you,' Straay said with a smile. He took a long pull on his cigarette and waited for her response.

'Well,' she hesitated. 'I think you've been very kind and generous, but I also think that's part of your plan. You're here to solve a murder, not to make friends. Ultimately, I believe that your kind nature and ease of manner is a ploy to get the guilty party to fall unsuspectingly into your trap, and then you'll have them. Am I right?'

He smiled brightly. 'I think that when you chose your occupation, you missed a greater calling. You could have very easily turned your mind to psychology.'

'I'm very good at reading people, Doctor Straay.' She gazed at him unblinkingly.

'Of that,' he said blowing a cloud of smoke away from her face, 'I have no doubt.'

'So is it my turn to get the difficult questions?' She seemed eager, a little too eager.

'Are questions ever difficult?' he asked locking eyes with her.

'If you don't know the answers they are,' she replied quickly.

'But the questions I ask aren't so difficult because I firmly believe that everyone here knows the answers. They just choose not to give me the information.'

'Meaning they lie?'

'Yes, meaning they lie. Are you going to lie to me?' He waited for her reply.

'That depends on what you may ask,' she remarked a little sharply. 'Understand that whilst I may answer all the questions of the Chief Inspector and help in any way I can, I'm not obliged and nor is anyone else here, frankly, to answer your questions.' She had turned a little red and Straay was pleased that he'd broken through the façade she had erected. Milly wasn't stupid and she had quickly learnt that Straay wasn't the type of businessman she was used to manipulating. However, he saw in her eyes that she realised that she had been sharp and had given herself away. He flicked ash into the large ornate ashtray beside him and looked away for a moment. Eventually he looked back and smiled.

'I meant no offence.' He was genuine with his reply. 'If you ask me to leave, I will go.'

'No.' She softened her face. 'No, of course I won't ask you to leave. I'm sorry. Ask me anything. I will do my best to answer you.'

'Truthfully?' He raised his eyebrows high on his head.

She nodded.

'Very well, I will ask you some simple questions then. Who killed Sir Laurence?'

'I do not know.' Her answer seemed truthful.

'Why do you think Sir Laurence was killed?'

'For his money, I expect.' This answer was constructed. She didn't really know.

'Are you in love with Desmond DuPont?'

'Yes.' Again, a truthful response.

'Is he in love with you?'

'I honestly don't know.'

'Did you love you mother?'

'Very much so.' Her eyes shone with fondness. 'Even though we didn't see eye to eye, I never stopped loving her. Lately… well let's just say I have found that I loved her more. I'd go so far as to say that I still love her.'

'What has changed in your perception to make the love for your mother increase?'

'Nothing changed, I simply learnt a little more about her recently.' Milly looked a little apprehensive. Straay hadn't missed it. The word lately implied more recently. Something had changed in the way she viewed her mother. It had to be some favourable new perspective of her mother that hadn't occurred to her before now. Somehow, he mused, the information she'd just given him was extremely relevant, so he filed it away in his brain for later analysis.

'Your aunt loved her sister very much, didn't she?'

'Oh yes, very much.'

'Enough to, perhaps, have a motive to, say, murder your father?'

'No,' she shook her head vigorously. 'Agatha didn't like my father it's true, and I'd not be speaking out of turn if I said she actually despised him, but murder? No… Besides, Aunt Agatha can't do much for herself, you know. Her maid is practically her right arm.'

'Ah yes, the faithful Mary…'

Milly nodded.

'Why do you think your mother and father fell out of love after he returned from the war?'

'The war made him angry, aggressive, uncaring in many ways. I suppose it was that change in him that caused my mother to dislike him. You should have seen them before the war. They were inseparable. My mother was very good at tennis, you know. She used to play with father at every opportunity. Agatha also teamed up with her, on occasion. The summer was always full of fun...well, for mother and father. Not for me, I was always stuck in the school or nursery.'

'Why didn't she simply divorce him?'

Milly looked out the window. 'Because deep down, I believe she felt it wasn't entirely his fault.' She turned back for a moment and tears began to form in her eyes.

'You also have to understand something about my mother, Doctor Straay. She wasn't the same as women are now. She knew her place. Yes, she was a powerful lady, rich and well established, but she was a wife also. A wife who made a vow—'till death do us part, isn't that it? Frankly, I think my mother would have been less miserable if my father *had* died in the war. She certainly wished he had on many occasions. It annoyed me.'

'It made you angry with her?'

'It made me very angry with her,' Milly snapped back. 'She was supposed to love him, but all she could do was pick holes, twist the knife. In my deepest, hateful moments, I used to think that she had changed after the war too. In the same way she accused my father of altering.' She stifled a sob.

He thought that this was a good observation. He liked talking to Milly because she was clear and precise. In many ways, her thinking was almost childlike. Whilst she didn't have a black and white view of the world, she certainly had a more profound understanding of it. He suspected that her experiences and her observations had shaped her into the intelligent and interesting person she had become.

Straay wasn't insensitive to the emotional turbulence that was just beneath the surface. He noticed the sadness in her eyes. He was aware how deeply this conversation had affected her.

'Thank you for answering me so honestly. I do not wish to cause you any further pain.' He modulated his voice with compassion. 'Sometimes, these questions, they can hurt. I have only a few more, but if you wish for me to stop, I can come back later.'

'No, I prefer to answer them now.' She wiped her eyes.

'Very well. Can you explain a little more about the relationship between your father and your aunt?'

'Like I said before, they didn't get along. I think he might even have hated her. They argued a lot about money, the house, and practically everything else under the sun.'

'Did they argue about you?'

'No… at least, not that I was aware. I was the one thing that didn't come between them.'

'What was your father's relationship like with Major Heskith and Doctor Powell?'

'Heskith was father's best friend. I only knew of one occasion when they had a heated discussion and that was shortly after some kind of accident on a shoot. Doctor Powell was also a good friend of father's. They often spent a lot of time together. It was Doctor Powell who introduced father to Desmond.'

'Thank you, now my last question. Who, in your opinion, had the biggest motive for wanting your father dead?'

'I did,' she said simply.

'Why?'

'Because with him gone, I would inherit most of the estate and his business and money.'

'Did you kill your father?'

'No I did not.'

'So then, if what you say is true, who next would have the motive to want your father dead?'

Milly thought for a moment...she thought very hard. Eventually she sighed. 'I suspect the person with the strongest motive, other than mine, would be my aunt.'

Straay sat for a moment looking out the same window. All roads lead to Rome, he thought, or in this scenario, to Lady Agatha.

ACT TWO

Chapter Sixteen

Drake Goes Fishing

Chief Inspector Drake had spent many hours reading reports on all of the suspects. He sat in his temporary office at the local station and sipped his lukewarm tea. The medical report still wasn't available and the medical examiner had practically thrown him out of the morgue. He was therefore content to wait and to fill that time by going through the background reports he'd had made up. The Home Office and Scotland Yard had come up with most of the information, which had been scarce at best. The rest consisted of local information, gossip, hearsay, and rumour gathered by a team of policemen and civilian staff during the course of the day. Three very efficient and meticulous secretaries had cross-referenced all the notes, typed up the profile documents and, whilst they looked neat, tidy and well presented, the bottom line was that they weren't very satisfactory. Drake decided to skip the extraneous information such as dates of schooling, rationing details, death duties, and childhood medical records etc.

The first file on the top of the pile was that of Major Heskith. The major had an honourable career in the Army, by all accounts. He'd been discharged at the end of the war with full honours. Two years after the war he had been awarded his OBE. The award had been helped by the backing of Sir Laurence and a few of his high placed friends and family. These connections in government had pushed the Major's name much higher on the very considerable list. It seemed that Sir Laurence even had the ear of the Prime Minister. None of this intervention suggested that the Major hadn't earned or indeed warranted the prestigious award. From what little there was in the records, the Major had a very straightforward career as an aspiring officer, rising to the rank of Major just before the war ended. Indeed, Sir Laurence himself had promoted him. His last few campaigns were classified as top secret, so the information on these was sparse. It is sufficient to say that these campaigns had resulted in the accolades and awards that ultimately led to him receiving an OBE. Everything checked out. Major Heskith was, basically, a model citizen who had served his country with distinction. Nothing in any of the official files, both from the Yard and from the Home Office, suggested any blight on his character at all.

The second file was that of Lady Agatha Geraldine Smythe. Here again was a perfectly good citizen with hardly any record of anything untoward. It was, however, empty of practically any information, which wasn't untypical for her class and the high society she moved in. Lady Agatha wouldn't have done much for herself; she would have had all her needs taken care of by her staff. The records showed all major jobs, outside of some personal matters, such as purchases, bill payments and the daily minutia of life, were performed by the dedicated staff assigned to her in whichever household she happened to reside in at the time. The only thing that showed up in the records from the Home Office was her clearance for active military duty as a nurse in St. Mary's Hospital, Dover. She'd spent four years, right to the end of the war, nursing at both the major burns units and the amputation wards. Evidently, she had seen her fair share of horrors in her time. This might go a long way toward explaining her dependency on drink.

Drake put down the second file and then picked up the third.

Milly Gregson's file had practically no information at all aside from the very basic birth records and schooling. She was by all accounts a well-liked woman who had been involved in many charitable affairs for the local community. There was nothing to indicate that she had been involved in any criminal activities and everything to suggest that she was, like the previous two, a model citizen.

He put down Milly's file and picked up the fourth.

Doctor Powell's history was that of an honest well-liked man who had performed his duties as a general practitioner with distinction. There were no complaints laid against him and nothing to suggest any ill treatment of patients. There was no evidence of any wrongdoing, medically, in his long career, and not a hint of killing off any elderly and/or wealthy patients and taking their pensions or being left legacies in their wills. The death rate during his time was in line with what one would expect from a local country community. To add to his character, he assisted as a volunteer doctor at St. Thomas' Hospital twice a week in the capacity of general physician, and devoted himself to his rounds and caring for his community without exception. Everything Drake had found on Doctor Powell in the official records showed him to be beyond reproach.

This file was neatly placed on the pile and he picked up and started to read the fifth, which seemed a little more promising than the last four.

Dawson, who was actually James Patrick Davies Dawson, was the son of Patrick Davies Dawson. His family had been in service for at least four generations. His father had been butler to the Smythe family before Lady Elizabeth had married Larry Gregson, as had his father before him. The younger Dawson had a criminal record for drunken behaviour and reckless endangerment. As a young man, he had been arrested for knocking a police constable off his bike while driving his master's car. There was a scandal at the time, but it was hushed up by the family, as far as he could tell. Interestingly, the young police constable at the time was now a sergeant at the station. He'd been very happy to give a full account to Drake about the incident. None of this information proved anything concrete regarding the murder of Sir Laurence. At worst, it was simply youthful exuberance. It hardly made Dawson a murderer. Again, Drake found himself sighing; it was all very unsatisfactory. Perhaps Straay could find more in these files than he had.

Lastly, he came to Desmond DuPont's file. In contrast, this file showed a number of interesting and conflicting statements associated with his name. There had been a question of checking out the legal degree, because his associate at the Yard had suggested it might not be the real deal. There was a note in the margin that said, "Checked with Trinity College, President wasn't available, said you would call, number below."

Drake picked up the telephone and dialled the number for the President's office. The call was connected and a very efficient young woman answered it.

'Trinity College, President's office, how may I help you?'

'Can I speak with the President please?' Drake asked politely.

'May I ask who is calling please?'

'Certainly, it's Chief Inspector Drake of Scotland Yard.'

'Hold for one moment while I connect you, Chief Inspector.'

There was a pause of about two minutes and eventually the young woman's voice was replaced by that of a man.

'This is the President speaking, how may I assist you, Chief Inspector?' He had a polite and articulate voice.

'I'm calling to check on the validity of a degree that was issued by your College three years ago, on September the fourteenth.'

'Ah,' he uttered, 'this would be for a…' There was a pause. 'Mr Desmond DuPont, would it not?'

'That's correct, sir.'

'It's doctor, actually. One of your chaps called earlier and left me a message. I had my secretary search the files and have the information here. Checked and double checked.'

'Can you confirm its validity?'

'I most certainly cannot, Chief Inspector. The degree is almost certainly a fake.'

'I see...thank you for corroborating that. You say almost certainly, doctor, not certainly. That's an interesting choice of words.'

'A linguistic mistake purely.' There was a slight hesitation, as if the President had just realised that he was talking to an intelligent man. 'I should correct it with: it is certainly a fake.'

'Again, thank you for your corroboration. May I ask if the issue number matches anyone else's award?'

'No, that degree doesn't match any on our records. It is complete nonsense. It does share the correct markers we use to signify a legitimate degree, but it isn't, I assure you. '

'I don't mean to be rude but is it possible that your records may be wrong?'

'We have just a little fewer than four hundred years of history at this College, Inspector…'

'Chief Inspector,' he corrected. 'Please go on.'

'Chief Inspector, my apologies. As I was saying, record keeping and maintenance was all ironed out quite a few hundred years back.'

'I see. So then, I can take it on your authority that this degree is definitely a fake?'

'You most certainly can. A poor one at that.'

'Hardly poor, doctor, considering it is on formal Oxford University letterhead and has all the correct seals.'

'You make an interesting point, Chief Inspector.'

'Has anyone with the name Desmond DuPont ever attended or signed up to your college within the last five years?'

'There is no record of a Desmond DuPont attending this college going back twenty years, Chief Inspector. I have been President for the last five.'

Drake made a quick note on the file. 'That is very helpful. May I ask you if you were acquainted with Sir Laurence Gregson?'

'He is on the board of trustees. You say were and not are. What has happened to him?'

'He was murdered yesterday evening.'

'Dear me, that is horrible. What is the connection to this Desmond DuPont then?'

'He is a suspect. DuPont was a lawyer working for Sir Laurence. They were close friends, I am led to believe. That is why I wanted to be absolutely positive that you hadn't come across him.'

'I am positive.'

'You see, doctor, it does worry me a little that here we have a member of the board of trustees at your College, and his close friend and legal advisor has a fake degree, which is also from your College. You can understand that concern, can't you?'

'I have no idea what you're suggesting.'

'You have every idea what I'm suggesting, doctor, because you're an intelligent man. You'd hardly be in your position if you weren't. Is it possible?'

'I refute the allegation in the strongest possible terms!'

'Noted. Is it possible?'

'No.' There was more hesitation in the voice. 'Well at the very least, on the face of it, I'd say highly improbable.'

'I see, but not impossible?' Drake persisted.

'What you're suggesting is impossible, yes.'

'What am I suggesting, doctor?'

'I think you're suggesting that someone here faked a degree at the request of Sir Laurence. I say someone, as I assume you're not in fact accusing me?'

'I am not accusing anyone at the moment, doctor. You are then still sure it is not possible?'

'I am sure.'

'Even if money was a motivating factor. It will be easy enough to check...I have a copy of Sir Laurence's bank statements in front of me.'

'Again, I refute the allegation. Sir Laurence was a benefactor of this college and, on occasion, he wrote us charitable cheques, but that action would not, and did not influence me, or my staff, in any way, to issue a degree fraudulently to any of his friends. It goes against all our principles and against hundreds of years of established procedures. Why are you assuming that the degree and letters were faked at this college anyway?'

'The letterhead and seals are genuine; so either we have an expert who is capable of reproducing genuine Oxford University documents and seals with precision, but is not capable of counterfeiting a genuine degree, or we have someone at the college who has produced a poor copy of a degree on legitimate stationery. It would need to be someone who had access to both the letterheads and the seals. Now I ask you, which seems the more plausible?'

'As you describe it, the latter. That isn't to say I believe it.'

'Thank you for clarifying that aspect. You can then account for the professional conduct of all your staff, I assume?'

'Well, certainly the fellows and scholars, I can account for their professional conduct, yes. I will not go on record saying I can account for their private and personal business.'

'Ah, so it is then possible?'

'No!'

'But if you cannot account for the private and personal business of your staff, then surely it follows you cannot answer my question with full knowledge?'

'It would be almost impossible to perform,' the President retorted hotly. 'I cannot see how it would be done and—even if I allowed myself to believe this had been orchestrated by a member of my staff, in the manner you suggest—it would be a feat of extraordinary fraud the likes of which –'

'So it is just possible then?' interrupted Drake.

'Yes, I suppose it is possible, but highly –'

'Improbable,' Drake finished. 'I understand.'

'At any rate,' continued the President, 'this college has awarded and continues to award honorary, that is, *honoris causa* degrees at regular graduation ceremonies. The term honorary degree is, perhaps, a misnomer because, generally speaking, a person who is awarded one would be entitled to the same standing and would be granted the same privileges as their substantive counterparts. This could have been *de facto* awarded, although that's not to say that they are just handed out. It is a formal and lengthy process and it takes time to finalise properly.

Now an *ad eundem* or *jure dignitatis* degree is sometimes considered honorary, although they are only conferred on an individual who has already achieved a comparable qualification at another university or by attaining an office requiring the appropriate level of scholarship. From what I understand this person has no such qualifications, standing, or office.'

'Well the answer is obvious to me, doctor. Time would seem to me to be the factor. There is always the possibility that your various committees would turn down the application, is that not so?'

'Yes, although we don't accept applications for *honoris causa* degrees. People are nominated by the university. It's feasible that Sir Laurence could nominate through an established scholar or fellow, but I assure you he didn't. We keep records of everything.'

'Not everything, it would seem, doctor.'

'We keep records of all legitimate practices then!'

'Then we're looking at, possibly, the oldest motive in the book.'

'Which is?'

'Greed.'

'I suppose you're right,' the President eventually conceded. 'I will look into the matter and get back to you. If I find anything, and that's a big if, you can be assured of a call.'

'I do appreciate your help, doctor, and if you would be so kind as to provide me with a list of all staff, their contact details and function within the college, I would be grateful. You say you keep excellent records so I would also like information on anything Sir Laurence attended, including guests and staff; dinners, functions, meetings, minutes of meetings. Anything connected to Sir Laurence.'

'It will be done, Chief Inspector.'

After the conversation was over, Drake put down the receiver and made a few notes on the file.

Chapter Seventeen

The Paper Hunt

Drake was pleased. Desmond DuPont definitely had not been awarded a legitimate degree by Oxford University, Trinity College. It was a fake. His legal secretary status was legitimate as were his other paralegal qualifications, these had already been checked out, but the degree wasn't. Drake also found it very interesting that Sir Laurence Gregson was a benefactor of the college. If Sir Laurence had put pressure on anyone for his associate to have such a degree, then there may be records in his bank accounts that proved it, although it didn't seem likely he would leave an obvious paper trail for anyone to find. Drake wondered if Straay had found out any more about the man.

Drake picked up the telephone and dialled. He spoke to one of the researchers at the Yard. He asked specifically for her to look into all legal matters DuPont had worked on because now that Drake knew he wasn't a qualified lawyer, he was under legal obligation to ensure the organisations who employed DuPont were also aware of his fraudulent status. It would be necessary to prepare a review of all their legal work, and inform their clients and other interested parties of the possible effects, once this information went public. He imagined a lot of very nervous directors and accountants and that thought made him smile.

Chief Inspector Drake had moved DuPont's file to the top of his pile, on the left of his temporary desk. Over the next hour, he made several other calls to colleagues at the Yard, but was ultimately disappointed, as there was nothing more forthcoming. He would yet again have to wait for answers.

◆

Drake was again alone with his thoughts. *What did this discovery mean in real terms?* Without a doubt, Desmond DuPont was a fraud. He had definitely broken the law and that alone necessitated a thorough examination of the man. Drake considered having him brought to the station but dismissed the idea. DuPont was currently under observation, and in a place where he was under the same pressure as anyone else there. Given his emotional state, it wouldn't be wise to move him out of a comfortable environment. DuPont was far more likely to spill the beans to Straay in conversation, than to Drake in a formal interview. In custody, he would likely shut up like an oyster and say nothing. Still, Drake couldn't help thinking to himself that things didn't add up.

Chief Inspector Drake sighed again and put down the file in disappointment. He had rather hoped to have more on the others by now. DuPont may be a scoundrel, he mused, but if it was by Sir Laurence's own hand or intervention that he had prospered, either via a fake degree or financially, he would be hardly likely to murder the man, let alone dress the action up as a suicide. It was not beyond the bounds of possibility that DuPont had orchestrated the crime for reason or reasons unknown. Drake just had that nagging feeling that emotionally he simply wasn't up to the task.

Drake was the first to admit he knew very little psychology but he was experienced enough with people to know a little about their characters. He had interviewed, charged, and been instrumental in hanging enough bold and inventive killers in his time to feel justified in his hesitance. On the little evidence he had, DuPont just didn't fit the picture. Hanging a person for murder was justifiable but hanging a person on the pretext of murder, based on evidence of him being a conman simply wasn't. He kept hearing that phrase, *'Don't bite the hand that feeds you."*

◆

Drake got up from his desk and stretched. He'd caught about an hour or two of sleep in the chair whilst the reports were being typed. He was still tired. He shook himself mentally. Even though he'd rested a little, he couldn't allow himself the luxury of proper rest until he was at least a little further forward. He checked his pocket-watch and noted the time, four-thirty. He planned to be over at the house that evening to sit down with Straay and swap information. There were still things he needed to do before that could happen.

He picked up the file marked gossip, rumour, and hearsay. The data had been collected from various sources, local shopkeepers, post office masters, railway employees, local pub gossip, and a few ex-employees. Drake read all the information gathered on each person three or four more times. Half the information was useless because there was no way of corroborating any of it. The rest was built up with half-truths, stories twisted over time, details of sordid love affairs, and blatant lies from disgruntled employees. There were, however, some possible lines of inquiry.

The distinguished Major might have been a bit of a "ladies man," from many accounts, and suggestions were rife that he had also been possibly courting Lady Agatha or even Ellie Gregson.

One nameless source stated that Doctor Powell had got a young woman pregnant and had "taken care of the child." By this it was implied the child had been terminated. There was no record of the name of the girl.

There was hardly anything on Milly Gregson, although the rumour mill in the town was that she and DuPont were romantically engaged. She was described as having many male followers, but there was no evidence of this. She was attractive, and it would be understandable, but it was mainly rumour and hearsay. Drake firmly believed the possible romantic link between her and DuPont was spot on.

Lady Agatha was hardly talked about by anyone, although some of the older people had mentioned her war background and, *"how nice it was that she'd been working in the hospitals, you know, like a real person."*

Dawson had the greatest amount of information attached to him. Most accounts seemed to suggest he was a heavy drinker. Played poker in the local pub once a week and was the source of all the gossip for the house. Three separate accounts suggest that he had apparently had a brother who had died early on in the war, which wasn't uncommon. Many families had loved ones who had perished in the conflict. A few reports indicated that Dawson had become quite well off in recent years. The sources said that he told them Ellie Gregson had left him a small fortune when she died. The will of Lady Gregson, however, told a different story.

Drake rubbed his eyes; none of this was helping him, but he knew from experience Straay would pore over this information before he even bothered to look at the official records. He understood why of course. Even if his training and procedure didn't allow *him* to see the importance of it, this information would give Straay a clue.

Drake sat back down and made a few notes.

1. DuPont – fraud. Find known associates and pull more information on them. Go over the background again.
2. Dawson – criminal record. Perform further checks into the reasons behind his behaviour on that night and his motivation, drinking habits, etc. Money: where did it come from?
3. Major Heskith – Lady Agatha and/or Ellie Gregson love interest.
4. Doctor Powell – possible links with abortion?

Drake then opened up the last file with the title: Lieutenant Colonel Sir Laurence Howard Gregson, VC, KCB, CBE. Underneath the name in bold red letters was the word, "Classified." He opened the file and was amazed to find only one sheet of paper in it. There were dates of service, dates of awards, and dates of victory campaigns, lists of voluntary work and a summary of his life leading to and after the war, but nothing else. Whatever his work in the war and after it was, there was no mention of it at all in this file. When he'd requested the file, he knew it would involve red tape. Superintendent Baker was able to give him a little bit of background from his personal experiences, which amounted to very little that he didn't already know.

The telephone rang loudly, breaking his train of thought. He answered it quickly.

'Drake. I see. Thank you, doctor, I will come down immediately.' He replaced the receiver and smiled; at last the medical examination was complete. Drake pushed back his chair and stood. He looked down for a moment and then rearranged some files. Nodding once, he left the room, turning off the lamp on his way to the door.

Chapter Eighteen

Doctor Carmichael and Mr Daniels

The medical centre was a short walk away from the station. It was an ordinary small redbrick building which had originally been a bomb shelter during the war, later modernised and extended. Drake approached with trepidation. In all his years as a police officer and detective, he had never entirely gotten used to the sights and smells of death. He took a moment to clear his mind and, as he entered through the glass doors into the clinical atmosphere, the overwhelming smell of formaldehyde reinforced that dislike immensely.

The room was tiled in white, with concrete flooring. It was clinically clean. Along the centre of the room in a neat row, he saw six stainless steel tables. All were empty, except for one. There was a body neatly covered with a clean white sheet that could only have been Sir Laurence Gregson. He approached it just as Doctor Carmichael came through an adjacent door.

'Ah, there you are,' the doctor said purposefully.

Carmichael came forward to meet him. He was a tall and efficient man, clean-shaven and well into his late fifties. His hair was grizzled silver-grey and thinning at the sides of his large tanned head. He wore a pair of large gold-rimmed spectacles with a chain looped around his neck. He was the type of man who never seemed to age. Drake suppressed a smile. *He reminds me of my grandfather, who looked the same from the age of fifty up to seventy.*

Like his grandfather, Carmichael had a very pleasant countenance and always greeted people with a smile. He removed his spectacles and allowed them to drop and hang on his chest. Without preamble, he began his report.

'My preliminary investigation into the death of Sir Laurence Gregson is now concluded, Chief Inspector. I apologise for the length of time it has taken, but with a case of this prominence it is something of a habit of mine that we double and triple check our findings.' He pulled back the cloth to show the head and pointed at the wound with a pen he had pulled from the pocket of his white coat.

'Cause of death was a single gunshot to the head, without doubt. You can see here that the bullet traversed the left side of the head, an inch and a half to the left of the orbital cavity. The bullet proceeded through the soft tissues of the face into the temporal bone. It expanded inward in a conical fashion. Several pieces of small curvilinear lead fragments were retrieved from this area. The bullet then proceeded through the left temporal lobe of the brain in an upward and forward direction to perforate the middle cerebral.' He turned the head. 'The bullet then exited through the left parietal bone here, causing, as you can see, extensive damage to the surrounding soft tissue.'

Doctor Carmichael allowed Drake to examine the body before continuing.

'The stomach contents consisted largely of partly digested meats and vegetables; I should say he'd eaten around three hours before his death, no longer than that. There was a mixture of alcoholic beverages in his stomach, suggesting he had consumed them probably no less than twenty minutes before death.' Carmichael pulled the sheet back further and replaced his spectacles.

'Now we come to the interesting bit.' He moved around the table so that he was facing the body from its right side.

'You remember I told you about the lack of blood secretion?'

'Yes, Doctor Straay said something about his blood pressure being low?'

'He's an intelligent man, Doctor Straay. I've read about him. He was also quite right. Look here,' he said pointing at a reddish mark on the right shoulder. 'You probably can't see it, but there is a puncture wound here which goes deep into the deltoid muscle.' Drake looked hard but eventually shook his head.

'I'll take your word for it, doctor.' He smiled at him.

'Well, that puncture wound introduced a poison into his system. We've identified it as curare. Symptoms of curare poisoning include paralysis of the extremities, which gradually moves in towards the victim's neck, arms, and legs, finally paralysing the muscles of the chest and lungs, which would eventually cause death. It's not possible to predict the actual dose injected, but it would have been a fatal one to be sure.'

Drake frowned for a moment. 'This was the reason that his blood pressure was too low to allow the head wound to bleed copiously?'

'Yes. If his blood pressure was that low, he really didn't have much time before his heart would stop. The poison would have done the job perfectly, so it makes no sense to me to put a bullet through his head at all.' Carmichael shook his head.

'Sometimes motives are clouded. What if the person who shot him didn't know he had been poisoned?' Drake realised the implication of that just as the doctor responded.

'If that is true, you're looking for two murderers. Well, one actual murderer and one person who was attempting to murder him. Either would have been successful in my opinion. Complicated stuff for you, what?'

'Getting more complicated by the minute. How long before the drug took effect?'

'Minutes. Once introduced, he'd have succumbed very quickly to its paralysing effect.'

'Perhaps the motive was to paralyse him and put him unconscious, but not kill him. It's possible the person who used it did not know it would kill?'

'Doesn't seem likely to me,' Carmichael's reply was quick and with authority. 'In my opinion, anyone who goes to the trouble of using poisons, especially this type, will know the effect it will produce. Curare isn't easy to obtain and I doubt a layman would consider it. It's the number one reason why people tend to use arsenic: because it's easily available. No, you don't use curare unless you know what it does. Like lead or mercury poisoning, they all have their own specific effects. He wouldn't have been unconscious, by the way.'

'No?'

'Oh no, he'd have been quite aware of what was going on right up to the end. Curare is a nasty poison. No, poor Sir Laurence would have been able to see, hear, and be completely aware, just unable to do anything about it. Pretty horrific if you ask me.'

'So it's not easy to get curare?'

'Certainly not. You can't pop into the local chemist and get some over the counter, that's for sure.'

'Where could you get it?'

'A few ways spring to mind. In its potent and raw form, you could get it direct from its source; it's a plant known as *Strychnos toxifera.* You would however need to travel to South America to get it. It's used as a poison by natives, for hunting. I know that some museums have it—you know, for display purposes. Recently, curare has been used as an anaesthetic in modern medicine because of its paralysing effect.'

'So a doctor could obtain it?'

'Technically, yes, or a nurse for that matter, but not easily.'

'That's very interesting. Anything else?'

'Just one thing. I don't know if it helps you or hinders you but Sir Laurence had tumours on his pancreas, and his liver was in very bad condition. Based on observation and the laboratory results we estimate that had he not been poisoned or shot, he probably would have had about three to six months to live; no more than six months, definitely.' He handed Drake the file. 'My full report is in there. You'll find initial observations on the body and full details of internal organ observations, weights, photographs and so on.'

'Do you think this illness was something he would have known about?'

'That's difficult to say. I would imagine, though, he would have been feeling pretty ill, judging by the state of his liver. It seems highly unlikely he wouldn't know anything about it, but a lot of people do put off going to see a doctor; it's the times we live in, eh, Chief Inspector?'

'Indeed. Well thank you, Doctor Carmichael.'

'A pleasure, Chief Inspector.' After a firm handshake, Doctor Carmichael covered the body and escorted Drake out of the building.

◆

Things were going off in so many directions. It was difficult for Chief Inspector Henry Drake to get his mind clear about what his next move should be. As he walked slowly towards his car, he found himself pondering a number of questions. The first and most important was: *who had the most to gain from Sir Laurence's death?* The second question that struck him was: *why was he poisoned before he was shot?* It was obvious that this murder had darker undertones than he'd initially thought. It was also a fact that, had Straay not insisted on investigating further, he would simply have classified it as a suicide and, had that happened, they might not have determined that Sir Laurence had been poisoned at all. Shaking his head slightly, he reached his car and got in.

Sir Laurence Dies

The journey to number thirteen Brunswick Avenue, Doctor Powell's house, took ten minutes with traffic. He pulled up outside the picturesque Victorian house and smiled. Wisteria and ivy climbed the side wall, right up to the chimney, and in every respect, it was exactly the type of house he imagined Doctor Powell would own. There were neat lawns on either side of a perfectly straight path leading to a pristine wooden front door. At the front were privet hedges and colourful rose bushes. Drake passed by the gate and entered number fourteen. As he entered, he noticed with mild interest that the neighbour was not as fanatical about his front lawn as the doctor was about his. In contrast to the doctor's house, his neighbour was slovenly.

Drake pressed the doorbell and waited patiently for a response. After about two minutes or so, he pressed again. Drake decided to walk around the house. He peered into a window and could see that the lights were on. He walked around to the back of the house and called out. There was no reply. He reached a gate that communicated with the back garden and gingerly tried it. It opened and again he called out to no reply. As he entered, he noticed a lawn chair and table situated a little way off the back porch. A man was asleep in the chair. Drake came forward and removed his hat.

'Excuse me,' he said politely.

The man jumped out of the chair.

'Who the devil are you and what are you doing in my garden.' The man had been startled awake and Drake noticed that mixture of anger and fear typical of being shocked awake. He apologised and produced his credentials.

'Sorry to barge in.' He put his warrant card away. 'I just wanted to ask you a few questions about your neighbour, Doctor Powell.' The man looked furtive for a moment and then indicated the back door.

'Well,' he stifled a yawn, 'perhaps we'd be more comfortable sitting inside.' He led the way into the kitchen and pulled out a chair from underneath a very untidy table. Drake sat down and placed his hat on top of a pile of books.

'Would you like some tea?'

Drake nodded.

Mr Daniels put the water on the stove and put a couple of spoonsful of dark tea leaves in a small pot. Taking a small tray from under the sink, he placed onto it a sugar bowl, a small milk jug, and some silverware and taking the tray in hand, he put it onto a tray-shaped space on the table. Clearly, this space was reserved for tea. He sat down while the water heated and said:

'How can I help you, Chief Inspector?'

'I'd be grateful, Mr Daniels, if I could just run through the statement you gave one of my officers this morning.'

'I see.' Just then the kettle whistled. He got up, poured the water into the pot, and then added this and two cups and saucers to the tray.

'Anything to be of help. Fire away.' He poured out two cups of tea, adding a little milk and pushed the sugar bowl towards Drake who declined.

'What time did Doctor Powell arrive home last night?'

'Well,' Mr Daniels took a sip of his tea. 'Certainly around ten...I can't be precise about the time. I was writing, you see. I heard, and then saw, the car pull up, but I don't have a clock in front of me.' He thought for a moment. 'I'd just made cocoa and that was at about nine-forty-five. Sorry I'm not being very precise.'

'I see. Did you actually see Doctor Powell enter his house?'

'Well,' he said again. 'It's rather difficult to be sure. I remember seeing him leave his car and he was carrying his coat and medical bag, so he must have, mustn't he?'

'You didn't actually see him go into the house though?' Drake took a sip of his tea. Mr Daniels' behaviour was odd. He fidgeted slightly, blinked a few times, and then smiled.

'Well,' he took another sip of tea. 'No, but the light came on a little while after he had come out of his car, so he was definitely home.'

'You say you were writing, it must be very easy for you to lose track of time when engaged in a creative activity like that, wouldn't you agree?'

'Well,' Drake inwardly cringed at the use of the word "well." Outwardly, he gave no such impression. 'It is easy, yes. I would have to agree with you there.' He smiled again.

'You lent the doctor a book, I understand. What was it called...?'

'*Cimarron* by Edna Ferber. It's an American book, but don't let that put you off, it's very well written.' Drake made a note in his pad.

'When did you lend him this book?'

'Well,' he paused in thought for a moment. 'I'd like to say a week ago, maybe two, it's so difficult to be sure of these things.' He poured himself another cup of tea and offered more to Drake, who politely refused.

'Did you see or hear Doctor Powell leave his house at any time after he returned home at around ten?'

'No, he didn't leave the house at all, not until this morning.' There was no hesitation this time.

'How can you be so sure?' Drake finished his cup and put it down on the saucer.

'Well...' Mr Daniels, thought Drake, had now quite definitely become the most annoying person he'd spoken to for some time.

'His car never left its parking spot. Doctor Powell never went anywhere on foot, he always took his car. He says it's because he spends so much time walking to and from patients that he likes the rest when he's driving. I'm sure I heard him talking to someone in his kitchen at around eleven, maybe a little after. Then later, maybe at around twelve, I was in my back garden smoking a cigar, as I often do after I finish my writing, and he was definitely out in his garden too. Mind you, you don't have to see him to know he's there. That pipe of his is always on the go and you can smell that tobacco before you see him. It's such a lovely smell.'

Chapter Nineteen

The Lawyer Speaks

The day was moving swiftly into evening. Straay had managed to talk with just about the entire household, with the exception of Desmond DuPont and Dawson. These two had been clearly avoiding him. That was okay. Their avoidance wasn't necessarily a bad thing because it meant that he was able to concentrate on some of the things he'd learnt during his previous conversations. *What had he learnt?* A few new threads had presented themselves during the day. There was a lot more information for him to process.

Lady Agatha knew a lot more about the relationship between her sister and Sir Laurence then she was letting on. Some of that reticence was probably due to her upbringing, he mused, but a lot of it was because Lady Agatha was actually very adept at making sure that people only discovered what she wanted them to find out. Or so she thought.

Milly was a keen observer of people and was very quick at adjusting to the intelligence level of the person with whom she conversed. She was also in love with Desmond DuPont, and she was quite attached to her Aunt. She was also definitely hiding something. Whatever it was went to the very heart of the matter, of that Straay was sure.

He didn't feel he'd learnt a lot more about the Major. He wasn't as black and white as he'd first thought; there was a hidden depth to the man. One he hadn't managed to reach yet. He would have to consider a different tactic in conversation to get to the layers beneath. That might be an interesting challenge, but was it necessary? Would he actually learn any more relevant details from this man? He suspected he wouldn't.

In contrast to the others, Doctor Powell was exceptionally easy-going. A pleasant man to debate with and highly intelligent, he didn't appear in any way to be bothered by Straay or his techniques. Powell was a man who was used to dealing with professionals. That made him one of the most likely suspects. If they were dealing with a psychopath, which seemed a reasonable theory, then the profile he'd built on the doctor certainly matched.

Doctor Straay put down his notebook, picked up the half-empty cup of black coffee, and drained it. The more he thought back over the day and interviews, he was sure that he was edging closer to uncovering something that would tie the many threads he had together. These people all had connections deeper than just being friends or family. They had a connection to this crime. It wasn't chance or just random actions, it was tangible. They were all intrinsically linked to it. The trouble was, although he could find a few crossed threads, they didn't all link up. There was something vital that he was missing, and that simply meant he had more work to do. He wasn't put off by failure or setbacks. He'd been statistically very successful in his career and this wasn't due to luck. He was a hard worker and he thoroughly enjoyed what he did. That alone made him probably the most dangerous person in the house.

◆

Straay looked up as the door softly opened. Standing in the doorway, unreadable as ever, was James Dawson.

'I understand you wanted to talk to me, sir?' Dawson's posture suggested he would rather be doing anything other than talking to him. This was going to be interesting. Straay smiled inwardly.

'Yes, I did. Please come in and sit for a moment.'

Dawson hesitated and then, making up his mind, he closed the door and walked across the room. He took the seat offered.

'I can't be too long,' he remarked quickly. 'Dinner will require my attention soon.'

'Of course,' Straay nodded. 'Why don't you tell me about yourself?'

'Anything in particular?' He looked sideways at him.

'Well, why don't you tell me about your youth and work forwards from there?'

'There isn't much to tell really.' He was pensive. 'My childhood was pretty ordinary...nothing special, you know. We lived in a house on the estate back then, before it was torn down to build a summerhouse. My mother was a housekeeper here and my father served initially as a footman and then went on to second, then first footman. Later he moved to the role of valet and ended as butler to General Smythe. Like his father had done before him.' He spoke with pride of his father's achievements. It was very clear that to Dawson, family was everything, and that the traditions of service were sacred.

'When I was old enough,' Dawson continued, 'I started working here too. I began my career as footman and in the same way my father had, worked up through the ranks until I eventually became butler. Back then, of course, there were a lot more staff. I am pretty much the House Steward now, although officially I never took on that role because it would take me out of service.'

'I see.' Straay understood what he meant. As a House Steward, Dawson would no longer be considered a servant but a professional man. 'You learnt the ropes from your father?'

'I learnt life skills here at this house from many people,' he replied quickly. 'My father was proud of my achievements. I suppose I learnt my father's trade in the same way he did before me. It was the way of things.'

'In fact it was expected?'

'Yes.'

'Do you have any children?'

'I have a daughter, yes. She will be nineteen at the end of the month.'

'Your wife is in service?'

'My wife died seven years ago. My daughter is living with my sister in Andover.'

'Do you see your daughter much?'

'I haven't seen her in seven years.'

'Why is that?'

'That's personal. It can have no bearing on your investigation.' Dawson said evenly.

'I didn't mean to offend you. When did you take position as butler here?'

'I became butler shortly after my father retired from service. Ill health forced him to slow down and as I had been groomed for the position, it was natural that I should take over his responsibilities. Shortly after doing so, my father died. My mother remained here with my wife and me, but she too eventually passed away. When my wife died I moved into this house. I have a room upstairs.'

'How did your wife die?'

'She died of an infection.' Dawson was being very tight lipped. His posture during the interview was strained. Either this was painful for him to discuss or, as Straay was more inclined to think, he wasn't being entirely honest.

'Can you tell me about the relationship between Ellie Gregson and Lady Agatha?'

'They loved each other very much.' The change of subject was appreciated and showed very clearly as his posture relaxed, just a little.

'They didn't always see eye to eye,' he went on, 'but that didn't affect the way they were together. Before Sir Laurence went off to war, both Lady Agatha and Mr David were regularly here for parties and so on. It was a much happier time. Sadly Mr David died in the war, along with my brother.'

Straay decided on a new tactic. He became remorseful. 'It was a dreadful time, wasn't it? We all lost loved ones; I don't know a family that didn't.'

'I thought your lot were neutral?' Dawson had clearly been speaking to the Major.

'The Dutch were neutral during the war, but not all Dutch people were living in the Netherlands. For me, growing up in Holland, it was very difficult. My father was a professor and he taught all over Europe. We moved from place to place. We had not long settled in Belgium when the war started. We were moved around so much as the war unfolded. I never really had a place to call my own.'

'You lost family too?' Dawson asked sympathetically.

'Yes, many.' Straay dropped his head slightly and sighed. 'Once my father realised that our nationality wouldn't save us, we had no choice but to leave. There was just my mother, father, and two brothers then, but we didn't stay in one place very long there. Wherever we went, the threat of occupation came, so we made it to the north of France and then over to England. I stayed here with my family until after the war ended. I went to school here. We eventually moved back to Belgium and I continued my education there. The one thing that always stuck with me was that our house was exactly as we had left it. Can you imagine that? It was very surreal. The small table in the kitchen still had the dinner plates on it. The house had been emptied of valuables of course. We never saw the family members who stubbornly refused to leave. To this day we still do not know what happened to them.'

'It does drive an arrow through your heart doesn't it? To have no control over events? It's as if you're watching your life in a picture house. You can see everything unfolding but you can't interact with anyone.'

Dawson had finally let down his guard, Straay thought, now I'm getting somewhere. 'That is a good observation,' he remarked, nodding as he did so. 'It is like that. You see the moving image. You see the participants in the story, but nothing you can say or do will allow you to influence them in any way. Tragedy begets tragedy.'

'It does too, sir. I remember when my brother went to war. Oh, we tried to convince him of the folly of it. He wouldn't listen though, had big ideas he did, head stuck in the clouds. Didn't want to be tied to a job in service.' Dawson spat the words out. '"What's wrong with being in service?" I asked him "Father would turn in his grave," I said.'

'You're right,' Straay nodded. He had found the way in. 'There's nothing wrong with being in service. We all are, in some form or another. Whether the butler to a household, or a policeman to a community, it's all a form of service, isn't it?'

'Exactly. You're so right.'

Straay pushed the point a little. 'I mean, your brother, he was thinking too grand I bet. Saying things like, "the bigger picture," I imagine, "for King and Country" that sort of thing?'

'That's right, he did. He didn't see that he was in service too, just that his master was an unnamed faceless politician, oh of course he'd have people in charge telling him where to go, who to shoot at, but that's not the same as actually knowing your master, is it? I knew exactly how my master wanted things done, better than he knew himself. I understood *what* was needed and *when* it was needed. Before things were asked for, they were ready and I still manage that to this day. The staff know what's expected, the household runs smoothly and all this because I know my place, and they know theirs.'

'Your brother didn't understand that though, did he?'

Dawson shook his head. 'No. He had these big notions. He wanted to make a new name for himself; he wanted us to know he was capable of doing the jobs that people above our station were. It was nonsense, really. I used to watch him playing tennis with Sir Laurence and his wife, as if he was one of them. We all have our place in the world. A Dawson's place is here, in this house. The station my father and his father before him built is respectable, coveted even. You have to look after the people you know; not a bunch of strangers you've never met or are even ever likely to meet.'

'So he answered the call and got enlisted as a Private?'

'A Private?' He laughed. 'That was far too low a position for my brother.' Dawson sneered as he spoke. 'Oh no, he was very resourceful. Had the ear of the General, did my brother. He managed to get him to write a recommendation so he was enlisted as an Officer! Imagine that?' Dawson shook his head in disgust.

'That is very unusual,' Straay commented honestly.

'Unusual?' Dawson looked at him aghast. 'It's a stain on my family that's what it is!' He was angry and trembling a little. 'Had he survived the war, he'd probably come out of it some sort of hero and maybe even be in a new class.' Dawson took a breath. 'Unusual isn't the right word at all. My father would have been—'

'Proud?' Straay suggested raising an eyebrow.

Dawson looked at him in disgust.

'What was your relationship like with Sir Laurence?'

'What an odd question. He was my master, I his servant. I did what was expected of me, and he was very happy with my work.'

'Can you think of any reason why he would have been killed?' Straay watched his reaction carefully. Dawson simply shook his head.

'No, sir, I cannot.'

'If you knew who had killed Sir Laurence, would you tell me?'

'No sir, I would not.'

'Thank you Dawson, you have been very honest with me, let me be equally honest with you.' Straay became stern and Dawson took notice. 'I will find out who killed Sir Laurence—of that you can be sure. I will also find out what the rest of this household is holding back. Something in the past affects the reason why this murder occurred in the present—of that I'm equally sure. Feel free to disseminate that information to anyone you chose. You may now go.'

Dawson stood smartly and with a nod of his head, he left the room and quietly closed the door. Straay smiled, that should do the trick. Now to find DuPont. It was time for some answers from the man; and he was in the mood for answers.

◆

Sir Laurence Dies

Straay found Desmond DuPont in the study, sitting at Sir Laurence's desk. The chair was facing the window and as the door fully opened, he turned and his face dropped slightly.

'Oh it's you.' It wasn't a very welcoming statement.

'You were expecting someone else? Milly perhaps?' Straay closed the door behind him and approached the mantle. He allowed his hand to run along the mahogany frame.

'How can I help you, Doctor Straay?'

Straay turned and looked at him, his arm resting on the mantle. 'You know the reason why I'm here, Mr DuPont. It's time for us to talk.'

DuPont sighed. 'I have nothing of worth to say.'

'I shall judge what is of worth. You do not yet know what questions I am going to ask you.'

'I can guess. Do I know who killed Sir Laurence?'

'Do you?'

'No of course I don't!' He half shouted the quick reply.

'I see. Well perhaps you can tell me something about yourself, so that I may understand you better.'

Once again, DuPont sighed. 'I'm not that complicated a person, really.'

'I hear that a lot when I'm talking to people, but in reality we are all complicated people, it's not in our nature to be anything else. We all try to—what's that expression—ah that's it, big ourselves up.'

'I'm not sure I follow you.' DuPont narrowed his eyes.

Straay smiled but said nothing for a minute or two. Eventually he turned back to the mantle. 'I think you do, Mr DuPont.'

'I'm telling you I have no idea what you're talking about.' It was an angry retort.

Straay looked back at him. 'You're quite an angry fellow, aren't you?' He turned his attention to the window and then went back to examining the mantle. He began picking at small bits of cotton left behind from the cleaning cloth. The act of seeming not that interested had done its trick. DuPont eventually broke the silence.

'I'm sorry, I'm just—' He looked at his hands. Eventually he said, 'He's going to find out, you know.'

Straay turned. 'I'm sorry, who will?'

'That awful policeman. Swan, or whatever his name was.' DuPont had nervously begun to chew his nails. 'He'll pry and prod and eventually he'll dig deep enough to uncover some little thing from your past. Then he'll twist it and turn it and before you know it you're on the end of a rope.' DuPont unconsciously rubbed his neck.

Straay thought about that. The worry in DuPont's face gave him reason to wonder. 'You believe that he will hang you for some past indiscretion?'

'Oh I know he would. Trust me these policeman are all just after someone, anyone. It doesn't really matter who it is, so long as they can bring someone to trial. Money changes hands, lawyers and judges connive, juries are directed to reach the desired verdict. In the end, it's your word against theirs. There are plenty of people dead who were innocent.'

'There are a lot more who were guilty too,' Straay countered evenly.

DuPont laughed. 'I expect you think I'm mad?'

'No,' Straay kept his voice neutral. 'I think you're upset and don't really know what you're saying. I hadn't understood that until now.' Straay began to believe that he had misjudged him.

'I am upset, my life is over now. Don't you understand that?' Tears began to form in his young eyes.

'No I don't understand it, not fully, but I'd like to. I really would. I'll ask you a simple question first: did you kill Sir Laurence Gregson?'

'No! No! No! I wouldn't ever kill him. I—' DuPont faltered.

Straay was confused for a moment and then it suddenly hit him. He'd commented before about his familiarity with Sir Laurence. It had perplexed him but his eyes were suddenly opened. He thought back to his conversation with Drake. "He works for Sir Laurence but he is not treated as an employee. He lied about how he met Sir Laurence" Now he knew why DuPont was as mixed up as he was. The answer was simple.

'You loved him,' Straay said, finally.

'Yes. I loved him.' DuPont sobbed uncontrollably for a minute and Straay took a chair and sat beside him.

'Did he love you?' Straay asked softly.

'I doubt it. I don't know. I would like to believe so, but what does it matter now?'

'It matters to you,' Straay began. 'If that's the only reason to want to know, why not believe it? Take something positive from this awful situation. Say to yourself, at least he loved me.'

DuPont rubbed at his face and cleared his throat. 'I could do, but it won't bring him back.'

'That's true, it won't.' Straay felt sorry for him. Sorry because he wouldn't be able to keep that secret. Sorry because he still needed answers. While he patiently waited for DuPont to pull himself together, he ran over in his mind the implications of what he had just discovered. Sir Laurence and Desmond DuPont were lovers. It didn't help him much at the moment, but he was sure that it would begin to.

'Did Milly know of your affair?'

'Heavens no!' DuPont was shocked. 'It was a secret. No one knew.'

'How long were you lovers?'

'Oh since I met him. It was clear what he wanted the moment we locked eyes.' Straay fought back his natural revulsion of such ideas, but the professional within him took hold and he nodded.

'You realise that Milly is in love with you?'

'Yes…yes… that was Laurence's plan all along. He wanted us to marry. I got cold feet, didn't want to go through with it, but he insisted. He even went so far as to say that if I didn't, he'd cut me off. Kick me out. The thought of that was enough to change my mind. Laurence was not a man you'd ever want as an enemy. I've seen the people he destroyed. So…so I was going to ask Milly to marry me today, at lunch, as we agreed… but then he died, and so it was no longer necessary.'

'This was his plan? To force you to marry his daughter?'

'Yes, it was so *we* could always be together.' He smiled slightly, his little brown eyes had lost their focus as his mind wandered off.

Straay thought that was a very odd arrangement. Why would Gregson need to marry off Milly to him? In order to ensure DuPont's loyalty perhaps? No. Sir Laurence would have known DuPont was at the point where he would do just about anything for him. It was interesting that he died before a marriage could be arranged. Very interesting.

'When did you have this conversation?'

'It was about two months ago,' DuPont replied.

'Was anyone else involved in the planning of it?'

'No. No, it was just between Laurence and me.'

'Where did you have this conversation?'

'In the summerhouse, why?'

'Is it possible that you were overheard?'

'No,' he paused. 'Wait a minute, now that you mention it I remember I did think we'd been overheard. I remember saying it to Laurence at the time. We both checked but saw no one. Laurence suggested it was probably a cat or something. I didn't think any more about it.'

'It is possible then that you were overheard, and it's possible that whoever overheard you would have a very strong motive for wanting Sir Laurence dead.'

'Good god I'd not thought of that!'

'You do understand the implications, don't you?' Straay's voice was firm. DuPont looked blankly at him. 'It is also a solid motive for *you* wanting Sir Laurence dead.'

'I didn't… I wouldn't. You must believe me, you have to believe me!' DuPont choked back tears.

'I'm beginning to,' Straay kept his voice softly modulated, 'but you need to be more honest with me. You're not a lawyer at all, are you?'

DuPont looked wide-eyed. 'How did you know?'

Straay smiled. 'I didn't. I suspected, based on a few things you've said to me.'

DuPont lowered his eyes. 'Laurence arranged for my credentials. I didn't ask any questions.'

'Interesting. I would imagine that Chief Inspector Drake has already discovered this. He is a very diligent investigator, and if your credentials are excellent forgeries, he'll likely want to talk with you further about them.'

DuPont closed his. 'Well… he'll have me in chains soon enough, then.'

'Actually, if he suspected you of murdering Sir Laurence, based on fraudulent credentials, you'd be in chains already. Don't confuse diligence with stupidity. Drake is one of the most intelligent and rational policemen I know. You say Sir Laurence organised it, through the college?'

'Like I said, I didn't ask any questions.'

Straay stood. 'You'll have to answer for the fact that you allowed yourself to practice as a lawyer, with fake credentials. I imagine that all the work you've done will be scrutinised.'

'There was never any work,' DuPont laughed a little.

'He organised for you to have the credentials but you were never to employ them?'

'That's right. He knew I wasn't good enough to be a lawyer, but he liked introducing me as one.' He rubbed his eyes. 'I think again it was part of a bigger plan to get Milly and I together. He said once that a lawyer would be regarded more favourably in the future; you know for awards and so on. He said that was something he would be able to arrange. I do think he wanted the best for his daughter. He went to a lot of trouble for her.'

'I wonder what Milly would make of it,' Straay remarked thoughtfully.

'Well one thing is for sure, I'm in a bit of a mess now.' He laughed a little nervously and looked up at Straay; there was desperation in his small brown eyes. 'Is my secret safe with you?'

Straay looked him firmly in the eyes and said, 'I'm sorry, no.'

DuPont looked down for a moment then took a deep breath and stood up. 'Well, I'd better get ready for dinner. Thank you for the talk, it has made me see things a lot clearer.'

Straay watched him leave and rubbed his chin thoughtfully.

INTERLUDE

◆

Desmond DuPont paced his room three or four times. His mind raced. That foreign detective had ruined everything and he was now far too exposed. He looked around the untidy room, which had been his home. His sanctuary. It wouldn't be long before they came for him. He had to do something but what? He couldn't escape the house, not with the police stationed at every exit. Where would he be safe anyway? He sat on his bed and looked out the window. Poor Milly, he sighed and then hardened a little. Poor me!

The door creaked just audibly enough for him to hear, and he turned and looked up. The face he saw in the doorway made the colour drain from his cheeks.

'What do you want?'

A flash of lightening played across the room.

The light flickered ominously.

The door was closed silently, as the storm began to rage outside.

◆

A few hours later the dinner bell rang. As they sat for dinner, Straay noticed one person missing.

'Where has Desmond got to?' Doctor Powell asked with genuine concern.

He wasn't the only one concerned.

Straay turned to Dawson.

'Show me to Mr DuPont's room….'

Chapter Twenty

Back to the House

Chief Inspector Drake had just finished putting together all his paperwork and clearing his office ready for his journey to Sir Laurence's house, when the telephone on his desk rang. He picked up the receiver and answered it.

'Drake... Oh hello, Straay, I'm just on my way over now… What! When? Are you sure? Don't touch anything and don't let Powell in there either. Yes, sorry, I know you know that. Sorry. I'll be over shortly.'

He put down the receiver. Superintendent Baker popped his head round the door.

'Everything all right, Henry?'

'I've just had word from Doctor Straay at the house. Desmond DuPont has killed himself.'

Baker shook his head and whistled. 'That's a complication.'

'I think I may know why.'

'You think he killed Laurence?'

'It's possible. We just found out all his qualifications were forged and the Yard have now confirmed that Desmond DuPont was in fact Harry Green.'

'Harry Green?' Baker frowned. 'The name is familiar.'

'It should be.' Drake's face had turned hard. 'Harry Green is wanted in connection with the murder of Captain George Warburton in the City.'

Baker clicked his fingers. 'That's right. Warburton was killed in Swinging Sword Alley, Blackfriars, not far from Temple, about six months ago. You think these murders are linked?'

'I have no idea, but it's an odd coincidence, don't you think?'

'That Temple is the legal sector of the city and DuPont or Green was posing as a lawyer? Yes, I agree. You'd better be off. I'll get the doctor to meet you there.'

'Right!' Drake collected his file and quickly made his way to his car.

◆

The bedroom of Desmond DuPont was in a mess. Straay sat on the end of the bed feeling mixed emotions. Not for the first time since he'd started this investigation, he felt his actions had led directly to a death. In the first instance it was Sir Laurence and now DuPont. He allowed his eyes to travel around the room. What was he seeing? The room was in disarray, true, but it was a semi-orderly mess, which wasn't the result of anger or grief. The room was this way because DuPont had wanted it so. It was a crafted mess. It reflected how his mind worked. It also reflected his personality; an example of this was the hasty dressing Straay had noticed earlier at breakfast. It all fit in with the untidiness of this room.

Straay resolutely looked up at DuPont. He was swinging gently by the neck from a belt he'd managed to tie to the chandelier hook. It was a sad and macabre scene. The weather had turned and a storm was now reverberating around the outside of the house. A dulled clap of thunder in the distance brought the rain down hard. A flash of lightning arced outside the window and cast eerie shadows around the room. Straay turned his attention to the window. He allowed his eyes to focus on two equidistant trees. Another flash briefly illuminated the garden, followed by a low rumble. The light played across his angular features. He thought back to when he was a child and how he used to be so afraid of the sound of thunder. Now, he was content to allow the sound of the rain to fill his world.

Straay's vision blurred slightly as his unfocused eyes continued to stare out into the garden. He found at times like this, he didn't need his eyes to see, he just needed his brain to think. Was it simply that DuPont's grief at the loss of a loved one, his certain knowledge that his affair and sexuality would be made public, and his fraudulent legal credential exposure were simply catalysts causing him to end his life, or was there more to it than that? These were questions he found difficult to answer.

Straay tried to clear his mind, but that last conversation with DuPont floated back to him. "Thank you for the talk, it has made me see things a lot clearer." Had there been a clue to his intentions in that statement? He certainly hadn't given any outward indication, emotionally or otherwise, that he had reached the moment of clarity and thought when he was more likely to kill himself. Straay tried to recollect DuPont's facial expressions and his body language but there was nothing there. It was true people did do things out of character when backed into a corner, he mused, but he never got the sense DuPont would seriously consider suicide. He hadn't the courage to pull off such an end. Straay sighed. He was annoyed that his impression was and continued to be that DuPont would never be able to go through with the act of hanging himself, even though the evidence was staring him in the face. Eventually, he reached the conclusion he had simply been wrong in his assumptions. It was a bitter pill to swallow. Even now, he couldn't shake off the feeling that it wasn't right, that every instinct he could draw on, every ounce of experience, was telling him DuPont would not do such a thing. Here he swung before him dead, and he still disbelieved it. If he'd been wrong about this, he wondered to himself, had he been wrong about anything else?

Straay thought over many conversations he'd had during the past day, but in the end, his mind was so full he had to voice something before it burst.

'So that was your clear plan, huh? To come here and kill yourself? Such a selfish act….' Even those angry and frustrated words held little comfort for him.

The door opened and Straay looked up. Chief Inspector Drake and Doctor Carmichael, whom he'd met earlier, entered the room.

'Bad business this, Straay, very bad.' Drake could see that his friend and colleague had been emotionally touched by this young man's death. He put a comforting hand on his shoulder for the briefest of moments, a simple gesture but a friendly one.

He crossed his arms and watched as Doctor Carmichael ran his eye over the body. 'I think you can cut him down now, Chief Inspector.' He stepped aside to let the constables into the room.

Straay pointed. 'He's holding a note in his hand; I didn't want to touch anything so left it in place.'

Drake uncurled the fingers and released the crumpled paper. 'It's a typed confession.' He handed it to Straay as the body was released from the belt and lowered to the floor. It read:

Dearest Milly,

There is nothing left in this world for me, I leave my legacy and other effects to you. I wish things could have been different and I'm truly very sorry. Sorry that I had to do it. I killed your father. My confession is necessary to save you. I only hope you'll find it in your heart to forgive me.

Love always,

Your Darling Desmond.

Straay read the note five times. Eventually he handed it back to Drake.

'Are you satisfied with this confession?'

'Satisfied? No, but I have to take it seriously.'

'Do you honestly believe that he had it in him to commit this type of murder then kill himself because of it?'

'I neither believe it nor disbelieve it at the moment. I will simply follow it up.' Drake turned to Carmichael. 'Anything?'

'Well he's quite dead, Chief Inspector, if that's what you mean.' Carmichael turned the head and examined the neck; he felt around the front and back. 'The neck didn't break, but he suffered what feels like compression of the second and third cervical vertebrae.' He opened the mouth and shined a pen torch inside. 'His airway was forced shut so it does appear he died from cerebral hypoxia. If that's the case, it probably took around four minutes for him to die. This is just an observation; I'll understand more once I've performed the post-mortem.' He stepped aside and allowed the constables to put the body onto a stretcher.

◆

When everyone had left the room, Drake re-entered and looked around at the disarray. He didn't know exactly what it was that he was looking for, but he had one of those "I'll know it when I see it" moments. Straay was also examining the room. Drake wondered if they were looking for the same things, then inwardly he reproached himself; of course, they weren't. Drake was looking for the tools of a murderer and Straay would be looking for something entirely different.

After around thirty minutes of searching, with very limited conversation, Drake triumphantly held up a shoebox with a number of items in it. Straay on the other hand had been carefully going through the waste basket. Whatever it was he was searching for didn't seem to be there. Straay cursed quietly to himself and looked up at Drake.

'It isn't here,' he shook his head.

'It would help if I knew what you were looking for,' Drake smiled at him.

'I'm looking for something that isn't here,' he said frustrated, annoyed even.

'That's not very helpful.'

'Nevertheless I must find it, no one came in here, no one took anything from the room, so where is it?'

'Where is what?' Drake snapped back.

'You don't know?' Straay frowned.

'If I knew… it doesn't matter, what are you looking for?'

'The old ribbon.'

'I'm sorry the old—'

'Ribbon… from the typewriter, the ribbon he typed that letter on is brand new, but I can't find the old one.' Straay emptied the drawers into small piles and sifted through the contents. Drake wasn't sure what to think.

'Why is it important?'

'Well, he wrote nothing else with this ribbon—just that note.'

Drake looked blankly at him.

Straay stopped what he was doing, aware now that he was unnecessarily keeping ideas and other important thoughts from his friend and partner. 'Let me explain. The desk is littered with work. All typed. He clearly liked his typewriter, probably the anonymity of it. He finalised the will that I signed, which he must have typed on this typewriter. There are letters written, dated yesterday and today, with the carbon copies. If he changed the ribbon this evening, where is the old one?'

'I see now what you mean. You think someone took it from this room?'

'It isn't here,' he said testily. 'I can think of no other explanation, can you?'

'Well, I can think of a few possibilities.'

Straay turned to him. 'Let me hear them.'

'He burnt it in the grate.' Drake walked over the fireplace.

Straay scoffed. 'It's June, it's very warm. This fireplace is clean and there is nothing to suggest he burnt anything in it.'

'Okay, he threw it out the window then.' Drake was tired, so was Straay and they were both getting irritated.

'Really? That's your idea?'

Drake held up a hand and pulled a pair of chairs together. 'Let's stop and talk for a moment. We both have a lot to discuss. We're both tired and we need some coffee too.' Straay nodded and stretched his back and neck, yawning as he did so. Eventually he sat down.

'You're right of course. It's been a long day. Let me hear your thoughts first, Drake, and then I'll tell you mine.'

Chapter Twenty-One

Widen the Search

A constable brought a pot of coffee and a couple of mugs. They sat and talked for well over an hour. When they'd finished the coffee and had gone through their various facts, statements and other titbits of information, they sat in silence for a while, reflecting. Eventually Straay turned to Drake.

'So, Desmond DuPont was a complete fraud—no such person exists?'

'Oh yes, it's confirmed that he is—was—Harry Green. That love affair between Sir Laurence and DuPont goes a long way to explain a number of things I didn't understand before, if it's true of course.'

'Oh I know that's true, Ellie Gregson herself told us that much.'

'She did? How so?'

'Surely it must be obvious to you now? She had either caught her husband in some compromising position, or she had good reason to believe he was seeking male company for his own pleasure; either way, she acted the only way she could.'

Drake seemed lost. 'I don't follow you.'

'She dismissed all the male staff, of course.'

'Yes she did. Well that makes a lot of sense now. I'd not put much stock in her actions before.'

'Ah but you see I'm looking backwards to find the answer, you're looking forwards.'

'Yes, I see what you mean. You think the answer lies in the past?'

'I think the answer as to why Sir Laurence died is intrinsically linked to his wife, yes.'

'Well, at least we're covering both bases.' A thought occurred to him. 'How did you know DuPont wasn't a legitimate lawyer anyway?'

'His actions, mainly, and the way he answered questions, his personality or lack of one, and his obvious lack of procedural understanding. You commented as much yourself. It didn't take a lot of working out, to be honest with you.'

Drake nodded. 'But what exactly drew you to that conclusion? How did you…' he tried to think of the right way to put it; then it came to him: '…piece it all together.'

'Ah, you want me to explain my methods in a way that you can understand the building blocks, the foundation of my analysis?'

'Well, yes. I think it will help me.'

There was a measure of deep respect in Straay's eyes. This experienced officer wanted to learn. He despised clichés, yet he instinctively thought, you *could* teach an old dog new tricks.

'Well, he made many errors. His inability to stay focused was a huge factor. Had he been the type of lawyer he pretended to be, he would never have succeeded in business. Had he been a junior clerk or maybe a legal secretary, he would not have piqued my interest. No senior executive would take such a man seriously. As a trained psychoanalyst, investigating the mind and the way a person thinks, I was able to come to a set of conclusions that led me to question his credentials. During your interview, he was petulant and rude, childish even. He was unable to think straight and he was nervous and agitated. These are hardly the traits of a trained and successful lawyer. He was barely able to keep his composure under simple questioning. Of course, I had already established that he was a liar, but that hardly disqualified him from being a lawyer.' They both laughed.

'Even his lying was sloppy, not thought out. A man of his supposed training and skill would have been able to stand up to your questioning. He would have been less likely to fold at a difficult question. Lawyers are trained to deal with difficult questions. Can you imagine this man in a boardroom? Can you imagine him being put under any pressure or scrutiny? No, I knew from the moment you pursued the relationship angle between him and Milly that he was a fraud.'

'It always seems so simple when you explain it.'

'Aren't all questions simple, once you know the answers?'

Drake chuckled. 'Yes. It seems we were both looking for different things, but came up with the same answers. I wonder if I could do it.'

'What, reading people?'

'Yes. I mean I'm experienced enough to know, by intuition I suppose, when something doesn't feel right, but is that really the same thing?'

'Essentially it is, yes. The only difference I can see between us is this; we both understand how people might react *to* a thing, but I am trained to interpret that reaction and place it into a specific category for analysis. I'm a people watcher. You can learn so much from people just by observing them. I figured out a long time ago that if I removed my procedural constraints and let myself imagine other possibilities, I could come to more informed and sometimes abstract judgements or opinions. Not all of them work, but now they lead me to avenues I would not have seriously considered before. In our business, certainly as investigators, we're trained to think in a linear fashion. We think like a train. We go on tracks and we stop off at certain stations, but we always get back on the train. Free of this constraint, I can not only get on or off the train, I can take a car or maybe a bus, possibly a boat...maybe even a balloon if I like. You see, I don't have to run on these preconceived procedural lines anymore.'

'That might work for you, but I'm constrained by procedure. I can't act on hearsay or other such gossip that cannot be used to either prove or disprove guilt in court. I have to follow the rules. If I don't, lawyers will poke holes in an investigation and criminals will go free due to what is affectionately termed "procedural mistakes." It's not easy when your own side look for ways to discredit your case.'

'You don't need to change anything to apply a little imagination. Let us try a little exercise. David Renwick was a dirty man who tinkered with engines. What can you tell me about him?'

Drake looked blank. 'Hardly anything.'

'Using your imagination, try and build a profile for me.'

'It's impossible, I need more. All I have is that David Renwick is probably a young man, maybe in his early twenties so he probably has long hair. He likes to tinker with engines, so he possibly wears a boiler suit or something similar and if that's the case, he'll probably be quite pale, and as he works with engines his hands may well be stained with grease and oil.'

'Bravo! You see. From one statement, you've already told me he was young, pale, and longhaired. His hands are stained with grease and oil. That was far more information than I gave you. You extrapolated this information from your own knowledge and applied it to the task.'

'Well, okay, I concede that, but what if he turns out to be fifty and dark skinned? It's not very practical is it?'

'You're thinking like a policeman again.' Straay waggled a finger reproachfully at him. 'The point is, he may be all these things, but you know from experience that younger men like to tinker with engines because it is the new craze. Engines, cars, motorboats, aeroplanes, all these things are so new, the young are putting aside their toy guns and dolls and picking up books on engines, or model car kits and so on. Where does it lead? The boy who is so keen on engines builds his first model car. Maybe he gets a job as an apprentice engineer, or goes back to school to learn more about engines. To conclude our exercise, we only needed "David Renwick was a dirty man who tinkered with engines" to start us on a theoretical path and our experiences, our knowledge and our imagination, allow us to construct a framework to work with. All you did was to think just a little differently.'

'I will try to remember that.' Drake was happy to learn these new techniques in bringing criminals to justice, even if he seriously thought they wouldn't be of practical use to him. Straay, however, wanted to move on.

'What do we know about DuPont?'

'Very little.' Drake pulled out a sheet of information from his file. 'The record states that he was a petty criminal, small time stuff. Theft, extortion, illegal gambling and so on, but nothing to suggest he was a murderer, that is, until the Warburton affair. After that, he disappeared.'

'What about forgery?'

Drake considered this and checked the file again. 'Well, there's nothing here, but that's not to say he didn't dabble. You think he forged his own credentials?'

'Well, only two people could reasonably answer that and they are now both dead. Either Sir Laurence had them forged or was able to obtain the stationery, or DuPont himself orchestrated the entire thing and pointed the finger at Sir Laurence who was unable to defend himself.'

'That's logical,' Drake mused.

'Conveniently, we only have DuPont's word for it that Sir Laurence organised it all.'

'Easy enough to point the finger, after the fact.'

'You said before that the forgery wasn't a good one.' Straay scratched his head. 'It doesn't sit right with me that Sir Laurence would have paid money for a bad forgery. If he were able to find someone to do this illegal thing, it would have been a professional.'

Drake concurred. 'We know a lot about DuPont and his background, but Sir Laurence's was totally clean. So if he was mixed up in criminal activities, they must have been a higher class of criminal.'

'It's possible then that if he was, as you say, mixed up in anything illegal, DuPont was his middle man.'

'Well that would make more sense. Sir Laurence was a leader. If he was involved in crime, he certainly wasn't the one performing it.'

'Then it had to be DuPont who forged his own credentials, but he wasn't well practiced in it. How he got the stationery is open for debate. The alternative is that he knew someone who could do it for him, but then again, I would expect that person to be a forger by trade and produce a far better result.'

'That's true enough and this business about being forced to marry Milly, you think there's any truth in that too?'

'I believed that was true.' Straay rubbed his eyes. 'It's all very difficult. Again, we have no real evidence to support it. In fact, we have nothing to corroborate anything he said to me. If his emotional state was a part of his act, then he should get an award. I don't know, Drake, this all feels contrived somehow. I'm sorry to say this but, given what we've just discussed, I'm uncomfortable believing that DuPont killed himself.'

'What about the suicide note? Surely that's evidence enough to show he killed himself?'

'You truly believe that? With all your years of experience? A letter, from a typewriter in an unlocked room? I could have typed that letter for all you know.'

'Well I didn't know it was an unlocked room,' admitted Drake, 'but we'll analyse it all the same. Typewriters are like fingerprints. They each have their own individual signature. No two are alike.' Drake studied the desk for a moment.

'We'll have it checked for fingerprints. It might turn up something, I'm not hopeful. If it does show his fingerprints on it, what then?'

'That just proves he used it, it doesn't prove that no one else did.'

'Well that's true enough I suppose. What about this ribbon anyway, don't the letters simply hit it and overlap?'

'No, this type feeds ribbon from one side to the other, it's very modern. Everything that was ever written on it is preserved on the ribbon.'

'I didn't know that.'

Straay picked up a notebook from the table and opened the index. It was an address book. He flicked through it for a few minutes and then saw something that made him exclaim. He handed it to Drake.

'Look at this!' Under "C" were the words "Coster – Paulus Potterstraat, Amsterdam."Drake just looked at him. 'I can't say that it means anything to me?'

'Coster is a diamond trader, world renowned. I've been there myself. Maybe we've found the reason for Sir Laurence's trip to Amsterdam.'

'Well, it could be just a coincidence,' Drake said a little unenthusiastically. 'It could be just one of DuPont's old contacts.'

Straay inclined his head. *Coincidence?* he thought to himself. Here we have one man who hid his true identity from everyone, and is now dead, and another who recently returned from Amsterdam, who is also *now* dead! The odds were enormously against this being a coincidence. However, he let it go.

'You think it's important?'

'I don't know.' Straay answered honestly.

'I'm inclined to believe that DuPont killed himself. I think he knew his game was up and this was his only way out,' Drake said firmly.

'We already have one murder in the house. Statistically speaking, the odds of a second one are extremely low.' Straay relaxed a little; he had shaken his melancholy now.

'Well, once Doctor Carmichael examines the body, we'll know one way or another.'

Straay persisted. 'DuPont was a man who already had two identities. I had assumed his actions were based on just the one. Now that I know he had alternatives, it changes my view of the man. Harry Green, who goes to a lot of effort to create the new persona of Desmond DuPont for himself, would have a back door if things got too hot. If I hadn't known about Harry Green, I'd have simply decided that I'd misread DuPont and left it at that. I'd have been the first to say, "I got it wrong". But now, you see everything has changed. I *do* know about Harry Green and so now I see something different, I see the man ending his life, for sure, but not in this way. I see him ending it by some other means. Something perhaps a little more artistic, something like leaving his clothes neatly folded up on a stone by the river and a note ending it all. DuPont is searched for but never found. You understand?'

Drake nodded. 'I see what you're saying.'

'What else did you find?'

'A metal tube—could be make-shift silencer—a silver pen, a hypodermic syringe, a bottle of curare and a notebook which looks like it matches the suicide note found by Sir Laurence,' Drake handed him the box.

Straay laughed. 'What a considerate murderer. He confesses his guilt, kills himself and leaves us, rather conveniently, all the tools he used as well. It's all neatly together in a box under his bed. I'm surprised it wasn't gift wrapped as well. You still believe he did it?'

Drake wasn't able to hide the fact that even to him this was all too obvious.

'No, but he has lied about everything and anything,' Drake conceded honestly. 'It's this business with Warburton...it's clouding everything, and it isn't going to go away.'

'Drake, it needs to go away, for the time being. We may uncover something that leads us to it, but until then, we have to keep it a separate investigation. You've pulled all the relevant facts on Green and we can use those, but from now on, we have to keep up the Desmond DuPont pretence. Don't you get the feeling we're being led somewhere else?'

'Yes I do. We are dealing with a very clever individual aren't we?' Drake stood and stretched.

'It's either a clever individual or maybe individuals.' Straay made his mind up about what he felt they should do next. All he had to do was to persuade the Chief Inspector to fall in with his plans.

'I have a suggestion.'

'Go on?' Drake saw a look on Straay's face he had seen the night before. There was a new light in his eyes and that meant he was about to suggest something out of the box, as he would put it.

'It is radical and you may not like it,' Straay said slowly. 'I urge you to consider doing it.'

'I can't make any promises,' Drake remarked evenly, 'but I'll listen.'

'I want you to release the household from house arrest.'

Drake stared at him for the briefest of moments. 'You're right,' he said, poker faced. 'I do not like it.'

'Well, I did tell you it was a radical suggestion.' He pulled out a cigarette and lit it. 'Here's my idea. Let them believe that the pressure is off. Let them think that DuPont was still DuPont and not Harry Green – let us forget this Harry Green. You don't need to tell them anything, just explain that they are free to come and go, but that it is still an active investigation and therefore they shouldn't leave the area.'

Drake still wasn't convinced. 'If what you say is true about DuPont's death being a murder as well, what's to stop the real culprit getting on the first boat out of England?'

'It's unlikely. Lady Agatha won't leave. Milly will stay in the house. Major Heskith has nowhere to go, nor does Dawson. The only fly in the ointment is Doctor Powell, and he isn't likely to go far either. In any event, if someone were stupid enough to bolt, you'll know definitely that you have a suspect worth chasing.'

'It's too risky,' Drake was outside of his comfort zone and he knew it.

'It is risky,' Straay agreed. 'But it will give us the space to continue our investigations unhindered and I can't do any more in this house. I need to get out and talk to people, to see places, visit houses, see graves and so on.'

'You've got hold of something, haven't you? Something I've missed?'

'I've followed a few threads as far as I can here; it is the way I work. I really think I've made some progress but I need more time and I need to get out of this house.'

Drake thought hard. 'Do you know who did it?'

Straay simply said: 'It's your call, Henry.' It wasn't often that he used Drake's Christian name, so Drake took notice.

'Will you take my advice?'

Chief Inspector Henry Drake weighed the consequences and then reached a decision. 'Only a fool ignores the advice of his doctor.'

'Thank you.' Straay relaxed a little. Now he could proceed unhindered. 'Superintendent Baker will agree?'

'I'll convince him.' It was devious but he could see the merit to it. 'Besides,' he waved a hand nonchalantly, 'Baker feels that Harry Green—Desmond DuPont—is the most likely guilty party. With the suicide note and this box of trinkets, it wouldn't take much to ensure he continues to think that way, at least for a while, but we have to be careful. You're putting my neck on the chopping block Straay, I hope you understand that?'

'I do and your faith in me is very gratifying. I think the results will alleviate any concerns but if we get nowhere we aren't any worse off than we are now.'

'That's true enough I suppose.'

'Can I take copies of all the background information you uncovered?'

Drake handed him the files.

'Thank you. After you have informed every one of your decision, I will leave this house and start my investigation proper.'

'Have you anywhere in mind to stay?'

Straay laughed, 'No, I hadn't really thought that far ahead.'

'You're welcome to stay with me. Mrs Drake would be very pleased to see you.'

Straay smiled. 'So you can keep tabs on me?' Drake laughed but said nothing.

'It is a fair thing you ask. I shall come and stay with you and Mrs Drake.'

'Excellent. Where will you go first?' Drake stood and put his chair back.

'Andover will be my first call.' Straay repeated Drake's action.

'Andover?'

'Yes, I go to see the sister and daughter of Dawson. I hope to be able to find something that he didn't want found. At the very least, I hope to increase my understanding of this complicated man.'

'Complicated? He seems pretty uncomplicated to me.'

'A phrase I have heard twice today. What about you? '

'I'm going to visit the President of Trinity College, Oxford University. I want to get to the bottom of this degree business.'

'I think that would be a wasted journey, my friend.'

'We'll see.'

'Honestly I think you'll regret it. It's important, I agree, but what will you achieve by following it up? You may discover that some stationery was stolen; that hardly helps us. If I were you, I'd think seriously about DuPont. There you'll find your answer, I'm sure. I also suggest that you put one of your men on Dawson as well—follow his movements and so on.'

'You think he's a serious suspect?'

'I think he, along with everyone else, is hiding something of value. I also think he's as serious a suspect as any of the others are—maybe more so.'

Drake agreed.

'Shall I have my men conduct a search for that typewriter ribbon?'

'I think it unlikely that it will be found, but I would appreciate it.'

'It's important to you, I can tell.'

'It's a key to a lock. I'd rather not force the lock if I can simply open it with the key,' he said cryptically.

Drake had no idea what he was talking about so he just called over a constable and issued orders for the house to be searched.

Chapter Twenty-Two

Mrs Talbot Speaks

The journey to the station had been a very welcome distraction. It was morning and Straay was very pleased to be out of the house. Chief Inspector Drake had informed everyone the previous night that they were no longer under house arrest and Straay had opted to stay the night purely because by the time he and Drake had finished together, it was midnight. Imposing on Mrs Drake at one in the morning would hardly endear either of them to her.

The journey via train to Andover had been relatively uneventful and Straay now found himself outside the small entrance, smoking. He was enjoying the bright sunny morning. There was no hint of the storm that had raged the previous night. It was his experience England was typically wet, even in summer, so it was nice to be in the sunshine, and take pleasure in the happy smiling faces of the people coming and going from the station.

Straay finished his cigarette and dropped it to the ground. He noticed a smart looking man, probably early thirties, wearing an opened shabby, high-collared tan overcoat over a neat blue suit. He was a hard-set man, with penetrating blue eyes. This could only be a policeman, Straay thought. Even in plain clothes, they still had a uniform.

'Doctor Straat?' He removed his hat as he spoke.

'Straay,' he corrected, extending his hand.

'Straay, yes sorry, I'm Inspector Jones. I got a call from a Chief Inspector Drake, telling me that you might need a lift?' He was courteous, but his body language suggested he wasn't keen on being a driver, and that was good because Straay wasn't keen on the idea of being monitored.

'That is kind of you, Inspector, but I can probably find my own way.'

'Well, I'm here now so no sense in turning away a good lift.' He led the way to his car. 'Where are you heading, anyway?'

Straay handed him the address.

'Oh that's just up the road. I'll drop you off on my way to the station.'

'Yes, I knew it wasn't far. If you drop me off, I'll come to the station after I've done what I need to do, there's no need to hold my hand, Inspector.' Straay was firm and Jones smiled.

'Fair enough, doctor.'

Straay memorised the journey back and took additional directions from Jones to the police station. The car drove off and Straay pulled out a cigarette. He liked to think and smoke; it was an old habit.

◆

The house was small, with a long path to the front door. He opened the gate and made his way along the narrow paving stones to an old wooden door. Before he could knock, the door opened and a small boy in dirty, ill-fitting clothes looked up at him.

'We ain't buyin' nuffin' mister,' he said, trying to appear far taller then he actually was.

'That is very wise,' Straay said sagely. 'It is also a good thing, because I'm not selling anything.'

'Wot-cho wants then?'

'I'd like to speak with your mother, if that's possible?'

'Maam!' The boy shouted over his shoulder, 'there's a toff at the door. Just you wait 'ere mister, she'll be coming.' He ran off into the house. Presently, he was replaced by a large woman in a flowery overall.

'Can I 'elp you sir?' She seemed a little suspicious but was polite enough.

'I certainly hope so, Mrs Talbot. My name is Doctor Pieter Straay, from Scotland Yard. I'd like to ask you some questions concerning your brother and his daughter.'

She folded her arms. 'Wot's ee been up to now?'

'Nothing definite; at least nothing serious,' he lied. 'I just need to speak with you. May I come in?'

'You got any 'dentification? Cos you can't be too careful, wot with them conmen being around these days.'

Straay produced his card and handed it to her.

'You ain't English are you?' She looked at the card and then realising that her question was particularly rude she quickly added, '...beggin' your pardon.'

'I'm Dutch,' he replied pleasantly.

'Consultant psychologist...wot's one of them, then?'

'I'm a private detective.' He felt that answer would be better understood.

'Oh! I see, so Psycho-wot-cha-me-call-it is Dutch for detective, then?'

Straay nodded.

'I was sayin' to George over the road, you mind who you let in, you can't be too careful.' She smiled at him and then laughed shrilly. 'Oh where's my manners, come in doctor,' she looked at the card again, 'Streye is it?'

'Straay,' he accented the longer "a." 'Thank you.'

'You 'ave to forgive me, cos I don't speak foreign. Come into the sittin' room.'

The sitting room doubled as a lounge and the dining room too, it seemed. Despite her appearance and that of the child, she was extremely house proud. The room was immaculate, and whilst the furniture was old and worn, it was well looked after. The arms of the chairs had neat white cotton covers.

He sat on the chair indicated. 'I'm just makin' some tea, doctor,' she didn't attempt to pronounce his surname. 'Would you care for tea?' She said this in her best approximation of what she would call a posh accent.

'I'd love some tea, thank you.' Mrs Talbot was very pleased because she liked to make guests tea.

'We don't get no visitors round ere, 'specially not foreign ones' she said loudly from the kitchen, 'not on Sundays, anyways.' She came back into the room with an elegant tea tray, adorned with what must have been her best china set. It didn't look like it had been used very often and Straay felt that he should be privileged that this poor woman was rolling out her best service for him. She put down the tray and he stood and stepped forward.

'Please, allow me to.'

'Well that's kind of you cos I don't get to sit down much durin' the day. See these feet?' She showed him. 'Ruined they are, look, and bunions? Oh, don't talk to me bout bunions, these are just killin' me.'

Straay made the tea and passed her a cup.

'You do speak good English, don't you?'

'Thank you. I was raised and schooled here during the war, so it is easier, yes.'

'That was nice. I ain't never been to no school, me, but that don't make me one of them illit-tree-ates.' She seemed quite happy at the use of a longish word. Straay inwardly smiled. He liked Mrs Talbot. She was plain speaking. Not quite easy to understand linguistically, but she wasn't trying to deceive him and he was grateful, considering the past few days. Mrs Talbot was a no-nonsense "what you see is what you get" type of woman.

'I'd like to ask you some questions concerning your brother, if that's okay.'

'Which one?' she slurped her tea noisily.

'How many do you have?'

'Two, well only one wot's alive, and ee might as well be dead for all I care.'

'Well it is James that I wanted to talk about, but perhaps you can tell me a little about both?'

'Well, there was Pat junior, Pee-Jay we called him. Ee was the oldest. Ee died in the war, early like. Shame it was, such a good soul. I still miss 'im. Then there's James. Ee's the snooty one. Thinks his own sh…' She was about to be vulgar and stopped herself. 'Well anyway, ee's all 'igh and mighty these days. Ee weren't that way always, but when Tony went to war it annoyed 'im. We fell out over it big time. I ain't spoken to 'im since.' She sniffed.

Straay looked at her with a comforting gaze. 'James said that when his wife died, his daughter came to live with you, what seven years ago?'

'Joycee don't want nuffin' to do with old Dawson,' she spat the words like bullets. 'Ee don't even go by James no more, just Dawson. Joycee came with me and she's been 'appy. Wot's this all about then?' Suspicion crept back into her voice and her posture stiffened.

'His employer, Sir Laurence, was killed on Friday. We're just following up the backgrounds of the household, you know, making the enquiries.'

'Oh, poor Mr Laurence! That's a real shame that is,' she was genuinely shocked by the news—he'd even go so far as to say saddened by it. 'Ee's been ever so kind to us, 'as Mr Laurence. Killed you say?'

'Sadly so, madam, sadly so.'

'You think Dawson done it?'

'We don't know exactly who did it, but we're following up all leads.'

'Well ee wouldn't 'ave done away with Mr Laurence. No, ee wouldn't 'ave done away with 'im.' She choked back a sob.

'Oh, poor Mr Laurence,' she put a hand to her breast.

'You seem quite sure that your brother wouldn't have killed him. Why is that?'

'It's 'bout the only thing I can be sure of.' She switched from being sad to laughing her shrill laugh then, realising it probably wasn't appropriate, she slipped back to being sad again.

'Poor Mr Laurence,' she sniffed. 'Ee's looked after us Dawson's since our father died. Ee sends me a cheque once a month for ten pounds and ee paid for Joycee to go to a proper school. I don't s'ppose there's anything, you know, like legacies and so on, not for me, oh no, but for Joycee?' She wasn't embarrassed to ask and he wished he could answer it.

'I do not know,' he evaded. 'The will has yet to be read.'

'Well, I s'pect 'e'll 'ave thought about us, cos ee was ever so kind. Wot with Pee-Jay dying and everything.'

'Was Pee-Jay the reason you and your brother fell out?'

'Damn right, if you'll pardon my French. Ee was a beast to me when Pee-Jay went off to war. I made ends meet, you know, wot with no money coming in and so on, then after the war, Mr Laurence set me up and bought this 'ouse for me, ee did.'

'That was very kind of him. You live here with Mr Talbot?'

'Oh no sir, Mr Talbot also died in the war. No, just me and Joycee and little junior.'

'Your son?' Straay finished his tea and replaced the cup on the tray.

'Yeah, but not from me if you know wot I mean. No, little junior was an orphan, weren't ee. They closed down the orphanage on the corner of Westbrook and ee was only two and such a little thing, so I took 'im in. Mrs Reynolds at number twelve 'ad a girl, but I always wanted a boy, so I called 'im Anthony, after my big brother.'

'Anthony?'

'Yea, my brother was Patrick Anthony Davies Dawson. So, I named 'im Anthony Davies Dawson Talbot, but we calls 'im junior cos ee likes that, ee's ever so sweet is our junior, just like 'is namesake.'

'Your brother was Anthony Davies? Lieutenant Anthony Davies?'

'That's right sir, ee didn't go by 'is first name, and after wot went on with Dawson, ee stopped using his family name too. When ee went off to war, ee was just Tony you see. Dawson didn't like the fact that ee was a proper officer, not one bit. The old General writ some fancy letter and Pee-Jay got made an officer, I was ever so proud.'

Straay was pleased. Very pleased. He'd just found a major link, probably the very information that Dawson had been hiding all along.

'You all right? You look like the cat wot just got all the cream!'

'Oh madam, you have been extremely helpful. Do you by any chance have a picture of your brother?'

'Yea, I got quite a few.' She got up and moved to the bureau. 'Ere's the last one ee 'ad before ee went to war, 'andsome fellow was my brother.' Mrs Talbot handed him the photograph. It was a perfect headshot of a man in uniform.

'May I borrow this Mrs Talbot?'

'You can 'ave it. I got four of em.' She smiled at him. He gratefully returned it.

'Such a shame about Mr Laurence,' Mrs Talbot said again as she escorted Straay to the front door. "'Im and Pee-Jay were close, you know.'

'He certainly took care of you,' Straay remarked casually, putting on his hat.

'Well after the accident I think ee felt it was 'is duty.'

'Accident?' Straay stopped dead.

'Yes sir, the one wot killed Pee-Jay. Mr Laurence said ee 'ad saved 'is life. So it was only natural that e'd look after us. E'll be missed by us sir, ee will.'

An idea began to form in Straay's mind, a big idea. He had to get back to Drake and he had to get back fast, but first he needed to speak with Lady Agatha. He bade Mrs Talbot farewell, promised to keep her informed of any legacies and so on, and hastily made his way towards the railway station.

Chapter Twenty-Three

A Revelation

Chief Inspector Drake sat in his office drinking a well-earned cup of tea. Straay was out in the field, which meant he'd be working his own agenda for a while, and he was following up on some leads the Yard had given him regarding known associates of Harry "Desmond DuPont" Green. There was a light rap at the door and Drake looked up to see Superintendent Baker.

'Busy, Henry?' It was purely a rhetorical question.

'Always.'

Baker nodded and closed the door. He clasped his hands firmly behind his back and walked over towards the large window. He surveyed the grounds of the station and looked up at the horizon. He kept his back to Drake.

'How's it going?' He observed Drake's reflection in the window.

'Slowly, George,' Drake replied evenly. 'There are a lot of things to do, information to sift and so on—you know the drill.'

'You're still working the Green angle?' He still hadn't turned.

Something in the way he'd said that made Drake pause. Superintendent George Baker was being very formal and his posture was tight. 'Yes, sir, so far we've not got much.'

At the use of the word "Sir," Superintendent Baker turned and looked at him hard for a moment, his face unreadable. Eventually he turned back to the window.

'Everything okay, George?' Drake felt he was missing something vital.

'That will depend on the next answer you give me.' Tight lipped, he turned and walked over to the chair opposite Drake and sat. 'Are you truly convinced that Green killed Sir Laurence?'

'Well,' Drake began.

'I see, so your reason for releasing the household and keeping me in the dark was...what?'

'We firmly believed that...that is to say, I firmly believe Green is or was instrumental in—'

Baker waved a hand at him, cutting him off. 'I'm disappointed in you, Henry.' He meant it. 'You should have spoken to me first; it was my call to make. Did you honestly think I'd be that easily swayed by your obvious ploy?'

Drake had been rumbled, and early on. Worse still, he'd upset his friend. He rubbed the back of his neck. 'How did you find out?'

'You know,' Baker said carefully, 'people often say to me, how did you know? How did you discover this? I'm Superintendent of this station, Henry. You think I won this job in a raffle?' He was stern and angry.

'No, sir. No, you didn't. I apologise. I didn't want to mislead you, but I have, and will accept whatever punishment you deem fit.'

Baker waved a hand again. It was clear that dressing down a senior officer and friend was not something he liked doing. 'It's done. You're a smart officer, Henry, a very smart officer, one of the best. You get results and you're my friend. Next time, don't leave me in the dark, understood?'

'Understood. It won't happen again, George.'

'It had better not.' He smiled a little. 'Where are you now?'

'Not very far forward, to be frank.'

'You're tailing Dawson, I understand?'

'Yes. I'm expecting a report within the hour.'

'Good. I'm expecting a report soon as well, from you. I hope I won't have to wait very long for it?'

'No, of course not,' Drake felt a little ashamed. 'I'm anticipating that Doctor Straay will be arriving soon. Once we've swapped notes, we'll have something definite for you. We're also waiting on Carmichael's autopsy results on DuPont/Green.'

'Excellent, I shall look forward to it.' He looked earnestly at Drake for a moment. 'Henry, I'm being pressured from upstairs. Some very important people are asking me some very difficult questions that I can't answer. I don't like not being able to answer them; I can only fend them off for a little while before they start interfering. We both know where that will lead.' Baker stood and re-adjusted the chair.

'We'll get the results for you, George,' Drake said with affection. 'You have my word.'

Satisfied with that, Superintendent Baker moved towards the door.

'Are we okay, George?'

He paused and turned. 'We're friends, Henry.' He smiled a tight smile and left, quietly closing the door behind him.

◆

The journey back to the house was slow and uneventful. For the first time since he'd used it, the train system had run very smoothly and since third rail electrification had been implemented, a few years back, it was actually a much more robust system allowing for faster and efficient travel. Straay needed to talk to Lady Agatha and this had to be done before he could speak to Drake. He had discovered something of significance, and Lady Agatha was the only person that could supply the additional information he needed.

Straay was pleased with the progress of the train; it was mirroring the progress of the investigation in his mind. It would eventually get there because it was on the right track, charging headlong towards its destination, with only a few minor stops along the way. However good the train system was, it still took some two hours to reach the house of Lady Agatha. It could no longer be called Sir Laurence's.

The door was opened by a footman and he was shown into the familiar sitting room. This time Lady Agatha greeted him with a smile.

'Doctor Straay, how lovely to see you again.' She held her hand out in the regal pose he expected and he bowed his head and kissed it.

'My Lady, I have not much time. I need to ask you some questions, and I ask you to be frank with me.'

She looked up at the footman severely. One did not discuss family affairs in front of the servants. 'Leave us and see that we are not disturbed.' When it was just the two of them, she turned to him, a little cooler now than her greeting had been.

'Ask your questions. I shall hold nothing back.' Straay was pleased with her attitude. He hadn't misjudged her resolve, or intelligence.

'Tell me about Anthony,' he said simply.

She sighed deeply. 'You know don't you?'

He nodded keeping eye contact with her. 'I know almost everything, my Lady, but I need a few answers.'

'Be specific with your questions, then.'

'Was he in love with you or your sister?'

She laughed bitterly. 'He was in love with *only* himself.'

'Were you in love with him?'

'No. I was fond of him once. So was Larry, but my sister wasn't.'

'You aren't a widow are you?'

'I believe I am, yes. As far as I'm concerned, the man I loved died in the war. Next to that, what does a bit of paper honestly mean? '

'Did your father approve of David?'

'No he did not.'

'You remember there was an incident involving a car and a police constable?'

'Vividly.'

'Who was driving the night Dawson supposedly ran down the police constable?'

'Anthony was.'

'Your father pulled strings didn't he?'

'Yes he did. He always did, and Dawson was ordered to take the fall. I hated him for that.'

'Your father?'

'No! Dawson. He should never have agreed.'

'Dawson is a servant. He knows his place. It's not in his character to disobey.'

'I know that,' she said sternly. 'That didn't make it right.'

'No it didn't.' Straay smiled at her. 'I will be back soon, I beg you to keep this conversation secret.'

She put a hand on his. 'Does it have to come out?'

'I am afraid it must.'

'For darling Milly's sake, I beg you not to do this.'

'The wheels are in motion already, they cannot be stopped now.'

She pulled her hand back to her lap and nodded. 'Then I will do as you ask.'

Straay left the house, content.

◆

The taxi deposited Straay directly outside the police station's main entrance and he entered quickly. The desk Sergeant recognised him immediately and called him over.

'Doctor Straay, the Chief Inspector is waiting for you. I shouldn't hang around. He's not in the best of moods.' The Sergeant tapped his nose theatrically. He thanked him and took to the stairs.

Straay followed the corridor down to Drake's office and when he reached it, he knocked on the door and entered. Drake looked up and there was relief in his eyes.

'Ah good, you're back. How'd it go in Andover?'

Straay sat in the chair opposite him. He looked pleased, Drake thought, very pleased with himself.

'It went better than I had hoped. I've made a remarkable discovery.'

'Well don't keep me hanging on to your every word,' he chuckled. 'Spit it out man.'

'Dawson's brother was Lieutenant Anthony Davies.'

Drake looked oddly at him, and then he pulled out a file from the collection on his desk.

'That's very interesting. You see I have a file here from the Home Office. It lists the personnel that died in the accident that Sir Laurence had survived. There were a few people involved, but one of the names on this list is Lieutenant Anthony Davies.'

'You see that's no coincidence and it confirms what I suspected.' He took the file and read the index very carefully. What he found made him smile.

'You're not the first person to ask for a copy of this file, Drake.' He handed it back.

'You're right. Lady Agatha requested it seventeen years ago.'

'Interesting and highly suggestive, wouldn't you agree?'

Drake had no context so just shook his head, 'It doesn't suggest anything to my mind.'

Straay looked at him for a moment. 'You do not understand the significance of my discovery, do you?'

'You got that from my lack of excitement, I imagine.' Drake frowned at him.

'I told you about the photograph that Lady Agatha showed me. I told you that she mentioned being very fond of this man.'

'Yes that's correct, I do remember that. It's probably why she wanted more information about his death. Natural enough.' Drake couldn't see why this information was important. Straay read that and was disappointed.

'Don't you find it odd that no one, not Dawson or Lady Agatha said anything about Anthony Davies at all, not in the interviews or in any conversations?'

'Odd, no. It wasn't really a topic for interview. They probably didn't think it was important. Didn't you say it was when Lady Agatha showed you a photograph that it became apparent?

'Yes that is true,' Straay admitted.

'Well it seems to me information like that is probably overlooked when you're being interviewed about a murder. I doubt anyone really thought it was important, especially because he died what, twenty odd years ago. Why is it important?'

'It goes to the heart of the matter, because he died early on in the war.'

'Straay,' Drake rubbed his eyes. 'I've not had the best of days, so if you could just be concise about why it's important, then perhaps I can be as enthusiastic as you seem to be.'

'What has happened?' Straay asked, feeling he'd need to address Drake's issue before he continued. Something was bothering him.

'Superintendent Baker.'

'Ah, he has discovered our ruse and dragged you over the furnace, eh?'

'Coals,' he corrected. 'Yes.'

'This has affected your friendship with him?'

'I don't think so, but it was awkward.' He paused for a moment, looking at Straay. 'Did you suspect he would discover it as quickly as he did?'

'I suspected that he would, yes, but it was still necessary.'

'As it turns out, I should have trusted him. He would have backed us up. Now he feels left out and, well, I could have handled it a lot better than I did.'

'Did your men get any information on Dawson?'

'Not much. He went to the shop, bought about four bottles of sloe gin, I assume for Lady Agatha, and some other miscellaneous items from the hardware store. I think he was probably aware that he was being followed, although Sergeant Peters says he wasn't.'

Straay smiled, 'He isn't stupid, Dawson. He knew. What about the ribbon? Was that ever found?'

'No, we searched meticulously. We didn't find it. You're convinced it was there?'

'It was there. The ribbon held something, something someone desperately wanted. I don't understand what, but I suspect it might have something to do with the Warburton business.'

Drake was thoughtful. 'That means someone else in that house was working with Green, or at the very least, had a connection to him and the crime.'

'Possibly, or someone outside the house came in after the house was released.'

'A conspiracy? On top of everything else?' Drake wasn't pleased by that.

'Two crimes are happening, I think. Two separate crimes. Solving the first might not aid us in solving the other; we have to be prepared for that.' Straay wasn't happy and Drake could see it.

'Would that change your position on whether DuPont had killed himself?'

Straay shook his head. 'It would strengthen my opinion that he was murdered.'

'You still want us to leave this aside? Every instinct is telling me we can't ignore this.'

Straay said, 'We must concentrate on the murder of Sir Laurence. The Warburton affair will always be there.'

'What about Baker? I've already concealed enough from him, now you want me to conceal this too?'

'We don't know anything definite. Besides, I don't want you to conceal it; just don't mention it. It's an ongoing investigation and won't help us with this current case, I'm sure of it. Make notes and be diligent. We'll get our chance. If Baker asks directly if there is a connection between Warburton's and Sir Laurence's deaths, you can say no with a clear conscience.'

Drake nodded, 'And...if it is proven that DuPont *was* murdered?'

'Then you can present what you know, but it isn't much is it?'

'No it isn't. It's leaving a bad taste in my mouth though. But okay, we'll move on.'

Straay thought for a moment. 'Get Superintendent Baker, this discovery I have made should be shared with him because I think we owe him that much.'

Drake was pleased. Whatever it was, he was glad to give George the heads up before he actually understood why it was important. It would go some way to fixing the mess he'd caused earlier. He left and less than five minutes later returned with Baker.

Chapter Twenty-Four

A Secret Revealed

'Doctor Straay, it's nice to finally meet you,' Superintendent George Baker said courteously. He pulled up a chair next to him. The two men then looked expectantly at him. Straay explained the conversation with Lady Agatha again for Baker's benefit and then detailed the revelation he'd just discussed with Drake. Baker rubbed his chin.

'So you think that there's a connection between Anthony Davies and Sir Laurence's death?'

'I think,' Straay said carefully, 'it's very interesting that no one mentioned that Anthony Davies was Anthony Davies "Dawson," yes.'

'I just can't see the connection,' Drake said. He and Baker looked at each other, and then back at Straay. 'Is there something more?'

Straay smiled. 'Oh yes. We know he died early on in the war, but as I was leaving Mrs Talbot's house, she said something like "Mr Laurence had been very kind to them, seeing as how he died in that accident." I asked what accident and then she said "the one that nearly killed Mr Laurence". Then to further corroborate this fact, Drake reveals confirmation of this from the Home Office files. Do you understand now?'

Baker leaned forward. 'Are you saying then, that this was the motive for Laurence's death? That Dawson had the best reason for killing him, and the reason why no one mentioned Anthony was because they already knew that Dawson had done it, so they were protecting him?'

Straay smiled and looked at Drake. 'What is your opinion?'

'Firstly, you said Dawson and Davies hated each other and this was corroborated by his sister.'

'There is truth to that,' Straay again nodded. 'Hate I think is a strong word, but there was a distinct rift between them that went far deeper than sibling rivalry. Davies had hurt Dawson's family pride deeply by his commissioning as an officer. It had caused the rift not only between his brother and himself, but with his sister too.'

Drake frowned. 'Then I find it hard to believe that he would have any such motive for wanting Sir Laurence dead. If anything, he would be upset. It doesn't follow, in my mind, that he had any motive for wanting to kill him. After all, Davies died in an accident didn't he? Or are you now suggesting it wasn't an accident?'

'Unless,' Baker cut in, 'unless Dawson and his sister are covering up for each other, maybe they are in collusion?'

'It's possible,' Drake conceded. It would explain a lot.

'It's a worthy point for investigation. Perhaps he isn't as dull as he made out. He could very well have telephoned his sister, explaining what had occurred, or maybe even to tell her the deed was done. That way when anyone came knocking, she could play her part.' Baker seemed very satisfied with this explanation.

'That's well reasoned George. We always believed that we were dealing with an intelligent murderer. It's quite possible he manipulated you, Straay. He knew you'd go to see her of course.'

Baker nodded. 'I strongly suspect you're right, Henry.'

'If what we're thinking is true,' Drake added, 'then perhaps DuPont was simply a casualty?'

'You mean he did kill himself out of genuine grief?' Baker asked.

'It's all pointing that way isn't it?'

'Yes and it's the best line of enquiry we have so far.'

Drake was conscious that Straay had been quiet throughout their deliberations.

'Don't you agree, doctor?' Baker clearly had been thinking along the same lines and articulated the question before Drake could.

Straay said nothing for a short while and then, as if making his mind up on some obscure points he asked them:

'When did Larry Gregson die?'

Neither one of them expected that question. He could tell by their expressions.

'Humour me.' He held up both hands. 'When did Larry Gregson die?'

'Okay, I'll bite.' Drake knew that Straay had his methods. They weren't always obvious, but they did get results. Baker on the other hand simply stared at him. Drake didn't need to consult any paperwork. He knew the facts of the case and the details from memory. 'Sir Laurence died Friday evening at approximately ten forty-five.'

Straay nodded. At length he said to them both:

'That is what we believed was true, based on everything we *knew* as facts, but things have changed. We know more. We have another death. There are threads that can't be tied together. So now, I ask you this. Are we *sure* of when he died?'

'Well we can't be precise about the timing, as you know. It was somewhere between ten thirty and ten forty-five.' Baker seemed confused by where this line of enquiry was leading. He was also a little irritated.

'I suspect it was much earlier than that.' Straay looked from one to the other.

Drake felt his headache returning. He rubbed his temples and Baker shot him a sympathetic look. Doctor Straay knew he could be infuriatingly unclear at times, but he had to let them make their own way. He would nudge them when necessary.

Superintendent Baker said firmly:

'Doctor Straay, we've already been over this, we know the timeline. It couldn't have been earlier than ten thirty, we've scientifically proven that.'

Straay understood their frustration, but he didn't want to hand it to them on a plate. What he had to tell them was far too important. He had to find a way to get them both to come to the same conclusion he had. He wanted them to see it, to appreciate the subtly of it, before he voiced it. He didn't want to tell them, he wanted them to work it out for themselves.

'I beg your indulgence. I realise I've confused you and you're a little irritated by my methods and it's late. It's been a long day for all of us, but let me try a different approach. Let us get back to the information regarding Anthony Davies. I said earlier that it was odd no one had mentioned this before now. Why was this information held back?'

'Perhaps because we never asked?' Drake offered.

'Excellent, yes, because we never asked. We can hardly expect an important bit of information like that to be handed to us, can we? I suspect that now we know, it will clear up many unanswered questions. It isn't just a case that this servant became an officer at the whim of an old General. This man had to be a close, personal friend of the family.

I asked myself, *what reason could there be for this man to be elevated far beyond his and anyone else's expectations?'*

Baker thought for a moment. 'You're quite right. Servants of his class aren't taken in by their masters and given the keys to the house. It's not impossible of course, but it's certainly not what would be considered normal behaviour.'

'You understand then my dilemma, Superintendent. Why was this man, the brother of the footman, later butler, treated this way? It isn't enough to say he and Larry Gregson were friends. Some servants enjoy a friendship with their employers, but there is a line that's never crossed. There were many servants in the household, people who had been in service for years, and they all tell the same story. In the background information, it is a popular theme that the General was extremely hard on people. He was very much top of the pole, head of the house. He never mixed with them and they never crossed him. In the same background searches, Drake, you discovered that Dawson had been charged for running down a police constable. It may surprise you Drake, but I suspect not you, Superintendent, to learn that it wasn't Dawson at the wheel.'

Drake raised his eyebrows in surprise. 'I interviewed the officer myself; he confirmed quite clearly that it was James Dawson.'

'There was never a court case was there?'

'No, from what I understand it was hushed up.'

Superintendent Baker had been fidgeting uncomfortably during their conversation. Straay smiled at him. 'The General's reach was long and hard, wasn't it Superintendent. What were you then? Sergeant?'

'Yes, but it's not quite what you imagine though,' Baker said slowly. Straay thought, *you have no idea what I'm imagining,* but let it go.

'I imagine,' he said carefully, 'it was very simple. The General suggested to your superiors that any investigation would be pointless. He probably made a generous offering to your Christmas fund, or am I off the mark?'

'No,' Baker said looking sideways at Drake. 'You're on the right track, actually. It couldn't be dismissed out of hand, so I was ordered to hand over all the material to my Inspector. He wrote the report and the case was closed.'

'Yes, but you suspected something wasn't right?'

'I knew something was fishy, but there was nothing I could do about it.'

Drake was stunned. 'So you were part of a cover up?'

'No!' Superintendent Baker shot back. He seemed appalled at the very idea. 'I was not. I was taken off the case entirely.'

'I know why.' Straay hadn't known Superintendent Baker long, but from the brief discussions Henry and he had and from his limited observations, he believed the man had a solid and honest character. He gave voice to it. 'It was because your integrity was beyond reproach.' Baker's anger subsided. 'It was simply because you were an honest police officer, and I think your Superintendent shielded you from what he knew to be a travesty of justice. The reports and investigation, they were all works of fiction.'

Baker silently thanked him with his eyes. 'My Superintendent was a good man, but like many people, especially leaders of smaller communities at that time, he wasn't beyond the reach of someone like General Smythe. It's different nowadays.'

Drake leaned across his desk. 'So who was driving that car?'

'It was Davies.'

'How could you know this?' Baker asked.

'I simply asked Lady Agatha.' Straay smiled an intelligent smile.

'This is all very interesting as a point of history, Doctor Straay, but it hardly helps us solve this particular crime. All these people are long since dead so there is no one to hold accountable.' Baker's statement held a firm authority. Straay looked at Drake and raised an eyebrow. He understood the meaning; *it's my move now.*

Drake and Straay both needed the formal support of the Superintendent because without it, they wouldn't get very far. Drake clucked his tongue and looked firmly at Baker.

'Henry, I always believed, as you do, that we had to centre this investigation on the here and now, not what happened in the past or in wartime.' He paused and, looking directly at Straay, he continued. 'Despite what Doctor Straay thought, I didn't seriously believe it could make any difference to our investigation. I wasn't interested in the things that happened in the past and I don't mean old crimes, because routinely we would try to link those. Family squabbles, movements of servants, staff, and the extraneous backstories weren't, I felt, that relevant. I read it all, but none of this information seemed to add any value to our investigation. They all happened such a long time ago.'

'But now you've come to re-evaluate your position?' Baker looked from one to the other. He wasn't stupid, Straay thought. He knew when he was being pressganged. It was clear from his expression, his body language, he didn't like it, but Straay knew he would listen to what they had to say, and Straay for his part was pleased, because he also knew that Drake still wasn't entirely on board with the idea, yet Drake had supported him. It boded well for what they needed to understand next.

'I'm forced to agree with Straay, sir.' Drake's use of the word "sir" was significant, Straay thought to himself.

'If we centre the investigation on the evidence we have, purely from the night in question, and ignore the profile and background information, however unreliable or likely it might be, we won't find the reason why Sir Laurence Gregson died and, as a result, we will not find out who killed him and why DuPont also died.'

'We don't know that the death of DuPont was anything but suicide, Henry; remember, only *his* fingerprints were on the items you found in the box.' Baker said evenly.

Drake conceded the point.

'So we're dealing with a sociopath.' Baker looked for affirmation on this criminal behaviour from Straay, but he simply shook his head.

'I thought so at first, but now I believe we're dealing with a psychopath.'

Drake seemed more confused than ever and Straay sympathised. Criminals were just lawbreakers to the policeman. He didn't understand all the fancy terms for being, what he would term, *not right in the head.* However, Straay knew that Drake equally wasn't a stupid man, and he was not averse to asking for more information about these terms, if he didn't understand.

Straay was vindicated when Drake finally asked:

'What's the difference between the two?'

Straay rubbed his chin in thought. 'It's not an exact science because there are still many things we simply do not know. As a rule, sociopaths tend to be nervous and easily agitated. They are likely to be uneducated, unable to hold down a steady job or stay in one place. They have no regard for society in general and in the eyes of others, sociopaths appear clearly disturbed. Crimes committed by a sociopath tend to be disorganized and spontaneous.'

'Sounds very much like DuPont to me,' Drake smiled.

Straay continued his comparison. 'Psychopaths, on the other hand, often have far more charming personalities. They are manipulative and easily gain trust. They learn to mimic emotion and appear "normal." They are often educated and hold steady jobs. Some are so good at manipulation and mimicry they can have families and other long term relationships without those around them ever suspecting their true nature.'

'Well, that makes it possibly anyone in the household,' Drake said.

Baker folded his arms defiantly. 'Well then it leads back to Dawson. He wanted revenge for his brother's death. Psychopaths carefully plan every detail of a crime and often have contingency plans in place. Well, that would explain his sister's evidence wouldn't it?'

'Or Lady Agatha's,' Drake said quickly. 'She knew Anthony Davies too, before the war, I mean, and she's holding back on many things.'

'Have we classified Lady Agatha as a psychopath now, Henry? Holding back information isn't the same as planning and carrying out a high profile murder.'

'We're trying to answer too many questions at once and defining or labelling people isn't the answer,' Straay interjected. 'Even if Dawson or Lady Agatha were prime suspects and fit our analysis, we still can't explain why DuPont was killed.'

'If he was killed,' Baker added sharply. 'It seems to me, you're assuming far too many things, Doctor Straay.'

'It was a poor choice of words only, Superintendent. I meant that whatever the motive, DuPont's death is a key factor in this crime and we can't ignore it, nor can we simply pass it off as extraneous. Whether he died by his own hand or by another's is yet to be discovered. Mystery surrounds this man and we already know he wasn't who he pretended to be.'

'Okay,' Baker said, giving ground a little. 'Let's say you're right and we do go back and look at something from the past, where do we start? It seems to me that, as most of the protagonists are now dead, we're running out of people to simply ask.'

'You are partly correct.' Straay tried to be as diplomatic as he could be. 'We don't need to ask anyone. We simply use what we already know.'

Drake pulled out his notepad. 'Let's do this logically. We know that Davies was a friend of the family, or possibly even more than a friend. He had the ear of the General. He was bailed out by him and his brother was forced to admit to his crime. Why was Davies treated with such affection from the General?'

Baker was thoughtful. 'Was he possibly blackmailing him?'

Stray said:

'It was my first thought, that, but it doesn't fit with the General's profile. This man would not have been blackmailed by a servant. This man would never have allowed such a thing to happen. He was so totally dominant that it's more likely he would have ruined Dawson in ways the man couldn't have conceived of, before he let him get away with something as crude as blackmail. So what other reason could there be?'

Drake clicked his fingers. 'He was in love with Ellie or Lady Agatha!'

'Yes, much better! We already know that the General was very fond of Larry, so his interest could only have been in Lady Agatha.'

Baker sat back and said:

'I still can't see where this is leading, but I can see that you won't rest until you've ironed out all the kinks and found the culprit. That alone convinces me you're worthy of my support. Even if that support means I will have to face very difficult questions if this all comes to nothing.'

'Thank you, Superintendent. I assure you, you will be rewarded for your support.'

Drake then said:

'Wasn't Lady Agatha already married?' He checked back through his notes.

'Not that I could find out,' Straay replied. 'She is Lady Agatha Geraldine Smythe, Drake. If she were widowed, as she led us to believe, then why is her name not that of her husband? Ellie Gregson isn't Lady Elizabeth Smythe, she was Lady Elizabeth Gregson.'

'Well, she could have simply gone back to her maiden name.' It sounded weak, but it wasn't that uncommon.

'Yes I agree, but not in the event of his death. This is usually the case in divorce. However, it is academic because I know that Lady Agatha was never married. She was deeply in love with David, yes, but the General favoured Anthony. According to Lady Agatha, David died in the war *before* they were able to formalise their union. The General being in favour of Anthony and not David would explain his affectionate regard for this ex-servant, wouldn't it?'

Drake nodded. 'It would.'

Straay continued: 'It's nepotism in the purest sense of the word. I firmly believe Davies had no interest in Lady Agatha. His interest was only to ensure his quality of life was maintained. With each bit of careful planning, his standing increased and as this continued, his position in society was elevated further. It wasn't enough though. I put it to you both that if marrying Lady Agatha meant that he could move up into the aristocracy itself he would have done it. She wouldn't need to agree to any of it, because it was a very different time. The General would have commanded and it would have been done, regardless of her personal feelings. You see, Anthony Davies was manipulative, ruthless, intelligent, narcissistic, and driven to achieve his goal by any means necessary. He was prone to both reactive and calculated aggression, lacked any emotional depth, and most importantly, did not experience a typical range of anxiety and fear. I believe these characteristics accounted for his lack of conscience. He was a psychopath.'

'You speak as though you actually met and interviewed the man,' Baker said with a chuckle.

'I have. We all have,' Straay said simply.

Drake frowned and then Straay saw it. The curtain was pulled from Drake's eyes. They now shone with the light of new knowledge. Straay had been trying to tell them for a while but they hadn't seen it. He had drip fed them. They had both been so fixated on the actual crime they hadn't seen what was practically right in front of them. Drake, he could tell, understood the significance of the build-up now. Straay had wanted them to come to the same conclusion he had, and it was a fantastic conclusion.

'My god….' Drake whispered.

'Yes, you see where I am going now?' Straay was happy.

'I do, it's fantastic… can it be proven?'

'Oh yes.'

'I don't like being gooseberry,' Baker said hotly looking at both in turn. 'One of you had better explain it to me.'

Straay handed him the photograph he had taken from Mrs Talbot.

'Who is this man?'

Baker studied it for a brief moment and looked up at Straay confused. 'It's Anthony Davies; it says so, on the bottom.' He handed the photograph back and then Straay came to his side. He put a hand partly over the face on the picture.

'And now?'

'God lord!' Barker looked up wide-eyed. 'But that's impossible. This is a picture of Sir Laurence Gregson.'

'No, Superintendent. It is a picture of both. This is Anthony Davies. There was no such person as Sir Laurence Gregson. The man who died in the war was Captain Larry Gregson. So now, you understand what I have been driving at. You see now why I said that I suspected he had died much earlier. Larry Gregson was not killed in his study last Friday at ten forty five because Larry Gregson was already dead.'

Chapter Twenty-Five

A Clear Direction

Drake re-entered the office with a pot of fresh coffee and some mugs. They all drank in silence for a moment. Straay cradled his mug in both hands, savouring the warmth of it.

'Did you know Sir Laurence regularly sent a cheque to Mrs Talbot?'

Drake nodded. 'Ten pounds, quite a sum. I had no reference or context for the payments before, but it was clearly in his bank statements.'

'I suspect that he loved his sister very much,' Straay said sipping his coffee, 'that was obvious. I honestly believe she had no idea that her "Mr Laurence" was actually her own brother; it is very sad.'

'You said that you could prove it?'

'The medical records and the autopsy files proved it. Once I had the idea, it seemed to me the most logical place to start looking.'

'This is a fine bit of work, Doctor Straay, and it changes everything!' Baker put down his mug resolutely.

'No, it mustn't.' Straay voiced that opinion with authority. 'No one must know what we know. It must stay in here, between us. This we must all agree on.'

'He's right George. If the household finds out we know, then we'll never get any further in the investigation. Worse, the guilty party might bolt.'

Baker was thoughtful for a moment. 'Okay, but I have to ask you to hurry it up, please. I'm being enormously pressured by the Home Office, now daily. If we don't come up with a suitable answer soon, I think we may *all* be enjoying our retirements a lot earlier than we'd planned!'

'I only require three more facts and I will have a complete case for both of you.' Straay lit a cigarette.

'You mean you've solved it? You know who did it?' Drake looked incredulously at him.

'I believe I do, but I cannot yet prove it.' Straay tapped his ash into the tray. 'I will tell you this much. Not only do I know *how* it was done. I also know *why* it was done. Why always leads me to whom. I only need now to tie up some loose threads to be able to offer you my conclusions.'

'Well whom *do* you suspect?' Baker lifted his mug to his lips.

'I suspect myself,' Straay answered a little dramatically, 'of coming to conclusions too rapidly!' He looked at their blank expressions and chuckled. 'It was a quote from your Sherlock Holmes. It seemed... appropriate.'

◆

The discussions were now over. It was late when Superintendent Baker left. The moon was out in full and the air was thick and warm. Chief Inspector Drake and Doctor Straay carried on their conversation as they walked to his car.

'What's our next move then?' Drake climbed into the driver's seat and closed the door. Beside him, Straay was sitting, hunched a little. He was a tall man, as a lot of Dutch are. His files, books, coat, and hat were all piled up on his lap.

'I need to think about that.' Straay watched the world go by from the passenger window. 'It's late, and I'm tired and hungry. A little food and sleep will revive my brain.'

'Mrs Drake has something hot for us. She's used to my time keeping by now, bless her.'

The car pulled into the driveway of the Chief Inspector's house. Mrs Drake greeted them as they entered the hallway and hung up their coats. Straay was almost overcome with the smell of something wonderful being cooked in the kitchen.

◆

A few hours later, when dinner had been eaten and both men had washed the dishes, they sat in a nicely decorated conservatory, drinking brandy, and smoking cigars.

'I've been thinking,' Drake turned to him. 'I've got an idea about who killed Sir Laurence that I want to run by you.'

'By all means.' Straay settled himself.

'Well I see it this way. We know that Sir Laurence was poisoned first, and that poison we've been unable to trace. The bottle in the box had only DuPont's fingerprints on, but that doesn't mean it wasn't wiped first. It's an odd poison to use, curare. Therefore, here's my theory. I think it's quite possible that Milly discovered that Anthony Davies wasn't her real father.'

Straay nodded.

'She may have been the person who overheard the entire conversation about the arrangement for the marriage between herself and DuPont. Maybe she heard DuPont say that he wouldn't do it. Maybe she heard Davies tell him he would kick him out and ruin him if he didn't. Now, she strikes me as a woman who would not be forced to marry anyone, but she also seems to me to be the type of woman that likes money.'

'Yes there is a lot of truth in what you say, go on.'

'What if it happened this way…? She approaches DuPont and confesses to having overheard everything. She tells him that she won't go through with it, but he convinces her that Davies would ruin them both. So she obtains the curare, injects her "father" when he's in the study and whilst he was paralysed, DuPont shoots him and then they dress it up as a suicide?'

'It's good, Drake, it's very good.'

'Thanks, I've been considering Milly as my prime suspect for a while. It fits the facts.'

Straay was quiet for a moment then said:

'Where did she get the curare from?'

'I don't know, but it occurred to me that DuPont could have got it from one of his criminal contacts.'

'That's entirely possible,' Straay admitted. It was a good explanation, it covered the facts well, but most of the evidence was circumstantial.

'A lawyer might argue that the box was planted. That there was no possible way to corroborate that Milly had overheard a conversation between two dead men. He may also say that DuPont's background wasn't enough to assume that he could get curare. DuPont himself may not know what it did, but I suspect Milly would. So then, what was the motivation behind poisoning him and then shooting him? You put the needle in her hand, but the gun in DuPont's. Whichever way you look at it, Milly is very unlikely to ever be tried and convicted as a murderer.

Conspiracy to murder perhaps, but from the way you just described it, DuPont actually killed him.'

'But we know that the poison would have killed him also.'

'Yes but it didn't. The bullet did. So what is there against Milly?'

'Well surely she intended to kill him, the dose was high enough.'

Straay stood and grabbed his own lapels. 'I put it to you, members of the jury, that Milly had no such intention to kill this man. She was frightened of this man; he bullied women. We already know he wasn't her father; we have clearly established that this man was a psychopath. So my client discovers his secrets and it appals and upsets her. Her father, Captain Larry Gregson, is dead in the war and this man, Davies, was posing as her father for all those years, pretending to love her, poisoning her against her own mother, her aunt. It was all too much. She is in this weak frame of mind, she isn't thinking clearly. This is when a notorious criminal, Desmond DuPont, sees his chance. He knows my client is in love with him, and so he manipulates her. He obtains the poison. He tells her it will temporarily paralyze but not kill him. Members of the jury, if she had intended to kill the poseur, she could have used any number of household poisons that would have done the job; she did not. Once she had gone through with it, DuPont came in carrying a weapon. She tries to reason with him, but he doesn't listen, he doesn't care. This vile criminal, this sociopath fires the weapon and kills him. He then tells her, we are both guilty. She is overcome by what DuPont has done, but what can she do? I put it to you that she falls in with his idea of making the scene look like suicide out of fear, not out of malicious intent. Therefore, members of the jury, if you believe that Milly Gregson intentionally meant to kill this man, then you should find her guilty. If however you believe, as I do, that she was tricked into performing this act by a criminal who was posing as a lawyer, as her friend, as her lover, a man who had already been associated with another murder, as yet unsolved, then you should find her not guilty.'

Drake laughed with good humour. 'Point taken.'

'It was still a good theory and I'm pleased your sterile police mind is opening up to fresh ideas.' He winked.

◆

Drake was reading the paper whilst Straay sat looking out the window. It was getting late and the doctor was considering going to bed, but his mind was so full of things, he knew that he wouldn't be able to sleep if he did. He sipped at his brandy, lost in his own thoughts.

'Loose ends,' Straay softly murmured.

'Sorry what's that?'

'Oh sorry, didn't realise I'd said that aloud. I was thinking about loose ends, there are a few that don't seem to connect.'

'Such as?'

Straay turned to him. 'DuPont.'

'What about him?'

'I'm still trying to figure out if he jumped, or was pushed.'

'I assume you're using a metaphor?'

Straay nodded. 'He is an anomaly in my reasoning.'

'You still think he was killed?'

'I believe he was killed, yes, but is that enough? Do I truly know it? If I know it then it categorically cannot be false. If I just believe it, that doesn't make it true at all.'

'I don't follow you.'

'How do I put it? I believe a bridge is safe enough to support me, and attempt to cross it; unfortunately, the bridge collapses. I *believed* that bridge was safe, but this belief was mistaken. It would be inaccurate to say that I *knew* the bridge was safe, because it was not. However, if the bridge supported my weight then I might be justified in saying I knew the bridge was safe enough to cross, at least at that particular time.'

'That's psychology?'

'No philosophy. Well… epistemology to be precise.'

'Oh.' Drake sipped his brandy. 'How does it help?'

'It doesn't,' Straay laughed. 'I'm just externalising my thoughts. I do it when I'm tired, forgive me.' He stood. 'When I start talking philosophy, I know it is time for bed.'

Chapter Twenty-Six

The Dream

Straay found himself totally in the dark. He couldn't see anything, not even his hand in front of his face. It was an unnerving feeling. He wanted to step forward but his body would not respond. He could neither hear nor see. The face of Dawson appeared, disembodied and directly in front of him, at some distance he couldn't directly gauge. It was a large face, far larger then it ought to have been. It was grinning madly. It floated in mid-air for a few seconds and then drifted to his left; the eyes never left his. In the centre, a new face appeared: that of Lady Agatha. In the same way, her head drifted off to the right. It was replaced by Major Heskith. Eventually five heads floated around him. They were all smiling at him. He tried to speak but he found no voice. When they eventually spoke, it was in unison. A mixture of phrases and statements that he'd either heard directly or read.

Dinner was at eight.
I so dislike brandy.
Have to think how you get the bodies off the battlefield.
You can't pop into the local chemist and get some, that's for sure.
You can smell that pipe before you see him.
Larry shot himself.
I was tired and went to bed.
The man I loved died in the war.
Major Heskith has a silver Parker pen.
We're dealing with a sociopath.
They were so alike.
Larry Gregson was already dead.
He was a peach before the war.
You don't cut off the hand that feeds you.

Straay awoke suddenly from the images of his dream. He blinked a few times in order to assure himself that he was actually awake. He looked over at the clock and it read seven thirty. It ticked so loudly in the room that it seemed to be the only sound he could hear. He had a word on his mind, a word that he couldn't quite remember. He thought hard. Then it came to him: a word that had more significance than its name.

'Pipe…' he said aloud.

◆

Drake was sitting at the breakfast table when Straay surfaced. He looked well rested. Mrs Drake smiled at him as he sat down and she poured him a fresh mug of coffee.

'Did you sleep well, Doctor Straay?' He gratefully accepted the coffee from her and took a mouthful.

'I did, yes. The bed was very comfortable.'

'Would you like some breakfast?'

'Toast, please,' he smiled at her.

'You all right, Straay? You seem a little distracted?' Drake folded his paper and studied him.

'I woke from a dream and I'm still trying to understand it.'

'What sort of dream?'

'A disturbing one. Full of images and faces, of phrases either heard or written. It was disjointed.'

'That happens to me too, when I'm on a case. I read all day and night, go to bed, and dream about it too. Sometimes, I can make connections from the dreams, you know, as if my subconscious mind is helping me unravel things. Sometimes the images aren't exactly real. It's difficult to put it into words.'

'I know that feeling. My mind is telling me something, I just wish it wasn't being so abstract about the way it chooses to deliver the information to me.' Straay drank his coffee.

Mrs Drake placed some toast in front of him. She had been listening to their conversation intently. She said, 'I remember once that I had a dream about a cat. I thought for the longest time that I was the cat, seeing the world from its perspective, but after a while I realised it was the other way around.'

'The other way around…' Straay whispered.

'Yes, that's right. You see, I couldn't be the cat and see the cat could I? So it had to be that I was part of the world looking down at the cat. Strange dream.'

'The other way around!' Straay stood, knocking over his chair startling both of them.

'What is it?' Drake stood too. He watched Straay laugh for the longest time, then pick up the chair and grab Mrs Drake by the hand.

'Oh my dear, Mrs Drake,' Straay twirled her around the kitchen. 'You, madam, are a genius.'

'Thank you,' she said breathlessly. 'I'm not sure what I said, though.'

Chief Inspector Drake looked at them.

'The other way around? What does that mean Straay?'

'I need to go to the house. There is some information I must get, but we're close, Drake, so very close.'

'Right, I'll drop you off there.'

Straay turned to Mrs Drake and said:

'Thank you, Mrs Drake. You have helped me more than you can know.' He kissed her politely on the cheek and she looked a little embarrassed by it.

'Get away with you; *both* of you,' she said laughing. Henry smiled at her and they went to their bedrooms to change.

◆

They sat together in the car for the longest time. Straay was now giving Drake some final instructions. Rain battered the windscreen and the small wipers were unable to clear it fast enough.

'You're sure about all this?' Drake wiped the inside of the window, which had misted up.

'Yes, I am sure. Did Doctor Carmichael say that his results would be ready today?'

'Yes, he said the post-mortem would be complete at ten, so I'll hang around the station till then and grab the results, then meet you at the house.'

Straay nodded. 'Good...until then. Remember, timing on this is critical. I'll only have one shot at getting it right.' He put on his hat and got out of the car.

'I've got your back, don't worry.'

Straay closed the door and walked off into the rain.

◆

With Straay in the house and with his instructions clear, Drake drove directly to the morgue to meet with Doctor Carmichael. The rain had stopped and the sun had now come out in full. The conversation he'd had with Straay played on his mind a lot but for now he had to get the medical results. Anything else would have to wait. Doctor Carmichael greeted him as he came into the room.

'Ah, there you are Chief Inspector.' He handed a file to Drake. 'It's all there. Everything you need.'

'Conclusion?'

'It was suicide, no question about it. Ligature marks were consistent with the belt, and his hyoid bone was still intact so we can rule out manual strangulation. It was a short drop so I was off in my timing a little. He probably took about five to ten minutes to actually die, but he would have been unconscious within five at the latest.'

'Did you do the comparison against the medical records I sent down?'

'Yes, there's no question about it. This was definitely your man Harry Green. Dental records confirmed that.'

'So he really did kill himself then.'

'That's my official conclusion, yes.' Doctor Carmichael put his hands into the pockets of his white overall.

'Doctor Straay won't like that,' Drake said shaking his head.

'Well, he can't be right all the time. What's his objection, anyway?'

'Something about it not being right, he wouldn't kill himself in this way according to Straay's character assessment.'

'You mean the psychological profile?'

'Yes, but I'm not that up on these things. The man was a coward and a fraud. I think he just couldn't live with the fact that he'd been caught out in a lie that would ruin his life. If you add to this that we know that he was also being sought for another serious crime and that he was in love with Sir Laurence...I'd say, from my experience and from just talking to the man, that he was perfectly capable of it.'

'Have you got any further in your investigation of Harry Green?'

'No, we've got nothing. The one thing I think is a little too convenient is that he died before we could interview him about it.'

'He probably had no idea you'd discovered who he was. Besides, it is all academic now. He committed suicide and there's an end to it. It's all in the file. Is there anything else I can do for you Chief Inspector?'

'No,' Drake shook his hand. 'Thank you, doctor.'

'As always, a pleasure, Chief Inspector.'

Drake left the morgue and headed to his next and possibly final appointment.

ACT THREE

Chapter Twenty-Seven

Smoke and Death

Once again, Doctor Straay found himself in the smoking room and, as on that very first night, all the people except for two were present. Lady Agatha sat back in a very comfortable chair with Milly Gregson beside her. Major Heskith stood at the window smoking a cigarette and Doctor Powell sat smoking his pipe. Dawson stood to attention by the door. Straay surveyed them all with a keen eye.

'Thank you for agreeing to see me this morning.' He bowed slightly.

'Well, I think I speak for everyone when I say that we have nothing to hide.' Doctor Powell's voice was carefully modulated. Heskith walked over to an empty chair and sat down.

'Doctor,' began Straay, 'if there's one thing I know for certain it is that everyone here has something to hide.'

'Where's your police friend?' Heskith eyed him sardonically.

'Chief Inspector Drake is at this very moment waiting for the medical examiner to conclude his post-mortem on Desmond DuPont. It is of DuPont I wanted to talk to you.'

'Look, he killed himself...boy was unhinged, that's all there was to it,' the Major said.

'Yes, he was unhinged, but not for the reasons you think. We discovered that he wasn't a lawyer at all. His credentials were faked.'

Milly was astonished. 'Unbelievable...and you think this is the reason he killed himself?'

'We do not yet know how he died.'

'I hope you're not suggesting one of us killed the boy?' The Major crossed his legs in defiance.

'Why not, Major? One of you possibly killed Sir Laurence. Why does it not follow that the same person possibly killed Mr DuPont?'

'For what reason?' Powell asked.

'The reason is complicated. First off, he was, as I say, a fraud. He was also being, in essence, blackmailed by Sir Laurence to formalise a union with Milly.'

Milly blinked, then looked at Lady Agatha. 'I didn't know,' she said. 'Poor Desmond. You say blackmailed, but why would my father do such a thing? You didn't know my father. He knew my feelings for Desmond; he wouldn't have forced him into marriage, that's just silly.'

'You are right, Milly.' Straay smiled at her. 'I didn't know your father at all.' Lady Agatha narrowed her eyes a little but said nothing. 'My observations of Sir Laurence were very limited. I didn't have enough time to get to know him, not like you all did.'

'Do you ever get to the point?' Agatha said, with a sigh.

'Eventually...when I am ready to. But you all know that I have come to a conclusion in this matter; that I have, if you like, solved the case. You know this because Lady Agatha knows it and she has told you all. I have no doubt about that. I am here now, in my private capacity and not with the police, because I wanted to be open, frank, and honest with you. My hope is, that you will be equally so with me, but even if you're not, I want you all to hear my thoughts and conclusions as a group, and then, once you know where I stand, I will take my conclusions to the police and let them do their job.'

'I'm looking forward to this,' Powell said, refilling his pipe.

'I'm not,' Lady Agatha whispered.

'As you know, I've spent a lot of time going over statements, revisiting the past and rooting through all the old and new files of Chief Inspector Drake for the past day or so, and it has led me to understand the motive for why Sir Laurence had to die. I already knew how it was done, but I needed to know why.'

The room was silent.

'So,' Straay said, smiling at everyone in the room. 'It comes to this.' He didn't reach any kind of point; he simply stood smiling at them. The silence in the room made everyone look questioningly at each other. Eventually Straay pulled out a little notebook and turned a few pages over. When he had found what he was looking for, he lifted his head and began to speak.

'You know,' he said evenly, 'it was extremely difficult to come to any kind of truth or conclusion in this matter. Both the Chief Inspector and I have hit many brick walls in this case. I expect that you all understand this feeling because it is largely thanks to you all that we hit them. The underlying problem we each faced was simply this: everyone here had a motive for wanting Sir Laurence dead. Each one of you was covering for another person who you thought had committed the crime. Once I realised this, I was able to sort through many of the inconsistencies in statements and arrive at the truth.' He paused for a moment to allow each of them to reflect upon the statement.

'I asked myself many questions: Why was Sir Laurence murdered? Why did his murder need to be discovered at a specific time? What was the purpose of the elaborate suicide fiction, and what was the reason for Desmond DuPont's suicide?' Again, a pause. The room was as quiet as it was before. He continued.

'Before I answer these questions, it is necessary to revisit the past; to go back twenty years: five years before the death of Ellie Gregson. When I first examined all the evidence, I had a feeling that I was missing something. Everyone had told me this and that, but more than one of you had told me all I needed to know. I didn't see it until I decided to ignore the evidence of everyone else and go back to examining Sir Laurence himself. You see, it occurred to me at the time that, either subconsciously or consciously, you were all trying to tell me about him. I realise now it had to be the former. You were all saying this man had changed; this man was different after the war. And then Lady Agatha showed me a photograph; a photograph that told me everything, not that I was able to understand it at the time. It was a lovely photograph, do you still have it?' He turned to Lady Agatha and she hesitated, looking briefly over at Major Heskith who nodded ever so slightly. She pulled it out of her bag and handed it to him.

'Thank you,' he said and turned it around for all to see. 'This photograph is old, it's faded, but in it are five people: Lady Agatha and her fiancé David, Lieutenant Anthony Davies, Ellie, and Laurence Gregson. The first thing that strikes me in this photograph is how happy everyone is. The second thing is how similar both Lady Agatha and Ellie Gregson are and the third thing is: why was there no female companion with Davies? This photograph doesn't really show any detail, as it is so faded, but this one...' he said, removing a second picture from his pocket, 'this one has much more detail.' They all looked at each other but no one spoke.

'This photograph was given to me by Mrs Talbot, the sister of Dawson. She told me many things, but most importantly, she gave me the clue that led to the discovery that Larry Gregson had actually died in the war.'

There was a collective intake of breath. Straay looked at Lady Agatha. She held his gaze unflinchingly.

Major Heskith just shook his head. 'I can't believe it. I knew Larry. Served with him! It's preposterous.'

'Yes I agree,' Doctor Powell said nodding. 'There's no way he could have been anyone else, I treated him, man and boy!'

Their responses were programmed, Straay thought. Even now, they are still using the collective defence mechanism that they had probably agreed on, should they be interviewed on this very topic.

'Major, you knew him *after* his accident. Doctor, by your own admission, he rarely needed or wanted medical attention. If you go back though all the evidence, it's right there for anyone to see. "He wasn't the same man that returned from the war," "My Larry must have died in the war," and "He was so scarred that anybody that knew him before the war would never recognise him." You see, there it was plain to see, everyone said it; I missed it because I had no context for understanding it. We all assumed that Sir Laurence was Larry Gregson, the police and I, but we were all wrong. He told me, you know, on our first meeting. As you know, I met him on the boat from Holland going to England. We were discussing crime fiction. It was there that he explained various absurd plots to me and one of them went: "A man goes to war then returns, different, bitter and war fatigued. He goes on to establish himself in some big country estate, but secretly isn't the same person who left it all those years previously".' He turned to Lady Agatha and smiled fondly, 'You knew, of course.'

Lady Agatha returned his smile. She seemed relieved. 'Yes I knew, but not right away. I put the pieces together eventually. My sister told me many times in private that he wasn't Larry. At the time, I didn't believe her. We didn't always get on, you know, so it wasn't easy to take her at her word.'

'As I suspected, you were aware but you could do nothing. Could say nothing. Is that not so?'

'Yes, a few weeks before Ellie died, she told me again and again that he wasn't Larry. Again I told her she was being silly. She was angry with me. She always intended for me to have the house because it was my father's, but then she changed her will. I didn't know at the time, so you can imagine the shock I got when I found that she'd left the house to me, but that Laurence would manage it. Effectively tying us together.'

Straay nodded. 'So you thought back on things and made a plan. A clever plan, to ensure that you would always have control.'

Lady Agatha hesitated a little. 'I'm sorry, I don't understand.'

Straay smiled a quick smile and said, 'You remember that I came to you and we talked about Anthony?'

'Yes of course I remember.' She looked into his eyes.

'You said to me *"You know, don't you?"* I said that I knew almost everything. You assumed from the way I phrased the answer that I had simply discovered the dual identity of Sir Laurence and this eased your mind.'

'Really, Doctor Straay, I fail to understand where this is going!'

'You made a mistake, a minor one, when I asked you if you were in love with him. You said *"No. I was fond of him once. So was Larry, but my sister wasn't."* You then said after a question about being widowed: *"As far as I'm concerned, the man I loved died in the war."*' She met his gaze, but he noticed tears forming in her eyes.

'Then a chance remark was made that changed the way I was looking at those answers. *"It was the other way around."* You see, the biggest revelation today isn't the fact that we knew Sir Laurence wasn't Larry Gregson. It's much bigger than that. Your mistakes were simple, but they all added to the puzzle. It was Milly who first told it to me with a simple word, and then you yourself slipped up and said it. You also confused yourself over your answer relating to Anthony Davies. *"I was fond of him once. So was Larry, but my sister wasn't."* and after I'd heard that chance remark, I asked myself, which way round was it. Who was fond of Davies and who wasn't.'

Everyone in the room looked at her and she clucked her tongue.

'What are you talking about? You're talking nonsense!' She was trying to maintain her composure.

'Please, My Lady,' he said holding up a hand. 'It is useless to continue the pretence. I know who you are.'

Milly took Agatha's hands in hers. 'It's okay… it's time.' That statement was enough to settle an unsettled room.

Chapter Twenty-Eight

The Final Revelation

'It wasn't Lady Ellie Gregson who died fifteen years ago,' he remarked, smiling at Milly, 'It was Lady Agatha.'

'You are far too clever, Doctor Straay,' Ellie Gregson said. 'What was the word?'

'Peach.'

She laughed. 'My peach….' She shook her head at the absurdity of it.

'Milly had told me you called him: *"My peach."* When I suggested to you that Sir Laurence's behaviour could have been related to the German ancestry of your father, you told me: *"He was a peach before the war."* Of course this could have been nothing, but given what I already suspected, I looked for more evidence to support the theory, and this was another piece.'

'How is it you remember the conversations you have quite so clearly?' Doctor Powell asked.

'It's easy when you have an eidetic memory.'

Doctor Straay walked over to the bar, pulled out six crystal tumblers, and filled each with brandy and a little soda water. He put them all onto a tray and went around, handing them out. He kept the last for himself. When this was done, he took up the story.

'You see the sisters were identical twins, the entire household knew it, but nobody suspected the switch. The photograph taken on a summer's day long ago, with tea on the lawn and all the protagonists showed it. I watched you run a finger over that photograph. You unconsciously caressed a person on it but it wasn't David, it was Larry, your husband. The man you loved. Here is what I suspect happened and please stop me if I get any details wrong.' Ellie Gregson nodded solemnly.

'Your husband returns from the war, but he is different. You expected this, because most men who came back were. When he finally arrived, the differences in him were huge but you couldn't initially put your finger on what they were. He was scarred horribly; no one recognised him. You didn't even recognise him. Was he really the same man? You set up a plan. You asked your sister to come and live with you, knowing that your Larry would be delighted by the arrangement. This man, however, was not because he wanted as few people as possible to share the house, lest his crime be detected. In some fashion, you suggested to your sister that the two of you should swap places, so that you could become Agatha and she could assume your identity. As you were identical, it would be an easy thing to do. Already you suspected Sir Laurence of being an imposter, but this action would allow you to observe him from the outside. Becoming Agatha was easy enough—as children you probably did the same to your parents—and it was a trick well played.

'In your new persona, you discovered that Sir Laurence was engaged in elicit sexual affairs with the male staff, specifically the younger men. You instructed your sister to dismiss them all, but leave the females. You also saw how Milly was being brainwashed by the man who was pretending to be your husband. It got complicated. There was no way you could rescue both your sister and your daughter, so you allowed Milly to follow her own path. As your sister became you, and you her, she made changes under your direction, but then the worst thing in the world happened. Your sister got ill. Your plan was in jeopardy. How could you switch roles? It wasn't possible. Quickly you wrote out a new will. You couldn't leave the estate to yourself, as Agatha, Sir Laurence would have easily contested it. You were also fearful for your daughter, lest she became a victim of Sir Laurence's future greed and lest he take murderous steps against her, so what could you do?

'It came to you in this way: You would leave the estate to your sister—you—but allow Sir Laurence to manage it. That was a stroke of genius. It ensured that you were not penniless and that you couldn't be evicted from your own family home. Your sister then died, but there was a scandal. She was pregnant. Despite being identical, Agatha had a rare illness that hadn't affected you. You'd already given birth to Milly with no such complications; Agatha had never borne a child, as far as we know. I do not know for sure who the father was, but Sir Laurence knew beyond doubt that it wasn't him – he had never slept with her.'

Major Heskith fidgeted slightly in his chair. Doctor Powell smoked profusely on his pipe. Lady Gregson nodded, and Straay continued.

'So you were trapped as your sister, watching your daughter become a woman, unable to come clean and tell her that her mother was alive. Your hatred of Sir Laurence grew and grew, and at every opportunity, you reminded him of little instances he should have been aware of, as a husband. Years passed and Milly's fondness for you increased. It's possible that the bond between mother and daughter drove her to you...she simply wasn't conscious of it. Whatever the reason, she sought you out frequently for advice and help. Sadly, you were more a mother to her as Agatha, than you were as her actual mother. You were more determined than ever to discover who this man was. With that evidence, you would be able to convince your daughter, and maybe then it would be possible to tell your secret. You told no one who you really were. How am I doing so far?'

'The detail is a little off at times, but generally you have it right,' said Lady Gregson; her white face made her eyes seem even larger.

'So then this is, I believe, the sequence of events. As Lady Agatha, you began having conversations with Doctor Powell regarding Sir Laurence's health. Is that not so doctor?'

Powell nodded. 'Yes that's right. We were talking about operations. Agatha said that Laurence hadn't ever had an operation before, but I said that wasn't true because he had an appendectomy scar. So obviously, he'd had this surgery.'

Straay looked at Ellie Gregson. 'But as his *wife,* you knew he'd never had an appendectomy so you used your sister's contacts in the hospital, called a few friends that she'd given you, possibly in a list, so that you'd be able to maintain your identity as Agatha, and asked them to get you his medical file from the Home Office. They sent you a copy and they sent the same copy to the Chief Inspector. In the index was a note that this file was a second copy. The file contained no record of an appendectomy on the body, but inside that file, you found the answer you were looking for. You found the names of the officers and men who had been in the same accident that had wounded Sir Laurence. Anthony Davies had been killed, you knew, in the war; it must have been a great shock to you, to find out that Davies had died in that very explosion Sir Laurence had survived.'

'It didn't take much for me to work it out after that.' Ellie was thoughtful, 'I knew Anthony before the war, but not as well as Larry did. Once I discovered the details, it wasn't hard to gather the evidence I needed.'

Straay looked over at Dawson and they followed his eyes.

'Anthony Davies was your brother; that we have already established, but you couldn't tell me anything about him because you feared you might betray the secret. Your sister gave me the clues I needed.'

Dawson looked broken. 'He stopped being my brother the moment he became Davies.'

'Yet he was still very fond of you. I wondered why he defended you so vigorously when it was suggested that you be a witness to the will. I put it down to your years of service at the time, but obviously Anthony loved you dearly.'

Dawson choked back a sob.

'You knew of course that he had established himself as Sir Laurence?'

'Yes sir, he was my brother. I knew it was him from the moment he entered the house. I agreed that I would say nothing and he promised to keep me on as butler. Nothing was more important to me than my position. As far as I was concerned, my brother had died in the war; I had no reason to want him alive anyway. It suited us both that way.'

'This explained your sudden financial gain. Your brother knew how much the family position meant to you. He had no reason to suspect any form of treachery from you at all, so long as he agreed to keep you in your position. I ask you then, who was worse?' Straay snapped his book shut, 'And what about your poor sister, hmm? What about the feelings of that lovely, hardworking woman, who still missed her brother so deeply? You know a psychologist's job is to report and not judge; but this act was so callous, so grotesque, I find myself disgusted by you both.'

Dawson said nothing as Straay continued to stare at him.

'You knew about his sexuality too, didn't you?'

'Yes. He was at it all the time, with other members of the household, even before the war. It was disgusting!'

'Was that the reason why you killed DuPont?'

'I didn't kill him, he killed himself!'

'You helped him though, didn't you? You suggested a way out. Probably said it was the best way, to protect Milly...but really, despite everything, you were still protecting yourself!'

'I was protecting my family honour! He killed himself. I never laid a hand on him.'

'You didn't need to. He was so emotionally broken, you could have suggested anything and he'd have done it. Family honour? You were protecting one person. You.'

Dawson looked down at his hands.

Eventually he turned back to Ellie Gregson.

'So, my Lady, through the presence of an appendectomy scar and the certain knowledge that this man wasn't your husband, you determined that Sir Laurence was, in fact, Anthony Davies. That was when you confessed everything to your daughter.'

Lady Gregson looked at Milly with a slight smile. 'I did.'

'My mother is the bravest woman I know. I was shocked to learn the truth, but I was angry too. A little at her for her deception and for allowing me to believe she was dead, but more so at him, this man who had taken over my father's place. My dear father who had died in the war. I had already developed a very tight bond with my mother, even though I didn't know she was my mother, but once she had told me all and expected nothing in return for her deception, I realised that everything she had done, had been to protect me.'

'That is how I imagined it.' Straay turned again to Lady Gregson. 'So then, the rest is simple. You knew that Sir Laurence was already jumpy. The accidents that had occurred were simply figments of his overactive imagination, his psychosis. There was never any real threat from them at all. He, however, was convinced by them, because you used a tool against him that he trusted over everyone, including over you, Dawson. He trusted Milly. Milly convinced him that things weren't right, here and there. Milly suggested he seek Doctor Powell's help and advice for fictitious health reasons.' Straay paused for breath looking around the room at everyone in turn.

'It was you, Lady Gregson, who overheard the conversation between Davies and DuPont regarding your daughter, wasn't it?'

'Yes, how did you know?'

'It was simple. The way you allowed us to believe DuPont was in love with Milly, when it was actually the other way around. You were protecting her!'

She said, looking at Milly, 'That *bastard* was trying to force DuPont to marry my beautiful girl.'

'Like Dawson, you were also aware of the love affair between DuPont and Davies?'

Dawson hung his head down further. Major Heskith crossed his legs tightly.

'Oh yes. I caught them in their little sordid affair,' she curled her lip and spat the words out. 'That summerhouse was his den of depravity. It had always been. I knew all about the two of them ever since he'd hooked up with DuPont. I knew the way he was with men, with boys. It was disgusting, but how could I betray what I knew, especially as my own daughter was falling in love with the man?'

'I understand. That was the reason you wanted us to believe that he was in love with her; why you kept up that pretence. It is as I said before. You were protecting her. Trying to deflect any attention from Milly and have it centre on DuPont.'

Her eyes met his. 'I knew you were a clever man, Doctor Straay. I made enough hints about the summerhouse visits, the male staff being sacked and so on. I never made direct mention of it, but I knew you'd come to the right conclusion.'

'You were kind enough to furnish me with no less than seven suggestions relating to this fact. I was aware that you were trying to tell me many things; that you were trying to lead me along a certain path.'

Lady Gregson simply nodded.

Straay held her gaze for a moment and then looked up.

'So the question is this: which one of you killed Sir Laurence?

They all met his gaze but were tight lipped. Now, he thought, now I play my card.

Chapter Twenty-Nine

Doctor Straay's Gamble

'No one will answer my question, huh? Very well, I will answer it. You all did.'

Straay put down his empty glass.

'This is how I believe it happened. Ellie and Milly, you both approached Doctor Powell and Major Heskith and explained the situation, showed them all the evidence. It was agreed among you that there was no way you could easily unseat him. The police wouldn't be able to help because Sir Laurence was too well connected. His family were all rich and powerful. That was the reason, then, that Sir Laurence had to die.'

Major Heskith looked at the others and there was a collective affirmation. Straay had known that the bond between these people was a strong one. He had hoped that by being honest, and showing his hand, he would be treated in kind. The silence in the room was finally broken.

'Once we had agreed on a plan, we set the date.' The Major's voice was firm.

'The only fly in the ointment was me?' remarked Straay evenly.

'That's right,' Doctor Powell nodded. 'There was nothing we could do once we knew you were coming, in fact we did discuss whether to change the date, but we couldn't agree. It was all or nothing, with us. We had no idea why Laurence had asked you to come, but we were quite sure that whatever suspicions Laurence had, he certainly had no idea about our plan. We all decided to simply carry on, but we weren't prepared for how clever you were.' Straay acknowledged the compliment.

'What you did next was to ensure that you would all be guilty. Doctor Powell, you obtained the curare. Milly acted her part of being drugged with a sedative to establish her alibi, and Lady Agatha's. Doctor Powell left the house and went home to establish his alibi as well. Desmond DuPont was quite innocent of this crime and had no realisation of what would occur next. Once DuPont and I had retired to bed, the plot was initiated. Doctor Powell, you returned to the house on a bicycle, but ensured your neighbour did not see you leave, thus continuing your alibi.'

'How could you possibly know that?'

'The wheelbarrow tracks of course.'

Doctor Powell looked perplexed.

'Chief Inspector Drake said he found wheelbarrow tracks by the summerhouse. I measured the tracks; they were an inch wide. All the wheelbarrows' wheels were nearly two inches in width. It suggested to me that someone crossed the lawn on a bicycle, and as everyone else was already in the house, the only logical conclusion I could reach was that it was you.'

'Clever…' Doctor Powell shook his head chuckling to himself.

Straay continued. 'When you arrived, Lady Agatha and Milly were fetched. I imagine that it was you, Major, who held Sir Laurence at gunpoint in this room?'

The Major nodded.

'Doctor Powell then injected Sir Laurence with the curare and within minutes, he succumbed to its paralysing effects. You moved him into the study; he was aware of what was going on but unable to stop you. You wanted him to know what was happening; you wanted him to understand what would happen next. Once you had positioned him, one of you broke the clock and set the time forward. A page from his diary was torn out to form the suicide note. To reiterate, throughout all of this preparation, Sir Laurence was aware of what was going on, but powerless...powerless to stop you. The rest was easy. Two of you left the room whilst one of you shot him from outside the window; the other person removed the bullet from the doorframe and placed it into the clock. The body was positioned and the gun was passed back into the room and placed into his hand.'

'Correct on all accounts,' Doctor Powell smiled at him.

'The only mistake was the damn cigar,' Major Heskith remarked and Straay nodded.

'That and the missing smell of gunpowder. I realised that you needed to give an impression that someone had entered the room via the window should the suicide ruse fail, but you were being far too clever. It led me to think beyond suicide. Had you not left the cigar in the room, I probably wouldn't have been able to convince Chief

Inspector Drake that Sir Laurence hadn't killed himself. Why was it left?'

'To make it look like Laurence had been in the room smoking,' Lady Gregson replied with a sigh.

'Was it then that you told Dawson?'

Doctor Powell nodded. 'I told Dawson.' He looked over at the old butler. 'He fell apart over it. He told me everything, but it just confirmed what I already knew. I told him it was in his best interests not to say anything and he agreed.'

'So this leads me to ask; which one of you shot him?'

Major Heskith smiled. 'It was I and I alone who actually killed him; the others aren't guilty of murder.'

'Nice try, Jonny, but we all know that I did it.' Doctor Powell gave a slight shake of the head.

'Ah, now we get to it.' Straay rubbed his hands together. 'You see I expected this, once I had discovered all the past information and analysed it properly. It really only led to one person. The cleverness of the crime, the subterfuge if you like, was in having you all involved. Each one of you could have done it, but you would all have done it in a different way. When I looked at this murder as one crime, I could place each person at the scene but my mind gave me a different result for each of you, it would not tie up to one person. Eventually it occurred to me that if I broke this down into a crime of Three Acts, I found I was able to answer all my questions. It made the crime more sinister. It made it carefully constructed.'

They all listened as Straay broke down each act for them.

'Act One: A rare poison is administered. This is typically a woman's weapon of choice, but not curare. That is a professional's choice.' He looked at Powell. 'A doctor perhaps?'

'Act Two: A shooting, such a dull and unoriginal method—definitely a man's choice.' He turned his attention to the Major. 'The simplistic view of a soldier perhaps?'

'Act Three: The construction of a suicide,' he turned to Milly. 'This was most definitely the work of an artistic, precognisant, and intelligent mind.'

Straay then looked at each in turn.

'Why kill him more than once? The answer is obvious; you can hide a murder inside another murder. It was the only way to ensure that the guilty person, the one who committed the actual murder, wasn't easily identified.'

They all looked at each other again for a moment and eventually Doctor Powell cleared his throat.

'We'll all take our chances in court.'

'You realise that, with the evidence I have, the police will charge you all with conspiracy to murder and leave it up to a good lawyer and jury to decide which one of you actually pulled the trigger?'

'Yes, and they will find me guilty,' Major Heskith said, 'simply because I will make them believe it. I'm an old soldier with nothing more to lose.'

Doctor Powell stood. 'Sorry, Straay, it's all or none.'

'It doesn't really matter,' Straay said, turning and walking over to the bar. He picked up an ashtray and walked over to a spare seat. He placed the tray carefully onto the adjacent table. He then pulled out a cigarette, lit it, and blew out the match with the smoke.

'I have enough evidence to have one of you charged with murder,' he said putting the spent match into the tray. He looked at them all. No one spoke.

'I know who did it. Will you make me say it?'

Again, there was no reply.

'Very well, I shall inform the Chief Inspector to arrest Milly Gregson.'

'What?' Milly said wide-eyed. 'I didn't shoot him!'

'You stupid foreign jackanapes!' The Major stood quickly. 'She didn't do it!'

Straay looked at him through the smoke he was exhaling. 'No?'

'No!' He stood shaking in anger.

'I can prove otherwise.' He maintained eye contact with the Major.

'Rubbish,' Doctor Powell said. 'You can prove no such thing, we made sure of that!'

Milly looked desperately at them all.

Straay took another long draw, exhaled slowly, and looked into Milly's eyes.

'Have you ever seen anyone hanged?'

Milly began to sob.

Ellie Gregson stood up quickly. 'You monster!'

Straay also stood and his eyes showed anger. It was an anger the likes of which none of them had seen in him before now. His six feet three inches in height looked even more intimidating. No one had really noticed how tall he was, until now.

'You call me a monster? Me! Me, who knows, *who knows,* who killed Davies. What does it matter to me that the real culprit gets away with it, eh? What does it matter? I will happily watch any one of you hang, I'll watch the life fade from your eyes and sleep soundly in my bed. You're all guilty! Again, I say, what does it matter if it's Milly, eh? I can make that happen. I *will* make it happen.'

Straay's outburst had silenced all but Milly. She was sobbing quietly into her hands.

Lady Gregson looked at each person in turn and then back at Straay.

'You truly know which one of us did it?'

'I truly know, but I'm not going to name them. I've decided.' He sat back down. 'I've decided that if the true culprit wants to avoid Milly's death, they will come forward and confess. Nothing else will stop me. Milly will go to the gallows, and you'll all spend the rest of your lives in prison in the certain knowledge that she was innocent of murder, a death you all could have easily prevented.'

'You're clutching at straws,' Powell said, but his furtive looks at Milly and the others showed that he wasn't sure of that.

'Are you prepared to put that to the test, doctor?' Straay stared the man down. 'Is anyone else prepared to see Milly die for them?' He looked around the room. 'Game, set and match to me, I think!'

'You leave me no choice then, I'll wring the life out of you…' Heskith darted towards Straay but Ellie put her arm out to stop him. The initial gentle touch didn't halt him, so she gripped more firmly, and he stopped. With every ounce of willpower, he took his blazing eyes off Straay and turned to face her.

'No John, no…'

He looked into her eyes and saw the resolution there. He fought to regain control and slowly backed off.

'It was I,' Lady Gregson said, briefly looking back at Milly. 'I pulled the trigger.' She turned to Straay and stood firm, her jaw set, her eyes wide and unblinking. 'I killed Sir Laurence Gregson.'

Straay smiled at her, all pretence at anger gone. 'Yes, Lady Gregson, yes you did. But it wasn't you who put the box of crime paraphernalia under DuPont's bed, was it?'

'No,' Heskith said. 'That was my idea. It seemed a good place to store it. We hoped you'd find it in the search of the house.'

'But as it happens, you missed it.' Powell added. 'Then he died and that gave us a perfect opportunity to type a confession on his typewriter.'

'I congratulate your ingenuity, the way you put his fingerprints on each item when he was already dead; it was artistic. What did you do with the original ribbon?'

'There wasn't one.' Heskith's answer was honestly given. 'I had to put a new one in.'

'So you sought to point the blame at DuPont, with this typed confession?'

'Yes, he was dead anyway so what did it matter?' The Major looked hard at him.

'What gave us away? Aside from the actual deed,' Doctor Powell asked with interest.

'Many things. An unintentional theft of a pen.' He pointed at the Major.

'Ah, that was the reason behind your sermon on the topic of theft. I did wonder.'

'Your alibi gave me pause too, doctor. It was over the top, making sure to leave your pipe smoking in the garden, so your neighbour would associate its smell with you actually being there, and then giving him back a book on the very morning you're asked to come back to the house. It was all a little too much. Then there was the pretence of alcoholism from Lady Gregson and her very clever turn around when I offered her a flask. You knew I hadn't been fooled by your acting, my Lady. Let's not forget the silencer for a gun which no silencer could possibly fit. That was a serious mistake. It occurred to me afterwards that my room and that of DuPont, being at the back of the house, meant that it wasn't likely we would hear a shot anyway. The Major then told us he heard a shot, but if it had been silenced as was suggested, how could he have? It all pointed in the end to a group involvement. I could go on, but truthfully I haven't the stomach for it.'

'What happens now?' Milly asked, wiping her angry eyes.

'Now I present my conclusions to Chief Inspector Drake and Superintendent Baker. You see, I knew that Ellie Gregson was guilty, but I needed her confession. I suspected I wouldn't get it, so I needed to use leverage.'

'You realise that we can simply deny it all,' Powell said deliberately. 'I mean, most of what you have is circumstantial, and we'll all testify as we agreed, so as to make it almost impossible for a jury to find any one person actually guilty.'

'Then I play my cards. Milly will be tried and hanged for murder.'

The Major's control finally broke. 'Not if I get to you first!'

Again, Ellie Gregson blocked his path. 'John, No!'

'Oh but you all failed to understand one thing,' Straay said with a smile. 'You've spent the last few days lying to me, so I felt it only fair that I should offer you that same courtesy. Do you honestly believe that I would come here and show my hand without backup?'

Powell frowned at him. 'But… you said… you came alone.'

Straay turned to the door. 'You can come in now, Chief Inspector.'

The door opened and Chief Inspector Drake, followed by five uniformed constables all filed into the room. The household all looked angrily at him. The Major finally snapped and lunged forward, his hands looking to find Straay's throat. They never made it. A Constable and Chief Inspector Drake wrestled him to the floor and handcuffed him. Straay stood unblinkingly looking down at the old soldier.

'So you weren't being honest with us after all.' Milly looked defiantly at him.

'No,' he said stepping aside as Drake and his men put handcuffs on the others and led them away. 'No I wasn't.'

◆

Once the suspects had been taken to the station and the servants were given orders to leave the house, a constable went around and locked all the windows and doors. He handed the keys to Drake and made his way to his sentry post outside the front door. Drake and Straay then drove back to the station.

'Well done, Pieter,' Drake said with great affection. 'What a fantastic result.'

'Thank you, Henry.'

'You got a bit angry back there…. Did you mean all that stuff about watching Milly hang?'

'You tell me, Drake.'

'I think you put on a good show. You did what they had done to us; you lied convincingly. We didn't have enough evidence to convict without a confession. So you made them think you were angry enough to see anyone hanged, as long as they thought that you knew you'd get the result.'

'I gambled, Drake. I could not know for certain.'

'I think I know you better than that, Straay. You knew enough about Ellie Gregson to be assured that any threat to her daughter would force her to confess. When you told me your idea, I admit I was uncertain how it would play out, but I trusted your judgement.'

Straay nodded. 'It's true the psychology led me to her, but the evidence was circumstantial. However, with that evidence and her profile, along with her confession, we have more than enough to bring her to trial. We did this together, Drake, you and I. We make a good team.'

'Yes we do, but I'm under no illusion, though. You did this. With a little help from me, but the credit is yours and yours alone. I may have eventually come to the same conclusion you did, regarding the identity of Sir Laurence. I am certain however, that I wouldn't have discovered that Agatha was actually Ellie Gregson. I'm equally certain that I wouldn't have been able to pin this on her, or anyone else. I'd have had a trial based on the circumstantial evidence and my charges would have been conspiracy to commit murder. I *may* have been able to cast enough doubt on one person—possibly the Major—but it's debateable whether I'd achieve a real conviction in this case. I suspect that's what they were banking on. They hadn't reckoned on you. You said before that Sir Laurence *knew* he was going to be murdered. Perhaps his reason for seeking you out in the way he did was to ensure that *when* it happened, you were there to figure it out. It seems to me that he would probably have loved the idea of you solving his murder, considering your discussion on the boat.'

'It's possible. He did give me the answer there and then.'

'Was it just that photograph that tipped you off?'

'No, the photograph in isolation was not what pointed me to the truth. It was the psychology. Her intelligence, her mimicry, her split personality, she was too clever for her own good. Agatha was the one with the dependency on alcohol. Ellie simply copied that character trait. In your own background searches, you found a number of conflicting statements over the Major—that he might have had a relationship with either Ellie or Agatha. I decided early on that it had to be Agatha, but not the Agatha we knew. They acted out their love interest for our benefit; the fleeting hand gestures, the looks—it was all false. I suspect the Major was the father of Agatha's child. You see, Ellie Gregson loved Larry Gregson. She loved him with such passion...she would never look seriously at another man, certainly not a one-dimensional character such as Major Heskith.'

Drake pulled into the station car park just as the suspects were being removed to the charge room.

'Well, there's a lot more to come out, I fancy.'

'There is, but they will not try to do anything stupid…' he turned to Drake with a smile. 'You said you could never read or analyse me, once. You were wrong. Only you know that I couldn't possibly allow Milly to be hanged for a crime she didn't commit, but they could never take that chance.'

Drake nodded and Straay exited the car.

EPILOGUE

◆

Doctor Carmichael walked his dog purposefully into the park, following the path around a small fishing lake. He had walked this route many times before. He entered a more overgrown area along a trail that was less used, and stopped at a fence partly obscured by a heavy bush. The dog sat patiently at his feet.

'How'd it go?' A disembodied voice said quietly. Carmichael didn't turn.

'It's done.' He reached down to pet his dog.

'Are you sure?' There was a little menace in that cold steel voice, Carmichael thought to himself. It sent a slight chill up his spine. As if reading his mind the voice said, 'There can be no mistakes, doctor.'

'There were none, I assure you.'

'Do you have the ribbon?'

'I do.'

'You had no trouble retrieving it?'

'No, I probably shouldn't tell you how I got it out of the room though.'

A gloved hand pushed through the bush and took the small cardboard box from him. It was then thrust back through, holding an envelope.

'Good work, doctor. We'll be in contact soon.'

'Thank you,' he said taking the envelope and pushing it into his jacket pocket. He pulled gently on the lead. He and his dog continued on their walk.

◆

The Old Bailey, London
February 1935

Doctor Straay, Chief Inspector Drake, and Superintendent Baker stood outside the Old Bailey smoking cigarettes. It was some months after the conclusion of the case, and now the result of all their hard work was about to be finalised.

The Jury was out and a verdict was due at any moment.

'It's not looking good for Lady Gregson.' Drake put out his cigarette.

'She confessed her guilt and she knew what the consequences would be,' Straay offered.

'Agreed,' Baker nodded.'It's out of our hands now; we've done all we can. Now we just have to wait.'

Drake shook his head. 'It's galling that we couldn't charge the others with murder, they were all guilty in some degree.'

'Conspiracy to commit was the best we could get.'

'You archived all the documents found in Green's room, I assume?'

Baker nodded. 'Yes, we have every scrap of paper being analysed. So far they haven't turned up much.' He anticipated the next question and pulled out a file from his leather case, handing it to him. 'Copies for you.'

'Thank you, I will look through them and see what I can discover.'

Drake rubbed his chin. 'Our work isn't finished, is it?'

Straay put out his cigarette. 'No it isn't. I have the feeling that Davies and Green were intrinsically linked to this Warburton case.'

Baker nodded. 'It's looking that way, I agree. You think Lady Gregson was part of it too?'

'No, I think in that we have at least a complete case.' Straay laughed. 'I guess you could consider this the twist at the end.'

Baker shifted his case back under his arm. 'I'll get all the Warburton case notes from the yard.'

'It's a good start,' Drake agreed.

'I have four questions. What was the relationship between Anthony Davies and Warburton? Where is the ribbon from Harry Green's typewriter? Who faked Harry Green's credentials? Lastly, what is the connection to an Amsterdam diamond cutter?'

'You've been giving this some serious thought, haven't you?' Drake smiled at him.

Straay said nothing. His mind turned over the fifth question that he didn't voice. *What was Sir Laurence doing in Amsterdam?*

'It's all pretty irrelevant now. I suspect we'll never fully know the answer to those questions,' Baker remarked solemnly.

Drake saw the look in Straay's eyes. 'You might not be correct in that assumption, George.'

A police constable came out and stood to attention. 'The jury is in.'

◆

Lady Ellie Gregson looked sombre in her black dress. She sat next to her lawyer. He had made an excellent case for her; eloquent even. She was unreadable as the jury entered the room and sat down.

The Judge waited for the room to settle before he spoke.

'Lady Elizabeth Gregson, you have been tried for murder. Lieutenant Colonel Sir Laurence Gregson, who was later discovered to be Lieutenant Colonel Anthony Davies, was shot through the head, in the study of his house. You were, at that time, under the assumed identity of your late sister, Lady Agatha Smythe. The police surgeon was able to ascertain that Anthony Davies had been poisoned prior to being shot. That poison incapacitated him, leaving it impossible that he could have shot himself. You were not an obvious suspect but when details of your own investigation into the true identity of the man pretending to be your late husband emerged, you became a suspect. The investigating officer, Chief Inspector Drake, discovered you had overheard a conversation between Anthony Davies and the now deceased Harry Green, posing as a lawyer under the name Desmond DuPont, regarding the marriage of your daughter. A gun found in the house, forensically proven as the murder weapon, belonged to Anthony Davies. Your family home and fortune, which rightfully belonged to you, were now in jeopardy and you purposefully enlisted the aid of your friends and family to assist you in covering up your crime, thus establishing your alibi. You therefore had the motive, the means, and the opportunity.'

The Clerk of the court said:

'Will the defendant please rise.'

Lady Gregson stood, along with her lawyer. She was unreadable, her head held high.

The Judge turned.

'Members of the jury, have you reached a verdict?'

The Foreman stood.

'We have, Your Honour.'

'In the murder of Anthony Davies, how do you find the defendant?'

The Foreman looked directly at Lady Gregson.

'We find the defendant guilty.'

Lady Gregson did not flinch, nor did she cry. She just stood there, almost as if she were carved from stone.

The Judge placed a black cloth over his ceremonial white wig.

'Lady Elizabeth Gregson, for the premeditated murder of Anthony Davies, I sentence you to be taken from here, to a place of execution, there to be hanged from the neck until you are dead.'

◆

A large group of people slowly filed out of the Old Bailey main entrance. Along with them were three friends: Superintendent George Baker, Chief Inspector Henry Drake, and Doctor Pieter Straay. They once again found themselves on the pavement outside, smoking.

A quiet voice behind Straay said. 'Good day, Doctor.' He turned to see the back of a silver-haired man casually walking towards a waiting car. Drake followed his gaze.

'Halloway?'

Straay nodded.

Superintendent Baker looked puzzled. 'A friend of yours?'

Both Drake and Straay laughed. Drake answered a look. 'Not exactly. I'll explain later.'

'Well, that's it then.' Baker lit a match and shared it with Straay. 'It's been a pleasure to have worked this case with you both.'

'She will get an appeal, of course?' Straay asked.

'Yes she will,' Baker answered quickly.

Drake straightened the kinks in his neck, 'But our job is done, unless they ask for more evidence. What are your plans now, Straay?'

'I've done my work at Scotland Yard. So I thought I might take a trip to Oxford.'

'Oxford?' Baker was interested.

'Yes, to the University—Trinity College, in fact. I think it's high time I looked into the matter of this business of the fraudulent degree.' There was a light in his eye.

Drake frowned at him.

'Wait a minute! You stopped *me* from doing that; you said it would be a waste of my time.'

Straay inclined his head. 'And I was right. In the matter of Sir Laurence's death it would have been a waste of your time. It won't be a waste of mine though, I assure you.'

Superintendent George Baker looked at Drake and then laughed. 'He's got you, Henry, admit it.'

Drake held his hands up in mock defeat.

'He has indeed.'

###

http://www.cdanabbott.com
http://www.jellingtonashton.com

Coming soon:
The Murder of Doctor Chandrix

23713864R00165

Made in the USA
Middletown, DE
01 September 2015